THE UNANTICIPATED BRIDE

COPYRIGHT © 2024 TINA.R.ABBOTT
ALL RIGHTS RESERVED.
NO PART(S) OF THIS PUBLICATION MAY BE STORED, REPRODUCED AND/OR TRANSMITTED IN ANY FORM AND/OR BY ANY MEANS MECHANICAL, ELECTRONIC, PHOTOCOPYING OR OTHERWISE WITHOUT WRITTEN PERMISSION FROM THE AUTHOR/PUBLISHER.

THE RIGHT OF TINA.R.ABBOTT TO BE IDENTIFIED AS THE AUTHOR OF THIS NOVEL HAS BEEN ASSERTED BY TINA.R.ABBOTT IN ACCORDANCE WITH THE COPYRIGHT, DESIGNS AND PATENTS ACT 1988

INDEPENDENTLY PUBLISHED

ISBN: 9798337554983

PLEASE NOTE THAT THIS NOVEL IS A WORK OF FICTION. ANY NAMES, INCIDENTS, LOCATIONS, EVENTS, AND/OR PLACES ARE EITHER USED FICTITIOUSLY OR PRODUCTS OF THE AUTHOR'S IMAGINATION. ANY RESEMBLANCE TO ACTUAL PERSONS, ALIVE OR DECEASED, IS PURELY COINCIDENTAL.

THE UNANTICIPATED BRIDE

Chapter One

Lorelei Whitworth was feeling rather splendid as she made her way down the street with her reticule clutched firmly in her hands. It had been raining quite enthusiastically all morning, but now the sun was peeking through the clouds and letting the powder blue of a perfect spring sky seep through the grey, brightening the scene before and around her. Rainwater pooled in lazy puddles scattered on the broken paths and nestled comfortably in deep crevices worn in the roads, but apart from that, the weather was turning out to be quite wonderful indeed.

Lorelei had woken early, hurrying from her home before she could be called upon by one of the servants, as was the usual occurrence. She needed time to herself and to take the air in her own stead. Just thinking about what may be deemed to be a small selfish act elicited a rather uncomfortable feeling. A pang of guilt flicked the centre of her chest with tiny forceful fingers, for it was the first morning of the week where she had been fortunate enough to have escaped the dreadful demands of her rather needy mama.

Of course, at the spinsterish age of almost thirty,

she no longer occupied the same home as her mother, but that did not stop the messages relaying back and forth from her childhood home to the house she now resided in.

Her home was a small yet elegant house, which she had purchased when her graceful Aunt Petunia had, on the lovely lady's demise, left her a substantial amount of funds to make her own way in life. Lorelei had to wonder whether her aunt had been all too aware of the hold her mother had over her, or perhaps the clever lady had known that Lorelei would never quite be good enough to be sought after as a bride. Now that she was well and truly into her spinster status, Lorelei did not feel the need to be offended by her aunt's assumption, for, in fact, it was quite the opposite because she was rather grateful that she had been so astute and thoughtful in her dealings in the matter. Lorelei dreaded to think of a life where she would have always been dependent on another.

Lorelei picked up the pace, her skin colliding with the cool breeze with even more fervour. The cool air caressing her body through the fabric of her clothes and running its fingers through the loosened strands of her hair felt as though it hugged her soul with strong arms of pure elation. The life inside of her was expanding delightfully within her chest. There was a sense of freedom in the morning that made her heart swell. It was exhilarating, thus increasing the vigour of her excitement at having the opportunity to pay the modiste a visit.

There was to be a garden party at the orphanage, Lady Howell had happily announced. Lorelei was a volunteer there, and she was rather looking forward to such an event, for Bernadette Howell organised the most wonderful parties. Although there had not been many, Lorelei had to admit that it was neither here nor there, for she considered herself rather fortunate to have been invited to each and every one.

It had been quite some years since Lorelei had been deemed a debutante; the thrill of the seasons had dwindled quite rapidly, leaving only the faintest of memories lingering in the back of her mind. It wasn't until she took the time to reminisce did she realise that she was now merely no more than one of the onlookers. She couldn't remember when she had first realised her new status. It could have been the third season, or perhaps even the fourth. To be honest, Lorelei had to wonder whether it had even been the first, for she had taken her seat amongst the wallflowers and simply remained there. The whispers had informed her that she was not of the feline-esque figure most commonly associated with the typical miss of the ton but rather that she had a womanlier physique, although it has to be said that it was never quite phrased quite as nicely as that. Lorelei shook her head amused at the thought, for now some, if not most, of the young ladies that had indeed been snapped up on the marriage mart were of a similar shape, and some even have what men may refer to as somewhat rather more generous curves.

Lorelei had always been blessed with ample bosom and curvaceous hips that flowed rather pleasantly, naturally cinching in at the waist. Her mother referred to it, rather crudely, as ripe for bearing children, but whatever her mother thought of her body—and anyone else, if they cared to have an opinion—Lorelei secretly liked it, and no, her opinion did not falter even when she was dismissed repeatedly when the dances came and went. Maybe that had been her mistake, she had wondered on many occasions when the silence filled her ears as she sat alone in the small parlour of her home with its rose-coloured fabric curtains and matching drapes, and in the moments when she could not sleep in the pitch black of the night, for her large, soft bed felt as though something or perhaps someone was missing. It seemed strange to her that she could miss what she had never had, yet that nagging and rather unwelcome sensation in her heart liked to show up on an occasion despite a lack of invitation.

Lorelei pushed the melancholy thoughts from her mind. It was a beautiful day, and she was determined to make the most of it. After all, an unmarried lady of her age was free to do whatever she liked. Gone was the chaperone; she was financially self-sufficient, and she supposed life really wasn't that terrible being an independent lady. Maybe there will be more like her one day, she mused, and who knows whether they may come to learn of her? Lorelei liked that idea, she thought chuckling as she shook her head with gentle self-mockery. "Far too fanciful, Lorelei," she whispered to herself. "You will hardly do any-"

Lorelei gasped as speckles of cold water splattered the side of her face and dress. The breathtaking, chilly drops of moisture had been propelled amongst the forceful, thick current of a dominant gush of air, momentarily pushing her off balance as a carriage sped past. It was certainly unexpected, and her gown appeared ruined with the filthy rainwater that seized the opportunity to seep into the fabric, but what astonished her most of all was that the perpetrator of the terrible deed had not even stopped to apologise or assist.

Lorelei huffed; a short growl scraped the back of her throat as she stared at the family crest emblazoned on the back of the carriage, shrinking slowly in front of her eyes as the vehicle continued its journey. "Rude," she grumbled, righting her bonnet and brushing away any dirt that felt kind enough to relinquish its position on her attire. Apparently, the filth was all quite comfortable and did not want to move. Lorelei inhaled deeply; there was no point in dwelling on what she could not remedy. She would simply have to continue her day slightly less pristine than she had been a few moments ago.

The modiste was not terribly far, and she was rather excited at the prospect of what the creative lady would suggest would suit her. She knew it would have to be something subtle yet not so subtle that it would be just like her other gowns. She wanted to feel beautiful. One did not need a gentleman to feel beautiful, for gowns, she believed, were the most convincing and never required anything in return for their opinion.

The modiste smiled as Lorelei entered, then quickly dropped her eyes to the pattern of dark splotches on her pale blue gown. She pinched her lips together and drew her eyes back to Lorelei.

"It is a very short and rather tedious story, Evangeline. Needless to say, I was splashed by a passing carriage." Lorelei tried to smile, but she was quite certain it did not even resemble what she had hoped. She rather imagined she looked like she was in a considerable amount of pain.

"Please sit down, Lori. I shall get Betsy to fetch you a cup of tea and some biscuits," Evangeline crooned kindly.

"Thank you, my dear friend. That would be lovely. I wouldn't mind so much had they at least stopped and apologised, but they simply carried on past as though it didn't matter," Lorelei explained as Evangeline poured the tea. "However," she grinned, accepting the welcome tea, "it does give me the perfect excuse to buy more than the one gown, wouldn't you say?"

Evangeline smiled. "Oh, absolutely, Lori. It would be quite rude not to.

"As to the dresses," the modiste continued, "I have the most wonderful sage green fabric that has just arrived. There are tiny flowers embroidered in a delightful pattern upon it. It really is rather exquisite. It would look an absolute dream on you with your dark hair and green eyes, Lori. Truth be told, you were the first person I thought of when I laid my eyes upon it."

"It sounds stunning, Evangeline. I would love to see it and, of course, any other fabrics you think I would like." Lorelei took another sip of her tea and cast her eyes around the shopfront. Evangeline certainly had an eye for detail, and her creations were second to none. It wouldn't hurt to buy a few dresses, Lorelei considered.

"We do have a pastel yellow, yet I do not feel that it would complement you as much as the darker tones will do, so I would suggest the stunning indigo velvet as well, perhaps a deeper green such as an emerald green, and the deep red," Evangeline said thoughtfully. "We do have an exquisite plum velvet. Perhaps we could try that against your skin, and you can tell me what you think."

Lorelei watched as the modiste exited from the room, returning promptly with reams of fabric stacked in her arms, followed by Betsy carrying a few more.

"Oh, heavens," Lorelei chuckled. "That is quite the collection." Lorelei stood, placing her tea on the small table at the side of the room, and walked over to the modiste. "They really are exquisite," she gasped, trailing the plum fabric over the back of her hand and gently against her cheek. "What do you think of the colour?" she asked, her eyes intent on Evangeline. She needed to know the truth and not to be pacified with kindness.

"I was not sure it would suit you, Lori, but seeing it against your skin tone and the depth of your eyes and richness of your black hair, there is no doubt that it is perfect for you. They are all perfect for you."

Lorelei grazed her teeth over her bottom lip. She really probably shouldn't order a gown in every colour, she thought, but before she could change her mind, Lorelei had ordered an evening gown in every colour and a day dress in every colour too. "Oh dear, is that greedy of me, Evangeline?" she queried. She knew most modistes would simply have said no because it was money after all, but she and Evangeline were dear friends, and she knew her friend would tell her the truth.

"Lorelei, when was the last time you bought yourself some new clothing?"

Lorelei thought for a moment. Recollecting the moment seemed to be a tad more difficult than she was expecting. "Well, I believe it was my very last season."

"I would have to agree with you. That means it has been six years." Evangeline smiled and patted Lorelei's hand. "If anyone deserves new clothes, Lori, it is you. You look after your dear mama, you tend to the children at the orphanage, and make sure your staff are well cared for, yet you always seem to forget your own needs. Let today be the day that you finally remember them."

Lorelei blushed at the kind words. It was true; she did tend to others whilst discarding her own needs, but she knew that if she didn't, then guilt would follow her everywhere and plague her every night. She was at her happiest when making others happy, but Evangeline had been right; perhaps it was okay to be kind to oneself now and then. "Very well," she beamed. "Then that is what I would like: a day dress and an evening gown in each colour."

Lorelei stepped out of the dressmakers in a new gown. It was not any of the dresses she had ordered, for, although Evangeline worked wonders, no one could expect her to create such masterpieces in the space of an hour. This gown was one that the modiste and her assistant had put together for another order, but—and quite luckily for Lorelei—they had cancelled. Evangeline had simply altered it a smidge, and Lorelei thanked the heavens for fussy women because it felt utterly divine against her body.

It was the red of wine. A simple muslin dress that tucked in under one's bosoms and flowed over one's hips. It made her feel secretly sensual, she thought, blushing as she swung her reticule at her side, hips swaying with confidence. She had forgotten how much new clothing could make one feel. It was rather wonderful.

The ground was no longer glistening with the residue of rain, and the sun was warm against her skin as the breeze whipped about her skirts. Her pelisse flapped and flicked up at the ends. Even though she sighed at the visible splatters on it, she could not quite bring herself to feel irked any longer, for she was not feeling as though she were twenty-nine but perhaps more in the region of her early twenties. The shopping excursion had done wonders for her frame of mind despite the mishap with her original dress. And as Lorelei prayed that she would not be splashed for a second time that morning, she held onto her bonnet and continued her walk along the street.

Chapter Two

Maximilian Lazenby, or Max, as he preferred to be addressed, did not realise what had actually occurred until he had observed the look of horror on the lady's face through the window of the carriage. A little stunned at the event, and thus speechless, he failed to alert his driver to stop in time, causing the man to simply carry on, oblivious to his misdemeanour. The fool drove straight past the shocked woman, who, by all accounts, appeared to be in the midst of coming to terms with the mess that the filthy rainwater had made of her gown and pelisse. Max tried to console his guilty conscience that was taking great satisfaction from pricking him with every inch he was carried further away from her, but he was running awfully late for a meeting with the bank, and even though he knew he should stop and assist the lady, he really did not have the time to turn around and pander to her attire. He would merely have to seek her out on his return, he assured himself, as though it would be a simple feat.

"Ah, Lord Lazenby," the gentleman behind the desk drawled as he stood abruptly, bending slightly at the waist in greeting. "It is a pleasure to see you."

"I will cut to the chase, sir," Max began. "I do not mean to be abrupt, but something has come up, which means I am pressed for time." He knew if he did not find her soon, he would not be able to concentrate for the rest of the day, and a man of his status had a lot to do without the burden of a guilty conscience plaguing him wherever he went.

"Very good, milord. I understand. Now, how may I be of service?"

"I would like to ensure that this," he said, slipping a scrap of parchment across the man's desk, "leaves my account every month. The detail of the beneficiary is noted above the sum. I assume you will be able to do this without any issue."

The banker relieved his face of his spectacles and began to clean them with what some may consider a great deal of pride. Max found himself quite intrigued, observing the significant effort the gentleman went to for such a menial task, only for the man's finger to smudge the pristine glass as he replaced them neatly back upon the bridge of his nose and pushed them up the length of it.

"Let me see," the banker muttered, holding the small piece of paper in front of his face. "Oh, my," he whispered, the realisation of Max's generosity finally settling upon him. "That is very generous indeed, milord."

"Yes, well, be that as it may, this must remain a private matter, sir. I trust you can keep this to yourself?"

Maximilian questioned, raising an eyebrow at the banker. "Your discretion is of the utmost importance."

"But do they not already know that you are a benefactor, milord?"

Max was not sure he appreciated the man's impertinence as the banker continued to question him on the matter. *Surely one would expect to have a simple transaction tended to without the necessity of having to satisfy the man's curiosity.*

"Indeed, they do," Max replied, trying to shake the thread of irritability that was currently tickling his veins as it was being swept along with the flow of his heated blood. "But I have only just made it through all that stuff and nonsense," he continued, "of constantly being thanked. It is not something I find terribly comfortable to endure, so this time it is my wish that the money be donated anonymously. Do you think you can handle that, sir?"

"I would have thought that it must be quite marvellous to be able to feel the gratitude of helping another," the banker mused aloud, completely ignoring Max's question as he stared at him quizzically across the desk.

The man was pushing Max to his limit with his ridiculous questions. He clearly could not understand why a gentleman did not wish to be gushed over. Max clenched his jaws, biting back the frustration with the fool. "One does not help another for reward, sir. If one helps merely for recognition, then I fear help has been given for all the wrong reasons. I give because I want to." Max allowed his words to hang in the air, waiting for some form of comprehension, then continued. "The satisfaction I feel comes from seeing the relief and joy it gives to others. I do not need to receive thanks. It is all rather unpleasant anyway," he added, shuddering. "I do not like to be fussed over."

"Absolutely, milord," the banker replied.

Max wasn't entirely certain the man understood, yet he did not have it in him to enquire further. "So, I am to be certain I can trust you with this secret?" Max drawled inquisitively, flicking an invisible speck off his pristine, deep grey coat.

"Of course, Lord Lazenby. Mum's the word," the banker replied, tapping the side of his nose as he unwittingly created another smudge on his spectacles.

Max rolled his eyes, then sighed with exasperation as he exited the room.

Max Lazenby strolled out of the bank into the busy street, revelling in the cool air as he tilted his face towards the sun. The warmth caressed his skin, washing away the remnants of his frustration with the banker. It was glorious, he thought, merely for the moment to be interrupted by a distorted image of the lady whose clothes he had inadvertently ruined as her face flashed across his mind, reminding him of what he needed to do next. "Ride slowly up the street, Barrett, would you," he ordered, "and as you go, you are to look for a lady with perhaps a puddle-splattered grey pelisse."

Barrett crumpled his face at his employer's request.

"Yes, I thought as much, Barrett," Max sighed. "You, my dear fellow, drenched a lady on the way to the bank, and you did not even notice," Max accused gently. "By the time I realised, we were a little away from her and, well… I suppose I am to blame for this part, but I knew I would be late for my appointment at the bank, so I did not alert you. It appears that we both have a responsibility to find her and make this right."

"Of course, milord," Barrett replied, the guilt etched in every line on his face.

"Don't look so forlorn, Barrett. It was not as though you did it on purpose. We shall find her and put it right."

Max quickly scanned the area around the carriage. "You know, I had hoped the banker would have been a little quicker off the mark," he mused to his driver, "but I am afraid it may have been an hour since the incident; therefore, we shall have to scan the streets with some considerable diligence."

"Very good, milord." Barrett began to get down from his seat at the front of the carriage.

"No need, Barrett," Max protested, not unkindly. "It is just wasting time. I am perfectly capable of opening and closing a door by myself at the grand old age of forty-five."

Max climbed up into the carriage and shifted as close as he could towards the window. It did not seem as though he would be able to see the young lady on the streets with much ease when he was couped up inside a box with such tiny windows, he thought. Having decided that he may as well have his eyes closed for all he could see from that ridiculous position, he quickly alighted from the carriage and climbed up to the very front of the vehicle, seating himself quite happily next to his driver.

Barrett's mouth hung open. Max had never sat next to him at the front. It all felt rather strange.

"Close your mouth, Barrett. Anyone would think you had never seen me sit next to you up here before," Max chided.

"I haven't, milord," Barrett breathed, utterly confused by his master's sudden demotion at his side.

"Really?"

Barrett nodded.

"Oh. Well now you have." Max grinned, then quickly schooled his features. "We have a young lady to find, Barrett. Drive on, but drive slowly," he instructed. "Remember, she will be wearing a grey pelisse, which should be rather grubby after all that palaver this morning." Max groaned and rubbed his face. "And perhaps her dress will be too. Oh, good lord, I have some apologising to do."

Barrett pulled gently on the reins, and the horses began a slow canter back up the street from which they came. Thankfully, it was not a terribly busy day, Max mused as his eyes scanned the ladies and gentlemen milling about. "Any sign of her?" Max mumbled to Barrett.

"Other than splattered dress and grey pelisse, milord, I'm not even sure what to look for," Barrett replied. "Grey pelisses seem to be the go-to item for most ladies; I am not even sure I can see a female without one."

The wind suddenly battered their backs, nearly lifting their hats off their heads, as they sat gazing around at the passersby. It was a squeal of what sounded very much like it lingered between amusement and something else that alerted Max to her, but there she was, the lady with the rain-splattered pelisse. She did not seem distressed in the slightest, he thought, involuntarily grinning to himself in awe of her as she gripped her bonnet. She was revelling in the force of the wind as it rushed towards her, pushing her pelisse wide open to reveal... Max gulped. He had never seen a woman so utterly delectable.

It did not matter that the breeze whipped her dark hair about her, nor that the ends of her pelisse flapped violently as she scrunched her features in an effort to protect her face from the sting of the winds. There was a broad grin brightening her tormented features as she appeared to laugh at the chaos of her situation.

"Stop," Max rasped, pulling on the reins, too impatient for Barrett to respond. As quick as a flash, he jumped down from the carriage and began a hurried walk towards her. "Excuse me," he called quietly. "My lady, may I be of assistance?"

The woman was still grinning as she dared to open one of her eyes. "Oh," she gasped, coughing as the air hit the back of her throat. "Please forgive me, sir. The winds are wild today." She laughed, trying to organise the layers of her skirts into an orderly fashion.

Max was relieved to see that her dress was unmarked as the wind died down, whispering curiously about their ears as though it were inviting itself secretly into their meeting. "They are indeed," he agreed. "May I have a word, my lady?"

"A word? With me?" she enquired, regaining her composure, which in turn saw to it that Max's did nothing more than crumble.

The rich wine-red dress hugged her bosom; her decolletage revealed subtly in a display of milky skin, ample yet not too much. It was elegant and tasteful, he thought, noting the skirts falling in a waterfall of lace and cotton from just beneath those tempting, soft, feminine mounds of pleasure that his hands were suddenly all too aware of. The fabric followed the contour of her well-rounded hips, sashaying gently around her legs.

Max's throat had gone dry, and his mind was devoid of sense.

"Are you quite alright, sir?" the lady enquired.

She gazed about her as though he was in need of help, and perhaps she too would need help to assist him in whatever it was that he was going through.

It was mortifying, Max groaned inwardly, for he must look a fine fool, he thought. He had stopped to apologise and to offer her a ride home merely to make amends, but now he was just standing in front of her, stunned by her beauty, yet the forwardness of it all did not permit him to utter such things in explanation when he had only just met her. It would be a tad more than a trifle awkward to be so bold.

"Sir?"

Max shook his head. "I apologise, my lady. I seemed to have lost myself in thought. Where was I? Oh, yes, that was it… a word. Shall we walk? The air is a little calmer, so we will be able to walk and talk. Or if you prefer, I can escort you to your home in my carriage."

"Oh, well," the lady began.

Max thought she looked torn between accepting and running in the opposite direction. "You will be safe, I assure you. My driver will be sure to boot me from the carriage if I so much as attempt to do anything to harm a lady's reputation." Max could see the lady was not a debutante, perhaps in her late twenties in years. Although she was most likely married, he considered. No man would be able to know her and not want to be with such a fine specimen.

She smiled and then nodded. "That would be most appreciated. Thank you, sir."

"My name is Lord Maximilian Lazenby, but you may call me Max, if you prefer. It would make me feel a little more comfortable."

"Very well, as I am not particularly partial to formalities, I shall call you Max. My name is Lady Lorelei Whitworth, but if I am to call you Max, I insist you call me Lorelei," she replied.

"What a beautiful name," he responded. A beautiful name for a beautiful woman, he thought. He was already becoming rather jealous of the lucky man who spent his days with her.

"Thank you, Max. But if you should ever wish to abbreviate it, you may call me Lori," she offered kindly.

"I feel it may be a waste to shorten such a pretty name."

Max and Lorelei walked a little further in silence. Max had never been silenced before by a woman other than his first wife, but that was for an entirely different reason. It was strange that even in his mid-forties he had discovered something new about himself. "Here we are," he announced as they approached the Lazenby carriage.

Lorelei stopped, her face almost identical to the first moment he had laid eyes upon her, only this time she looked considerably peeved. *"You?"* she began, her cheeks brightening into a delicate pink. *"It was you?"*

"Well, yes, that was what I wanted to talk to you about." Max swallowed as he watched her tremble. He didn't know why, but he could almost see the anger rising within her like the tiny bubbles in a flute of champagne—overexcited yet perfectly in control. If she hadn't looked so dreadfully serious, he may have chuckled.

"You knew that you had splashed me, and you did not even stop?" she asked incredulously. She was scrunching her hands around the fabric of her skirts.

"It was extremely remiss of my driver and inconsiderate of me to have neglected you as such. I wanted to apol-"

"I was drenched," she growled, her voice restrained for fear of alerting passersby to their minor conflict.

"As I was saying, I wanted to apologise. I still want to apologise, if you will allow me to." Max looked at her beseechingly. How anyone could become more fetching as anger simmered beneath their skin, he did not know, but she had certainly managed to perfect such an act. It sent a tickle through him until he could not help but smile at her, rather wolfishly.

"Is this amusing, Lord Lazenby?" she snapped.

"Not at all, Lady Lorelei. Perhaps it is a little bold of me to say, what with you being married," he began.

She did not correct him.

"But you are rather splendid to behold when you are angry."

Lorelei huffed. "I do not see how making one angry is anything to find amusing, whether you think them splendid or not, Max."

Max noted how she had ceased with the full extent of his name.

"I apologise, my lady. I seem to be getting it all rather wrong today, do I not?"

"Yes, quite," she sniffed.

"Please won't you let me escort you to your home, Lorelei?" he asked.

Chapter Three

Lorelei gazed up at the sky. Her lips were pursed as she made an effort to portray that she was giving the gentleman's offer some consideration. It was paramount that she did not appear too eager, for one did not want to seem overly keen even when the gentleman in question was rather dashing. "It is still rather sunny," she said thoughtfully, "but I do have to admit that my feet are rather tired, so I shall accept your offer, Max. It is most appreciated."

The man in front of her smiled and offered her his arm. Lorelei was not used to such attention; it was all rather unnerving, yet when she allowed her gaze to rove over his features, she thought it all rather thrilling, actually. She could dream, couldn't she? she pondered, although she knew it would be a fleeting dream, for there had to be a Lady Lazenby waiting for him at home.

Lady Lazenby, Lorelei thought, was most likely one of those annoyingly petite, slim, feminine creatures that she always failed to stand a chance against when her seasons came and went in her younger years. Max was much older than herself, she assumed, but she wondered whether she would know his wife if she were to meet her, which of course she never would. That would be ridiculous, for no sensible lady would want to share the time they had between the *ton* and this delicious man.

Lorelei blushed as she realised her thoughts. '*Wonderful*,' she thought sarcastically. '*Blushing, Lorelei? You may just as well have told him what you were thinking.*' She groaned.

"Is everything alright, Lorelei?" he enquired, looking rather amused as he leaned back lazily in his seat opposite her.

She placed her face against the cold glass pane of the window, trying to cool the burgeoning heat in her cheeks. "Absolutely," she replied rather stiffly. "I am feeling a little warm, is all. It must be the excitement of the morning."

Max shuffled back in his seat, straightening his spine so that his broad body looked astoundingly more magnificent and regal. "I would like to pay for a new pelisse for you and anything else that may have been damaged by the rainwater this morning," Max offered. "I see that your dress is untouched, but your pelisse still bears the mark of our mishap."

"This is a different dress, Max," Lorelei informed him pertly.

"Oh, I apologise. Please forgive me, for I must have quite ruined your day, Lorelei. I will pay for it all, I assure you."

"There really is no need, Max. I was on my way to

the modiste to order new dresses anyway. Your mishap, as you call it, probably gave me the encouragement I needed to order more than one. It has been many years since I have been quite so extravagant."

"That is indeed very generous of you, but what about your pelisse?"

"It will simply wash out, I assure you."

Max was looking at her with an intense blue gaze. His eyes were the hue of a perfect summer sky, she realised, absentmindedly licking her lips. Lorelei shifted on her seat and turned her gaze to the world outside the carriage. It was getting dreadfully warm between them, but they were almost at her home. "You may stop here," she announced, not wanting him to know where she lived. "I live just there," she added, flapping her hand around in a fashion that would give him absolutely no sense of direction.

He was laughing again, but this time it infuriated her even more than the first. "I am glad I amuse you so," she snapped. "I thank you for your hospitality, but I really must go."

With that, and without the aid of a footman or Maximilian, Lorelei made her way out and away from the carriage, leaving Max staring after her, mouth agape, amidst the struggle of what she rather thought appeared to be his temporary inability to speak.

Lorelei wondered whether she could have handled matters with Lord Lazenby perhaps a little more graciously as she slid the key into the lock of the front door. Distracted momentarily, she looked at the key between her fingers, surmising that she could have simply knocked, but it seemed such an overly aristocratic thing to do when she possessed her own key and was quite capable of letting herself into her own home.

By the time the lock clicked, the satisfaction of rendering Lord Lazenby silent, whilst all he did was stare as she alighted from the carriage, had apparently lost its sparkle. In its stead, there was a horrible, nagging sense of guilt; after all, he had sought her out to apologise and had even been as kind to escort her home.

"Everything alright, m'lady?" Florence asked as Lorelei stepped through the door.

The young maid was what Lorelei wanted to refer to as a mere slip of a girl, but certainly didn't, for she had only ever heard that term used by ladies much older than she, and she refused to enter into that stage of her life quite so early. Florence had been her mother's maid, but to put it lightly, her mother had quite terrified the girl, so when Lorelei moved into her new home, she made certain that Florence would follow.

Her mother's current maid was the type of lady who would not bend quite so easily at will, which meant Lady Whitworth would have to find it in her to conjure a decent volume of pleasantries or her days may become somewhat infuriating.

After only a few months, Lorelei noted whilst looking at the young maid standing in front of her, she had to wonder if indeed Florence was the same girl, for she had quite come out of her shell.

"Yes, thank you, Florence. I have had a wonderful morning." Lorelei unbuttoned her pelisse and slipped her arms out of the sleeves.

"Oh, m'lady, your dress is lovely," Florence exclaimed kindly. "It brings out that deep red sheen that I adore about your hair."

"I have red in my hair?" Lorelei enquired. She had always believed it to be a simple black.

"Why yes, m'lady. It possesses a deep red that seems to glide over the surface in certain lights. I have always admired your hair." Florence was blushing. "I hope you don't mind me saying, m'lady?" she added.

"Not at all, Florence. It is a rare occasion that one receives a compliment as lovely as you have given me, especially when I have always been quite envious of your beautiful golden curls. Thank you, Florence. I think you have indeed made my day."

Florence blushed. "I'll just fetch some tea, m'lady, shall I?"

"That won't be necessary but thank you. I believe I shall visit my mother. I have no doubt that the note on the table over there is from her." Lorelei eyed the small, polished chestnut table where a folded piece of parchment sat. Even from a distance, she knew it was from her mother, for there was nobody else she knew who would seal their correspondence with ivory wax.

The woman refused to pay any extra for what she called fanciful and unnecessary colours.

The young maid smiled her commiserations as she picked up the letter and handed it to Lorelei.

"I will just find a clean pelisse and will set out to visit her. Hopefully, I shan't be long."

Sitting in the parlour with her mother, Lorelei's body pressed against the back of the chair as though the intensity of her mother's stare was pinning her to it.

"You have a new dress," Lady Whitworth remarked accusingly.

"I do," Lorelei replied, halting her words as she placed her lips to the teacup in her hand. There was usually only one way the conversation would go, so she braced herself for her mother's critique.

"It is rather bold for you, is it not?" Lady Whitworth questioned, one eyebrow arced as she stared at her daughter.

"Well, I quite enjoy the colour, Mama."

"It is a colour for young women, not for women of our age," her mother retorted.

Lorelei coughed as the tea caught at the back of her throat. "Mother, I am not the same age as you. I am merely nine and twenty."

"Almost thirty, Lorelei," Lady Whitworth reminded her. "You are a spinster. You should act and dress accordingly. Always stick with browns and greys, and if you really must have a colour, pastels are much better. You give the impression that my daughter is one of those strumpets. You know the ones I am talking about." Lady Whitworth was holding her arm up and wiggling her finger in the air as she tried to think of the correct word.

"Courtesan?" Lorelei enquired calmly.

"Yes, that's it. A courtesan."

Lorelei gritted her teeth. Her mother's words may have affected her had it not been for the butler who stood silently behind the woman, shaking his head in disagreement. Lorelei adored Jenkins; he had been with the family since she was a little girl and had always managed to turn a sour moment into a softer one. Without him, she wondered whether her grieving mother would have made her into quite the miserable wretch.

Lorelei nodded and smiled secretly at the butler. "I will take your advice into consideration, Mama," she offered. "Now, tell me how have things been? You look well, I must say."

Lady Whitworth coughed lightly. "Well, yes, I am, apart from this terrible cough, of course. I think I shall take to my bed soon."

Lorelei held the teacup to her lips again, accidentally blowing a bubble in her tea as her inability to hold back her laugh saw to it that it burst from her mouth and hit the liquid.

Lady Whitworth glared at her.

"Oh, I do beg your pardon, Mama. Perhaps I too have developed a cough."

Lorelei kept her eyes averted from the butler. She could see his body rocking in silence and knew if she so much as looked at him, she would not be able to contain her amusement at her mother's all too convenient onset of an ailment. "Perhaps I should call a doctor, Mama?" she queried. "He may be able to give you something for it."

Lady Whitworth coughed again.

"Oh, it sounds quite dreadful, Mama." Lorelei knew that it would be rather ridiculous to even contemplate calling her mother out on the matter, so she simply played along like every other time.

"Oh, it is, I assure you, Lorelei. Although I expect if you moved back home, I shan't suffer quite so much," Lady Whitworth muttered.

Lorelei rolled her eyes and decided that the best course of action was to simply ignore the comment and divert the conversation, and it just so happened that she had the perfect topic of discussion to do just that. "Have you ever met Lord Lazenby, Mama?" she asked. The man seemed to have made quite an impression on Lorelei's mind because she couldn't help but be somewhat curious about him. She hadn't even heard of the Lazenby's before today. It was as though he had appeared out of nowhere.

"Lazenby, you say?"

"Yes, Mama."

"And why are you asking about him? He's married, you know, so don't go getting any funny ideas," Lady Whitworth snapped. "Besides, you are well past your prime, my girl. It is better for you to accept life as a spinster and to spend your days with your dear mama while she still continues to breathe." Lady Whitworth coughed for effect, then dabbed her embroidered handkerchief at the corner of her eye.

Lady Whitworth was in her prime. One would have thought she was a fragile lady by the way she spoke of herself. If one did not know her but only her words, one would have been forgiven for believing the lady would quite easily blow away in the breeze, but Lorelei did not inherit her robust feminine curves from her father. She already knew what she would look like when she was sixty years of age, for she only had to gaze upon her mother to see.

"Of course you are correct, Mama," Lorelei replied to pacify her mother. "I am merely curious because I met the gentleman today and, until now, had not heard of the family before."

"Ah, you must be referring to Maximilian Lazenby. I was thinking of his father, but of course he passed some years ago." Lady Whitworth took a biscuit, slowly carrying it through the air towards her mouth.

"Are you sure you should eat that, Mama?" Lorelei enquired wickedly. "Surely, the crumbs will only make your cough much worse," she added smugly.

Lady Whitworth stared at the biscuit longingly,

realising the error she had made. "Yes, I suppose you are correct," she sighed, returning the sugary, golden shortbread to the plate with a wistful, longing glance. She could not take her eyes off it.

"So do you know anything about the Lord Lazenby I met today, Mama?"

"Hmm? What?"

It appeared her mother was sorely regretting the sudden onset of a cough, for she was struggling to tear her eyes away from the plate of biscuits.

"Maximilian Lazenby?" Lorelei encouraged.

"Happily married."

"I wasn't enquiring about his marital status, Mama, but only if you knew him." Lorelei groaned. If her mother did not eat that biscuit soon, then she would be hard-pressed to get a coherent word out of her. Although, Lorelei pondered, that could give her a rather fine excuse to take her leave.

"Must have moved back," Lady Whitworth mumbled.

Lorelei brushed down her skirts. She was not going to get any conversation from her mother today, so she may as well return to the comfort of her own home. "You look rather tired, Mama. I shall leave you to your rest. I am sure Jenkins will see to it that you are well cared for."

Lady Whitworth nodded.

Who knew shortbread held such power? Lorelei mused as she gave the butler a knowing smile. He bowed and began to escort her to the door. "No need, Jenkins, but thank you. Perhaps you can see that the biscuits are removed from temptation," she said with considerable volume to cut through her mother's longing state.

"Of course, Lady Lorelei."

"Thank you, Jenkins. I will see you both tomorrow."

Lorelei closed the door behind her and waited as she listened silently outside the door.

"Do not touch those biscuits, Jenkins," Lady Whitworth snapped, "or you shall be out on your ear. Do you hear me?"

Lorelei sighed, chuckling quietly to herself. "A cough indeed," she whispered, shaking her head. A severe case of overacting, she thought, but that was all.

Smiling broadly, she took her leave.

Chapter Four

Lord Maximilian Lazenby stepped down from the carriage with the enthusiasm of a man half his age. Something rather strange and energetic had woken up inside of him, he thought, as he gave Barrett brief but strict instructions to wait for him further up the way. The man obediently led the horses and the carriage down a discreet side road where the rather obvious vehicle would not be detected.

Max wondered whether he had taken leave of his senses, for he had never been as riddled with curiosity about a lady as he was about Lorelei—not even once in his entire forty-five years of life. And no, not even about his late wife either.

Max and Henrietta's marriage had been one of convenience, arranged at a rather early stage in both of their lives by two sets of amicable and somewhat delusional parents who had, wholeheartedly, believed their plan was rather a good one. The whole affair was indeed quite brusk as far as Max could remember, for he had just finished his education at Eton, and Henrietta did not even bother to throw herself into the usual requirement of attending a season—her father had informed her that it would be a dreadful waste of money when she was already betrothed. Of course, neither Max nor Henrietta had been permitted to have an opinion on whether one would like to marry the other and vice versa, but such was the way, apparently.

Max did not want to stomp over his late wife's memory, he thought, for he and Henrietta had had a perfectly respectable friendship—apart from that thing she did, he huffed to himself—and, considering the birth of his two daughters, there had never been any concerns between them with regards to the marital duties, yet it all seemed a rather mundane selection of memories in comparison to the sudden rush of desire he was experiencing for the dark-haired, green-eyed stranger who said her name was Lorelei.

The feeling that was delightfully tormenting his body and his brain as he pressed against the cold wall of a building, keeping out of sight, had taken Max rather off-guard. Although, he had to admit, it was not quite enough to deter him from his current pursuit of finding out exactly where she resided. One might even say it was what had spurred him on in his endeavour.

Staying close to the buildings and trailing behind pedestrians wherever possible, Maximilian followed Lorelei. His mind was telling him that he looked like an utter buffoon. And had he been observing himself, he was quite sure he would have had to agree, but on this occasion, he simply brushed off the annoying and rather unhelpful commentary in his head.

Max leaned back against a wall. "Minx," he whispered wickedly, observing the way her hips undulated subtly as she walked. It did absolutely nothing to break him from the extremely obvious web of enchantment in which she had him ensnared, nor did it diminish the rather wolfish grin he hadn't realised he was wearing.

Lorelei's pace began to slow. She was fumbling incessantly in her reticule. It was perhaps a good sign if she was searching for a key, he mused, studying her from beneath the shadows of his top hat. What exactly did a lady keep in her reticule anyway? Max pondered as his eyes followed her every step. Surely it had to be a key, and if it was indeed a key, then it could only mean that they were not far from her home at all.

As if on cue, Lorelei swept around the corner, her skirts swishing about her legs and ankles—they were rather lovely ankles too, if anyone cared to ask for Max's opinion—as she momentarily disappeared out of sight. Max pushed his relaxed body off the wall with a newfound enthusiasm to follow her and thus continue with his rather thrilling detective work. His feet began to pick up speed, his legs taking long strides until he rounded the corner and stopped again.

Scanning the road, he searched for a dark-haired vixen whom he knew would haunt his dreams, but the city life had bled into the road, hindering his vision, he realised, releasing a groan of annoyance. The throng of citizens seemed to blur the scene as each person became merely the backdrop of a large painting and Max was beginning to think he had lost her, but then, like all superb art, the muse reveals herself at the centre of everything—never quite obvious to everyone but everything to those who know of her beauty—just as Lorelei was doing in a swish of burgundy skirts and that dreadfully dull and ruined pelisse as she quickly disappeared through the entrance of a house and closed the door behind her.

Lord Lazenby remained still for a few minutes more, pondering as he smiled gratefully at the rather fortunate meeting. However, he abruptly reminded himself, she probably had a husband within those four walls, and even he would not stoop so low as to destroy a marriage. Yet, he considered with a morsel of hope, that his assumption of her marriage could be quite incorrect, for if he were a widower, why then would it not be possible for her to be a widow? It certainly wasn't unheard of, and although he did not wish the demise of a man, it was a rather tantalising dollop of a dream for his imagination as far as the lovely Lady Lorelei was concerned.

Making a quick note of the name of the road and the number upon the door, he headed back towards the awaiting carriage.

"Cassandra, you are simply being catty," Katie snapped as she glared at her older sister. "You knew I wanted to wear that particular dress for Lady Howell's Garden party."

"Yes, well, you shall have to find something else to wear then, won't you?" Cassandra retorted smugly. "Truth be told, you should actually be thanking me, Katie, because I have probably saved you from quite the embarrassment. After all, it is not difficult to see that this gown looks much better on me."

Katie sighed. She knew rather too well that it was best for one to simply ignore her sister over something so petty as a gown. After all, it was not as though she did not have other beautiful gowns to wear.

"Why don't you visit the modiste tomorrow, Katie?" Maximilian offered as he strode into the drawing room.

"Oh, Papa. Really?"

"Of course. It is about time you had some new dresses to wear. Perhaps you can take your aunt with you, so she may help you choose."

Max sauntered over to the inviting pot of tea on the table and lifted its lid. Steam curled in a silky, seductive dance that briefly kissed his skin, informing him that it was indeed a fresh pot and, more importantly, exceedingly hot as he always preferred it. "Lovely," he whispered, then poured himself a cup and settled back into his favourite wingback chair.

Max's daughters' gazes followed his every movement. Cassandra had set her deep brown eyes upon him, narrowing them until they appeared almost black from her apparent disdain, whilst Katie's blue eyes glittered as they widened from an obvious sense of gratitude. "Thank you, Papa," Katie sang, pressing a kiss to her father's cheek.

"What about me?" Cassandra bit off, the shade of her skin heightening to a rather vibrant red.

"Yes, Katie. Don't forget to give your sister a kiss," Max jested, keeping his eyes averted from his eldest daughter.

Cassandra's throat emitted a subtle growl in annoyance. "You know very well what I meant, Papa. Don't *I* deserve new dresses too?"

Max bit his bottom lip to halt the chuckle lodged in his throat from working its way out of his mouth, then simply stared at her. "I thought you were happy to wear your sister's dresses. After all, you are wearing one of them now, are you not?"

Cassandra sighed dramatically. "I only have to wear them because I do not have anything else," she lied. "If anyone should be rewarded with a visit to the modiste, it should be me," she added bitterly.

Katie rolled her eyes as she stood behind her sister. "Anyone would think you were younger than me," she chided, "what with the way you behave. I am quite certain that Papa would not buy me dresses and not you. Isn't that correct, Papa?"

"Indeed, it is, my darling daughter. And as I am in an exceedingly good mood, you both may purchase as many dresses as you like." Max closed his eyes and gave into his grin, leaving his eldest daughter, Cassandra, revelling in the prospect of fine gowns, but his youngest daughter, Katie, was merely observing him with a rather curious expression, wondering what—or rather, who—his smile was for.

Katie Lazenby would openly admit that she positively lived for romance. It was what occupied her mind for most of the day, if not all. Although only seventeen years of age, she had spent her days wrapped up in the arms of knights, kings, dukes, and princes, all hidden in the worlds of her favourite novels. It was the very reason that she was quite certain she knew that particular contented, lazy smile on her father's handsome face. She may not have seen it on his face before, but she had seen it on the faces of others—she had witnessed her lady's maid don a remarkably similar yet somewhat more smitten version—and she was desperate to know more.

Seeing her sister remain sitting quite comfortably amongst them, Katie pocketed the information for later, when perhaps she would be able to practise her interrogation skills on the man. She did not know how Cassandra would respond to such a subject, and if her father confessed to what she thought he would confess to, then she did not want her sister to spoil it.

"Did you have a good day, Papa?" she enquired.

Oh, don't be so disappointed, for one is allowed to interrogate a little, aren't they?

"It was splendid, my dear. Did you?"

"We did, didn't we, Cassie?" Katie replied, looking in the direction of her sister.

"Err, pardon?"

Katie shot Cassandra a withering glance. The faraway look in her sister's eyes revealed that the young lady had proceeded to design an array of new gowns in her head, which obviously meant that she did not have time for idle chit-chat, Katie assumed, rolling her eyes. The expression on her sister's face made Katie wonder whether her father had been wise to have been so non-specific when he had said *as many dresses as you like,* for she was sure that Cassie had designed at least twenty in the last five minutes.

"I said we had a lovely day," she repeated.

"Oh, yes," Cassandra replied, then swiftly went back to her daydreaming.

"I'm glad," Max replied. "I can't say that I revel in the fact that I do not seem to have much time with my daughters between the business matters I have to attend to."

"Papa, we are young ladies, and we understand. It won't be so long until we shall have to marry. You need to keep busy, Papa, for I should imagine this house will feel rather lonely if you do not." Katie suddenly felt rather melancholy at the thought of her father alone in Hawethorne House. Of course, there were the servants, but everybody knew there was a rather gigantic divide between the members of staff and their masters or mistresses. "Perhaps you should consider marrying again too, Papa?" she suggested.

Katie could feel the burn of her sister's glare on the side of her face. She knew Cassandra did not want their father to remarry, but it had been ten years. The man had devoted his entire life to them, and if they were to leave him alone to make their own ways in life, she would love nothing more than to know that he would be happy with a lady who would love him as he deserved to be loved.

As Cassandra maintained her seething silence, Katie looked to her father for his feelings on the matter.

"Perhaps," he replied casually. "You never know what luck one may have. There is, of course, the season's frivolities for you two, and many a stranger thing has happened at such events, even for us old, wrinkly ones." Max chuckled

Lord Maximilian Lazenby had a new, rather dazzling twinkle in his eye, Katie noted happily as she smiled. Even her sister's swift exit following a rather dramatic short and sharp exhale couldn't extract the lustre from it.

"Oh, that is wonderful, Papa," she beamed. "It would make me so very happy to see you happy."

"Mmm," Max hummed thoughtfully. "Perhaps."

Max rose from his bed a little later than usual. His night had been a rather restless one, much like it had been for an entire week where he had been haunted by dreams that were always pleasantly filled with Lorelei. Although his dreams were rather scandalously wicked and secretly thrilling, he was a tad annoyed at how his physical body would wake rather invigorated—more so in some areas, it had to be said—yet his mind was more often than not, heavy with exhaustion. This very fact had led to the man, who insisted upon waking before eight in the morning, to rise only a minute or two before ten.

He would probably have to arrive late, he realised, for Max had promised to attend an important garden party at the home of Lady Howell, who ran the local orphanage. He was their newest benefactor, and it was to be the first event he would attend there, but now his tardiness had left him hardly any time to do what else he had intended to.

Maximilian pulled back the coverlet and positioned himself at the edge of the bed. He had been used to nights of perfect slumber before he had met the raven-haired beauty by chance, for no one had ever taken up a prime position in his mind as she had. It was rather peculiar for a stranger to etch themselves quite so comfortably into his thoughts, and he was not sure whether he was entirely happy with the fact.

"Good morning, milord," his valet drawled, setting about his usual duties. "I have reheated the water for you, sir, for I could not rouse you at your usual hour."

Max caught the man's gentle exhale of displeasure and his signature side-eye glance that was always like a reprimanding slap in the face. "Thank you, Henry. I do appreciate your assistance."

Henry nodded. "Is there anything else I can assist you with?" he enquired, standing with such rigidity that it looked as if he had pressed his body up against an invisible wall.

Max caught a glimpse of the solider the man had once been and pondered as to whether it was beneath Henry to tend to a person's needs, specifically one who had never so much as picked up a sword let alone rode boldly into battle as he had. "No thank you, Henry."

"Very good, milord." The valet bowed deeply, then turned on his heel to leave.

"Henry," Max called.

"Yes, milord?" Henry replied, turning to face him.

"Remind me to raise your wages. You deserve more than I give to you," he said, eyeing the man thoughtfully.

Henry's eyes widened, glistening as he evidently suppressed his emotions in a visible swallow. "Thank you, milord," he rasped, flushing, then quickly bent at the waist in a bow to hide the sudden onset of crimson in his skin. "That is indeed very generous and kind."

"You have earned it, Henry. There is nothing kind or generous about it."

Henry offered a tight-lipped smile and left the room.

"Good morning, Papa," Katie smiled, watching Max walk regally down the wide staircase towards her. "It is rather unlike you to sleep until this hour," she remarked. "You have not seemed quite yourself this past week, I must say. Are you feeling alright?"

"Is a man not allowed to sleep in a little later than usual, Katherine?" Max retorted somewhat snippily, whilst raising an inquisitive eyebrow at her.

Katie frowned, a little caught off guard by her father's unexpected and rather unusual onset of tetchy behaviour. "Of course, Papa. I was simply asking about your well-being. I did not mean to come across as rude or impertinent."

Max watched the twinkle in his younger daughter's eyes fade, and he knew it had been entirely his doing. Guilt rose up into his chest. He had no idea why he had been so inconsiderate of her feelings nor unnecessarily rude, for it certainly had not been her fault that he had overslept. In fact, it had not been anyone's fault other than his own. "I apologise, my darling," he sighed. "You shall have to ignore your grumpy papa this morning. It appears waking up later than usual does not agree with me."

Katie's eyes brightened, relieved at the dissipation of tension between them. "It is quite alright, Papa. I believe we are all allowed to be a little lacking in sunshine sometimes."

Max chortled. *"We are all allowed to be a little lacking in sunshine, sometimes,"* he repeated. "I like that, Katie. It is quite poetic."

Cassandra confidently strode past, cutting a path directly between the two of them without a word. She was dragging with her what appeared to be a rather thunderous rain cloud, lingering precariously above her head.

"Perhaps some lack a little more sunshine than most," Katie whispered, eyes wide as she watched her sister storm towards the parlour.

"Cassandra Lazenby," Max called, his voice sharp with an edge of warning.

Cassandra stopped, her fists clenched at her sides, shoulders high. "Papa?" she offered, keeping her back to him.

"I will not have you upsetting the household like this."

Cassandra spun on her heel; a look of utter astonishment splashed across her face. "How am I upsetting the household?" she demanded. Her eyes were fierce and frantic, set deep within her face, her features morphing rapidly into a stony sculpture of defiance as she pursed her lips with considerable vigour.

Max kept his eyes fixed on his obstinate daughter, briefly flicking a glance at the maid, who was sensibly hurrying away from where they were standing. The poor young woman displayed an obvious air of panic from her previous interaction with Cassandra.

Cassandra's pursed lips were a picture of pure spite, Max observed. They were so tightly puckered from her anger that her skin had paled considerably around their edges.

"Apologise," Max demanded.

"I apologise, Papa," she sniffed haughtily. "I suppose I am merely annoyed that I do not have my new gowns yet," she offered begrudgingly.

Katie watched the interaction carefully, knowing all too well that her sister may have just made a dreadful mistake.

"Not to me, Cassandra Lazenby," Max bellowed, "but to Annie, your lady's maid."

Annie seemed to teeter on the tips of her toes as she paused, halted by the sound of her name as it lingered in the air.

"Annie, please come here," Max encouraged, "for my daughter has something she wishes to say to you."

Annie walked back towards the small gathering, consisting of her employer and his two daughters. Her demeanour oozed a desire to be anywhere but that spot in that house at that particular time with those particular people. Max was quite sure that if someone merely breathed in her direction, she may actually disintegrate from fright.

"Cassandra," Max warned.

"Annie," she mumbled. "Please forgive me for my mood this morning. I did not mean to upset you."

It was lifeless and lacking heart, but when Annie looked as though she may possibly swoon, he simply gave her an apologetic look and allowed her to escape the scathing tension of his eldest daughter.

"You had better be more gracious at the garden party this afternoon," he forewarned Cassandra. "It is to be a small event, but nevertheless, I am sure they do not need your sour glances and poisonous words to spoil it."

Cassandra looked shocked, as though it were utterly befuddling that anyone could think her less than angelic. Max could see the temptation almost tickling the tip of her tongue as she struggled to maintain a denial of her vicious personality traits.

"I will, Papa," she promised.

"I am pleased to hear it. Make sure you are ready by midday, for we shall be leaving then."

Chapter Five

Lorelei exited through the grand doors of Lady Howell's home and stepped out into the sunshine, admiring the exquisite beauty and magnificence of the grounds. Beyond where the eye could see, Bernadette Howell had built a rather different type of orphanage than England was used to, and Lorelei, over time, had become somewhat of a regular visitor, insisting that she may help in anyway Lady Howell required.

Today was yet another fundraiser, for they were indeed the lifeline to maintain such a splendid residence for the poor children, and the lady of the house had worked wonders once again. The décor was simply exquisite and elegant, or maybe just exquisitely elegant, Lorelei mused, drinking in the scenery. There were several tables scattered around the edge of the main garden as well as random, neatly piled bundles of soft blankets with all the necessities for an elaborate picnic. Apparatus for a game of croquet had been arranged at the centre of the lawn to entertain those easily bored, and from the gazebo, a sweet symphony drifted with elegance upon the gentle breeze from a violin as the gentleman's bow met its strings. Everything simply oozed a splendid air of romance, Lorelei thought as her eyes fell upon the delightful addition of white lace that draped rather poetically over the prettily decorated tables.

Lorelei looked down at the emerald-green skirts of her gown. Evangeline had worked her magic once again, and Lorelei felt quite superb in it. The comfort of the bodice and the way the skirts fell lightly over her hips was as though she were wearing nothing more than clouds, she thought, blushing briefly as she pushed such an image from her mind.

Observing the ladies and gentlemen walk arm in arm around the garden ignited a swift, sharp pinch at the centre of her chest. Although she was indeed content to be a spinster, Lorelei was quite aware that she was not altogether numb to her dreams. However fanciful and lovely they were to imagine, she reminded herself, it did not and would not benefit her in the slightest to even consider such a ludicrous possibility. Like her mother had said, she was almost thirty, and she knew that if a man was looking to marry, it would not be to a lady such as herself in appearance, nor quite as old. *Once a wallflower, always a wallflower,* Lorelei thought, walking around the edge of the lawn and heading towards the lake in the distance.

Lorelei leaned against the rough trunk of a tree and gazed out across the water. The sun was caressing the lake's surface, conjuring prickles of light that danced and glittered upon the ripples of water. "Scattered diamonds," she muttered quietly to herself.

"I beg your pardon?"

Lorelei pushed her body away from the trunk of the tree and turned quickly to see a tall, broad figure of a man smiling curiously at her. It was Lord Maximilian Lazenby.

'Max,' her mind whispered with a sigh as she smiled inwardly, quite unexpectedly astonishing herself with her somewhat misguided romantic reaction. She pulled back her shoulders and cleared her throat. "Scattered diamonds," Lorelei repeated. "The way the sun kisses the ripples of the water," she continued, offering an explanation, "looks like scattered diamonds."

Rose petal pink nestled in the apples of her cheeks as Lorelei groaned silently, for she could have used any word other than kisses. There must be hundreds of them, she thought, mentally berating herself, but she had let her poetic side get carried away, and now she had said it to one of the most handsome men she had ever met. To make matters worse, he was smiling at her, one of those smiles that makes one wonder what it is they are thinking, especially as his gaze kept dropping to her lips every few seconds. "It is a pleasure to see you again, Lord Lazenby," she offered, trying to break the stifling moment of... of... well, she couldn't quite describe it, other than it was stifling yet a little exciting at the very same time.

"Max," he corrected her.

"Max."

"It is a pleasure to see you again, Lady Lorelei. What brings you here?" Max enquired, his voice whispering over her flesh.

"I am an acquaintance of Lady Howell and like to volunteer whenever I can." Lorelei smiled, trying not to gaze quite so intensely at his mesmerising blue eyes. "It really is a wonderful cause," she added.

"Indeed," Max agreed, regarding her thoughtfully.

Lorelei began to fidget under the scrutiny of his hungry gaze. "What brings you here, Max?" she asked, trying to steady her voice. The way his blue eyes drank her in warmed Lorelei from within, yet she knew, as there was sure to be a Lady Lazenby, she should not even entertain the new sensations fizzing beneath what she hoped was her well-schooled façade. She had had many years to perfect such emotional nonchalance and had assumed one could not perfect her stance beyond what she believed to be perfection, but she had never been quite so taken or intrigued as she was with this man. It was taking her considerable effort to maintain a level of control over her reaction to him, she noted with a little exasperation, as heat remained stubbornly evident on her cheeks.

The rather brooding and sophisticated gentleman before her possessed a wonderfully masculine voice with deep rumbling, resonating tones, Lorelei thought whilst feeling a little misty-eyed, and it had, for some rather peculiar reason, made her far more aware of the shape of her body than she had ever been. Her dress seemed to feel more snug over her bosom, the delicate layers of her skirts seemed to tickle the bare, sensitive skin of her legs, and she noted every rise and fall of her chest as though she was willing him to gaze upon her décolletage. Even the sensation of the fabric of her undergarments as they brushed her skin had somehow believed that it was all relevant to the moment.

Lorelei's heart began to thud, the beat becoming louder and faster beneath her ribcage. She wondered whether Max could see every pulse through her flesh as his eyes roved over her body approvingly.

The rise and fall of her chest broke its steady pattern as her breath staggered with a sudden intake of air. They were too close, far too close, for there was a proximity of no more than a few inches between them. Lorelei stepped backward, afraid that she would say or do something that would be deemed inappropriate, as she marvelled at her hands that were suddenly itching with an overwhelming desire to be placed upon his broad chest. She let out a little squeal as her heel caught in the tiniest of dips in the lawn, thus causing her knees to buckle beneath her. Lorelei was certain she would hit the ground, utterly mortified at herself for being so clumsy, but before she could finish her self-chastisement, two strong arms had wrapped themselves around her and cradled her against their owner's body.

The warmth of Max's body radiated through every

layer of fabric between them as the rich, woody fragrance of cinnamon that he wore filled her senses with its intoxicating and alluring powers.

"Are you alright, Lorelei?" he enquired.

That exquisite, deep rumble of his voice vibrated against her. It travelled from his body, banishing all laws of physics as it passed through her flesh and entered her chest, tightening her stomach muscles in a peculiar curling sensation that she could only describe as pleasurable, which, she had to confess, was somewhat alarming.

Unable to draw words from the depths of her brain—muddled by a bout of rather unnecessary exertion due to pondering scandalous thoughts—she simply nodded.

"Papa!" a young woman called, smiling.

There were two young ladies. The one who had referred to Max as her father appeared to be approximately seventeen, perhaps even eighteen, Lorelei thought, smiling at the way she seemed to ooze vivacity. She had dark curls with blue eyes similar to her father, but the other lady with the rather acidic scowl permanently poised on her face had blonde hair and brown eyes. Lorelei pushed her body away from Max and stepped back carefully as she brushed her hands down the front of her splendid gown. Max looked a little taken aback by her sudden departure from his arms but said nothing; he simply smiled a smile that said he was a little disappointed that they had been interrupted.

"Ah, Katie, Cassie, this is Lady Lorelei. Lady Lorelei,

these young ladies are Katherine and Cassandra. They are my-"

The blonde-haired lady pushed forward in front of Max, a pleasant smile stretched uncomfortably across her face as she falsely announced how much of a pleasure it was to meet Lorelei, deliberately cutting off the man whom she was now clinging to before he could finish the introduction.

Lorelei noted how the lady did not curtsey, but nevertheless, Lorelei decided that she would. She may have felt a veritable fool, being as she was the older of the two, yet good manners forced her to offer the unreciprocated gesture whilst silently contemplating whether Cassandra Lazenby was indeed Max's wife, what with the way the young lady was practically pinning herself to his side.

She was young, it could not be denied, but it wasn't unheard of for a gentleman to marry a much younger bride, and Lorelei would guess that the woman before her was in her early twenties. Perhaps a second marriage for Lord Lazenby, she considered, remembering the other young lady who bore feminine similarities to her father.

Perhaps Max sought Cassandra out to produce an heir, she wondered.

Lorelei suppressed the burn of disappointment and humiliation beneath her ribcage as she quickly dismissed her musings, then turned her attention to the friendlier lady of the two.

Katie was still smiling. She looked as though the joy inside her would overflow at any moment from her petite frame. Lorelei liked her, she thought, returning her smile. "You must be Katherine," she said, offering another curtsey, which the young lady mirrored.

"Oh, please call me Katie."

"Katie," Lorelei repeated. "You can either call me Lorelei or Lori, whichever you prefer."

"Oh, that is a difficult one. They are both so very pretty," Katie breathed. "Perhaps I shall use both."

Lorelei chuckled, comforted by the young lady's kindness.

"Lorelei, these young ladies are my…"

The sudden sound of Max's deep voice re-entering the conversation startled Lorelei, only for him to be cut off by Cassandra once more as she feigned a wave of recognition, flailing her arm in the air at someone in the distance. "Oh, look who it is," she crooned. "Do you see them?"

Cassandra began to tug Max's arm, desperately trying to pull him away from the spot where they were gathered.

"There is nobody there, Cassandra," he bit off. Max ground his teeth together, the muscles in his jaw twitching with annoyance. He pulled his arm away from her.

Lorelei observed the sudden onset of pinched lips as she glared at Max. "Why won't you come with me?" she snapped.

Lorelei had never seen a lady react to her husband in such a manner. She found herself feeling nothing but sympathy for the man.

"Cassandra Lazenby, you are being extremely rude. I did not pay for your years of tuition so that you may treat a friend such as Lady Lorelei with such disrespect."

Lorelei unashamedly listened to their interaction as their tangled words slowly unravelled, allowing her to piece together the puzzle of what their relationship was to one another. It appeared that Cassandra Lazenby was not his wife at all but his daughter.

"I apologise, Lady Lorelei. It appears that my eldest daughter has forgotten her manners," Max offered, confirming her thoughts. "Apologise now, Cassandra, or I shall only pay for Katie's gowns, which will mean you will have no other choice but to wear your old clothes for the season."

Cassandra was seething. Her face had paled, and her eyes were glittering with the sharp shards of anger that were cutting a fierce, pointed glare at her father as she clenched her jaw.

"Cassandra," Max warned.

The young lady let out a breath. "I do apologise, Lady Lorelei," she sang, a bitter tone laced into her words. "Papa tells me I am like Mama. She *is* rather demanding like me. It is something we share."

With that, Cassandra walked off, not even allowing Lorelei to respond.

Max groaned. "I must apologise, Lady Lorelei. Cassandra can have a vicious tongue, unlike her younger sister. She is correct to say that she is like how her mother *was*," he emphasised, "whereas Katie is very much like myself. Perhaps a little too laid back for her own good though."

Lorelei smiled. The burning in her chest had subsided, she realised with some relief, as she unintentionally sighed. "Do not worry, Max. She could not be any worse than my mother, I assure you," she promised. "One has learned to harden a little to it all."

Max frowned. "Yes, well, one would hope to think that after ten years as a widower, one's daughters would offer a little grace when one is in the company of ladies," he replied, sighing. "One day, she may have to accept that I may wish to marry again."

Lorelei could feel heat rising up her neck. "I imagine you will be attending many a ball this season, for Cassandra and Katie will be wishing to find husbands," Lorelei observed, trying to divert her mind from the way he was looking at her. "Perhaps you will find a lady suitable there," she quickly added, wondering why she felt the need to say such things to a gentleman who she would very much like to know better.

Maximilian Lazenby's mouth tilted at one side, a devilish smile lighting up his handsome features with an air of mischief as he leaned forward. "Perhaps I already have," he drawled in her ear.

His breath whispered against Lorelei's sensitive

skin, fluttering down the length of her neck, causing her to shiver. *Oh, heavens, she did not know what she was supposed to say to such a statement.*

"...our generous benefactor, Lord Lazenby!"

Lorelei secretly thanked whoever it was who had called Max's name, for his eyes had been so intent on her that her brain had become a bundle of confusion as she seemed to have lost her ability to offer a witty retort. No gentleman had ever succeeded in rendering her silent, most probably, she mused, because no gentleman had ever complimented her as he had.

"They are calling you," she rasped, watching him as he brushed his mouth against the inside of her wrist. His soft lips drew the breath from her body as she found her lungs staggering to draw it back in as a pleasurable shiver skittered up her arm.

"I heard," he replied with a teasing grin. "If you will excuse me," he breathed, trailing a finger softly over her cheek, "it appears I am required."

Lorelei watched, lacking the ability to speak, as Max strode away from her towards Lady Howell. Bernadette was standing in front of the guests, attentive pairs of eyes following Max as he walked towards her. 'Good grief,' she thought in horror, wondering whether the array of guests had seen her and Max together. 'Lorelei Whitworth, you are ridiculous,' she chastised herself inwardly, for she probably should have been paying attention to the event rather than behaving like a debutante, fluttering her eyelashes at the most eligible gentleman in London. She had never behaved as such a wanton in her entire life.

Lorelei shook her head to break her free from her mental meanderings. She very much doubted she would see him again, and even if she did, nothing would come of it, for there were plenty of young ladies he would prefer. He was merely toying with her, she decided. But as the crowd raised their glasses of champagne in a toast, he caught her eye. She was trapped, she realised, ensnared by this beautiful man, but as the blonde at his side pierced their moment with a vicious scowl, she knew it was extremely unwise to hold out much hope.

Chapter Six

Max was going to personally throttle the banker next time he was passing that way, he grumbled inwardly to himself. He wouldn't allow anyone else to do it for him because the thought of causing the man considerable pain with his bare hands had suddenly become rather an appealing prospect, he mused as he reached Lady Howell's side. Despite specifically insisting that the man did not divulge the details of who was the benefactor for the additional sum every month, it appeared that Lady Howell was quite aware of his generosity, for he found himself being thanked profusely for the additional contribution to the orphanage in front of all the guests.

"Please, there is no need," Max mumbled as the lady poured more and more gratitude on him. "I'd really rather not-"

"Pffft," Lady Howell huffed. "You, Lord Lazenby, have been very generous indeed. You deserve recognition. It is the least we can do, and, of course, we would all like to thank you," she added, smiling at him in a manner that informed him that he really had very little choice in the matter, if any.

As Lady Howell made her speech, Max kept his eyes on Lorelei. She was a happy diversion from the discomfort that riddled his body from the pairs of eyes fixed intently upon him. Lorelei had kept herself back beneath the shadow of a tree where he had left her only moments before. Her beautiful oval face was eloquently expressive, and he knew she was thinking about him as he was thinking about her. Max could still feel a tingling on the tips of his fingers where he had caressed the softness of her face, and he wondered whether his touch still lingered upon her skin.

He lowered his head as a glass of champagne was placed in his hand, and as they raised a toast to the success of the orphanage, Max met Lorelei's eyes. He knew then that if he were to marry, there would be no other lady for him than Lorelei Whitworth.

"Tell me what you know of Lady Whitworth," Max demanded as he leaned forward and urged his friend to remove the newspaper away from the front of his face.

"I don't really know very much about her," Marcus replied, lowering his newspaper, "other than she is a spinster, of course."

"Are you sure?" Max queried. It seemed remarkably strange that someone such as she had not been married. "If there is no Lord Whitworth, then surely it is because she is a widow?"

"Oh, there's definitely the deceased version of a

Lord Whitworth, but had she been married to the man, it would have been most incestuous indeed, for he was her father," Marcus retorted with subtle sarcasm. "The lady you speak of was a wallflower from the start, if I remember correctly. And I am known for an exceedingly excellent memory for detail, I will have you know. She is a little *too* voluptuous for wife material, would you not agree?"

Max ignored him, even though he felt very much like breaking the man's nose for the snide comment about Lorelei's wonderful curves. "This is very good news," he mumbled, getting to his feet.

"I beg your pardon, what did you... Oh, are you going so soon, old chap?" Marcus asked, looking rather astonished.

Max supposed he could have stayed a little longer with his friend, but he was not feeling very sociable with the man after he had assumed that every man in London was ludicrous enough to not consider such a desirable woman to be his wife.

"I'm afraid I have just remembered a prior engagement," he replied. "Do excuse me."

If the men in London had no taste in women, then he certainly did, Max mused. In fact, he believed he was rather grateful for the gentlemen's lack of refined taste in the fairer sex, for perhaps if they were born with any sense then she would not have been free for him to attempt to court.

Max was determined to win Lady Lorelei's heart,

and to do so he would need to be where she would be, he decided, remembering the abundance of invitations he had received. Surely, he would find her at one of those events, he thought hopefully.

Max spent the next week socialising amongst dukes, duchesses, viscounts, and marquesses, exchanging polite conversation about weather and politics whilst exhausting his patience as his eyes continuously peered over shoulders and round corners for a glimpse of her. However, it seemed that Lady Lorelei's status as a spinster meant that she did not appear at the top of any host or hostess' list of desired guests. It was all terribly disappointing and a shame that they did not seem to note the lady's worth as he did. Their attitude was rather rude and inconsiderate, he thought begrudgingly, as he began to miss her delightful presence. Her title alone should have seen to it that she would have mingled amongst the ton. Unless, of course, she did not wish to mingle amongst these people. That was indeed a worthy explanation, he considered, for Max was quite sure he would have gladly swapped many a yawn-inducing conversation with the pompous aristocrats for even the tiniest of glimpses of the lovely Lorelei.

Finally, after the last brain-numbing supper held at Lord Bartholomew's manor, he had the definitive impression that none of his associates had even an inkling of how one was supposed to enjoy themselves, and he had left the party quite aware that he would have to take matters into his own hands, for what he had attempted so far was obviously not working at all.

Lord Maximilian Lazenby would host his own party, or perhaps a ball, he considered. That would indeed ensure that Lady Lorelei was invited. It was an excellent idea, he thought, feeling quite smug that it was he who had thought of it. He supposed he would have to invite those he had spent the last week with, but maybe it would do them good, for they could learn a thing or two from him of how to host an event that was at least the tiniest amount enjoyable, he thought with a wry smile.

"Is everything alright, Max?" Ava queried as she entered the drawing room, her mind quite obviously and curiously assessing her brother as he sat across the room, looking more thoughtful than she had ever seen him.

"Hmm?"

"I do not believe I have ever seen you quite so lost in thought before," she offered playfully. "Do tell me that there is a lady involved."

Max simply offered her a mischievous smirk.

"Oh, there is!" She was beaming at him, her eyes glittering with wonder and excitement.

Ava reminded Max of Katie when she smiled. It was as though they were the same person, born twenty years apart. When they stood together, it was utterly uncanny, yet he rejoiced in their likeness and the fact that the Lazenby genetics had been quite successful where his youngest daughter had been concerned. Even their delight in the possibility of him finding happiness again was the same, but as for Cassandra, she seemed to have that damn vicious streak her mother had. He didn't know whether she had inherited malice from her mother or a bitter streak of jealousy. Either way, she was proving to be an obstacle where Lorelei was concerned. Had he not met Lorelei, and the subject of marriage was merely a thought, it would not have bothered him so, but the woman he intended to court and eventually marry was very real indeed. He didn't know how he was going to get around the inconvenient attitude of his eldest daughter.

"Indeed there is, Ava," he sighed.

Ava noted the exasperation in his response and could not fathom why someone who was considering marriage would ever feel as he portrayed to her in that long, drawn-out exhale.

"Why do I feel like you have created a problem for yourself with regards to this lady?" Ava asked. "I hope you are not feeling like you shouldn't, Max. It has been ten years since their mother passed."

"It is not that I have created a problem but merely that there is a problem... a very blonde problem."

Ava frowned in confusion, and when she realised what he meant, she raised her eyebrows in acknowledgement. "Oh, I see," she crooned softly, her face stretching in a grimace.

"Indeed," Max replied. "But that is not the only

problem, for I do not seem to be able to be in the same place at the same time as she is to speak with her. There have been two times so far, but they were merely by chance."

"You have met her twice?" Ava exclaimed excitedly.

Max shot his sister a withering glare. "May I continue?"

Ava bit her bottom lip, stifling the giggle of glee from rising. "Oh, yes. Please do go on, brother," she encouraged, settling herself back in the seat opposite him. The maid had just arrived with a fresh pot of tea and clean crockery, placing it between them on the low table, prompting Ava to busy her fidgeting hands by pouring the tea for them both. She had so many questions, wanting to know so much more about this lady who had caught her brother's attention. She was fit to burst with curiosity.

"As I was saying," Max grumbled gently. "I have only managed to be in the same place as her on two occasions. I thought that by attending parties and suppers—exceedingly tiresome ones, I might add—I may have seen her again. But, as yet, I have been entirely unsuccessful, for everywhere I am, she is not." Max leaned back in the chair and reached for the teacup at his side. The tea was not hot enough, he noted grimacing as he placed it back down and rang the bell.

"Oh, that really is a bother," Ava commented thoughtfully. "I do hope you will not simply give up on her, Max, for I believe you really are quite taken with the lady, aren't you?"

"I certainly do not intend to give up on her, Ava."

Ava noted how he failed to respond to her last question, but she simply dismissed it. She did not believe she even needed to hear the answer, for it was evident in his eyes, in his obvious distress, and even in his voice.

"I believe that if I cannot go to her, I may know a way that she will come to me," Max replied, smiling, regaining his sister's piercing expression of curiosity. "I think I shall have to organise a party of my own and invite her. She has connections to Lady Howell's Orphanage, so perhaps I could organise a ball as a charity event," he explained. "I do not believe she could possibly decline an invitation to an event for such a worthy cause."

"Maximilian Lazenby, are you telling me that you have an ulterior motive for helping raise funds for a charity?" Ava gasped mockingly. "What on earth would our mother have said?"

"I know it must sound like that, and perhaps in a way it is-"

"Oh, it most certainly is, Max," Ava chided playfully.

"However," Max ground out, not unkindly, "it would still be beneficial to the orphanage. Besides, I was going to arrange something similar eventually to help raise money. I do not see why I cannot merely hope she will attend."

"I think it is a wonderful idea," Ava announced, elated.

"I do too, but," Max began, his smile faltering, "as I have said, Cassandra may be an issue. She is quite adamant that I do not marry. Only the other day at Lady Howell's garden party, I think she tried to pass herself off as my wife!"

Ava's mouth fell open. "I beg your pardon? Did you just say she tried to make this lady believe that she was your wife rather than your daughter?"

Max nodded. "It is not quite as sordid as it may sound. She simply clung to my side and interrupted every time I tried to introduce her as my daughter."

Ava's lips pinched. "That is incredibly naughty of her, Max," she remarked. "But you have to realise this is not your doing, for you are a wonderful father. You have spent the last ten years alone other than Katie and Cassie, and, as much as Cassandra is displeased at the thought of you remarrying, you have every right to find happiness for yourself."

Max picked up his tea and began to drink. The maid had brought a fresh, wonderfully hot cup whilst he and Ava had been talking, and he wanted to consume it before it started to cool like the last one. The thought of another drop of luke warm tea touching his tongue was not pleasant. "You would think so, wouldn't you?" he chuckled.

"She and Katie will marry eventually," Ava continued. "Most probably this season, if I have anything to do with it. After Cassandra's last season, I am quite sure that she may even feel a little jealous that you may marry before she does, which, I might add, is not only ridiculous but extremely selfish and unkind. You must not allow her to dictate your life, Max. You must go after this... this..."

"Lorelei," Max interjected, his voice soft with the memory of her.

"Oh, what a charming name," Ava whispered in awe. "I think I may be a little in love with her, simply because of it," she giggled, her eyes twinkling.

Max grinned. It was rather boyish and endearing, Ava mused as her heart swelled with fondness for her older brother.

"As I was saying, you must pursue this Lady Lorelei. Don't give Cassie another thought. Leave her to me. I am sure Katie will be a dear help in controlling any outburst from the young lady. And whilst we are doing that, you, my dear brother, must concentrate on seeking out this lady with the loveliest name I have ever heard and sealing your own happiness."

Max rose from his seat and walked over to his sister, placing a kiss on the top of her head. "What would I do without you, dearest sister?" He smiled joyfully.

"Perish, no doubt," she quipped, chuckling. "Now let's write that guest list, shall we?"

Chapter Seven

Lorelei slid the invitation off the silver tray and turned it over in her hands, admiring its obvious elegance. Such correspondence rarely, if ever, was delivered to her address, and she was most intrigued indeed. There was to be a ball in aid of Lady Howell's Orphanage, which Lorelei thought was a splendid idea. There was never a better time where the ladies and gentlemen of London proved to be frivolous with their finances than when their personalities were softened with the hazy golden glow of champagne and fine wine.

Of course, just because she rarely received such invitations, it did not mean that Lorelei never left the confines of her home. She had helped organise many events for the orphanage, and then there were the invitations issued out of pity, or perhaps politeness, from her mother's acquaintances—the elders of the ton were prone to believing that a woman would never quite be enough without a husband—but this invitation was solely for her and rather exciting indeed.

Lorelei wracked her brain for who the M.L. could be. It was on the tip of her tongue; she knew it, but she simply couldn't remember. Never mind, she thought, for she was meeting Lady Howell for luncheon, so she could ask her then. If anyone would know, it would be Bernadette Howell.

Lorelei stepped down from the carriage and sighed with a sense of satisfaction. She had been blessed once again with the warmth of the sun as it caressed the side of her face, causing her to smile as she remembered how Max's fingers had languorously trailed a similar delicious heat upon her skin in the very same place. As she removed her rather annoying bonnet, the sun continued its intrusive exploration, stroking her hair with its heated fingers.

Lorelei had another hour until she was to meet with Lady Howell at the tea rooms, but Lorelei was Lorelei, and she had planned her time with precision. The hour was ample for what was required of her, as it was the day she was to collect the finished evening gowns and day dresses from her dear friend Evangeline. The timing of Evangeline's correspondence, delivering the news of their completion, could not have been more fortuitous, what with the charity ball coming up. Although, Lorelei mused, she now had the dratted task of deciding which gown she would wear. Perhaps she could ask Evangeline, she considered.

Evangeline beamed as Lorelei entered the shop. "Good morning, Lori."

"Good morning, Evangeline." Lorelei let out a little squeal of excitement as she smiled profusely. "Are they really ready?" she queried as she closed the door behind her.

"They are indeed. I cannot wait for you to try them on. You are going to look fabulous."

"I hope I do them justice, Evangeline. You know I adore your designs."

"Do you trust me?" Evangeline enquired.

"Absolutely," Lorelei replied sincerely.

"Then let me show you."

Lorelei gasped at the woman in the looking glass. For a spinster, she did not look very spinsterish (whatever that may look like) at all, she thought. Lorelei, although usually modest, had to admit that she looked like an elegant lady. She was thrilled.

The deep plum colour accentuated the rich tones of her black hair and drew out the green of her eyes, even highlighting the depth of the hue of her lashes. Her lips appeared to be a deep dusky rose, and she felt positively divine. She did not need to ask Evangeline which dress she thought she should wear for the ball, she realised, because instinctively she knew it was this one.

"What do you think?" Lorelei asked.

There was only silence.

"Evangeline?" Lorelei turned to see the modiste's eyes wide.

"You look exquisite, Lori," she breathed. "I knew it would look lovely, but I have never been quite so lost for words when a lady has tried on one of my gowns."

Lorelei blushed, then quickly grinned.

"The most important thing is that you like it, though, Lori. Do you?" Evangeline enquired.

Lorelei could hear the hope in her friend's voice, but she knew she needn't have feared her reply. "I don't simply like it, Evangeline, for I adore it. I don't believe I have ever felt so lovely in a gown before."

Evangeline's elation was evident on her face as she took in Lorelei's words. "Now to try the others," the modiste exclaimed, passing Lorelei an evening gown in sage green.

Lorelei could have spent the rest of the day in the dressmakers, chatting and trying on the remainder of her day dresses and evening gowns, but sadly she knew that could not be. After she had tried on another evening gown and a day dress, Evangeline packed all of her purchases up nicely and helped her carry them to the carriage.

"Would you like me to take you to the tea rooms, m'lady?" the driver called down from the front of the carriage as she closed the door, concealing the stack of her purchases behind it.

"That won't be necessary, Bentley, but thank you. The tearoom is only over there," she replied, nodding to the other side of the street. "Do you mind waiting for me, though? I should only be an hour or two with Lady Howell."

"No problem, m'lady." Bentley secured the reins and eased himself back in his seat, placing his hands behind his head as he reclined a little. "It is the perfect weather today, m'lady. I shall be only too pleased to wait right here for you."

Lorelei smiled wryly. "I thought you might be." She chuckled. "I will see you in no more than two hours."

"Right you are, m'lady."

Lorelei wondered whether she ought to have put her bonnet back on as she entered the tearoom. It appeared she was the only lady who did not wish to wear such an item on a day as lovely as it was. In fact, the tearoom was awash with an array of bonnets, ribbons, gowns, and chatter, so much so that she nearly did not see Lady Howell, who was tucked in the corner, hidden slightly by the menu she was perusing.

"Good afternoon, Lady Howell," Lorelei breathed, offering a gentle curtsey. "I apologise if I am a little later than planned. I have been across the street at the modiste."

"Good afternoon, Lorelei. You are hardly late at all. A minute at most." Lady Howell smiled, gesturing to the seat across from her so that Lorelei may take the weight off her feet. "You may desist with the Lady Howell title here, Lori, for we are not at the orphanage now."

"Thank you, Bernadette. It is merely habitual, so please bear with me if I forget." Lorelei lowered herself into the chair and gazed around the room. "It is rather busy today, is it not?"

"A little, but I am sure the ball will be a tad busier," Bernadette remarked. "How fortunate we are to have such a prestigious event in the name of the orphanage."

"Oh, yes," Lorelei breathed. "I must admit that I am rather looking forward to it. And now that I have new evening gowns, I do not have to worry about what I might wear."

"That sounds rather intriguing." Bernadette leaned in. "Do tell."

"Evangeline is incredible, Bernadette. I simply will not do her work justice if I describe it. Although I can tell you that I bought several and the colours are sage green, emerald green, deep red…"

Bernadette's eyes widened, and her brows rose with a look of surprise and approval. "Go on," she encouraged.

"…indigo and an exquisite plum shade." The memory of the plum evening gown lit up Lorelei's eyes until they sparkled. "The plum evening gown is my absolute favourite. I believe I shall wear that one for the ball."

"They sound exquisite, and I have no doubt you will look divine in them, Lorelei.

"It is very generous indeed of Lord Lazenby to go to so much trouble. He is a regular benefactor, but he has never done anything like this before."

Lorelei sipped the tea that had been placed before her whilst she had thoroughly immersed herself in her talk of gowns and dresses. The initials M and L were starting to make sense now that Lady Howell had divulged that Max Lazenby was behind the upcoming ball. "I remember him from the garden party," Lorelei muttered, trying desperately to keep the heat from her face as her mind whisked her off to the moment when he'd stepped in front of her to assist her. She thought herself the most silliest lady, for she had been plagued by his image in her mind every day, yet she had not even considered that the initials M and L were his.

"Yes, that's correct," Lady Howell replied. "I suppose it is most probably because he has only recently moved to his London residence, whereas before he was residing in the country."

"That would certainly make sense," Lorelei offered thoughtfully. "Either way, it is most considerate and kind."

"And even better," Lady Howell announced, "I do not have to do anything except turn up to the event. I do not think I can remember a time when I have not had to host. Maybe I shall be whisked off my feet across the dancefloor by Lord Howell." Lady Howell laughed. "Poor Edward. I do not think he will be best pleased to find out that he may have to dance." She giggled, turning her eyes to the sandwiches as she selected one daintily. "Always knows how to crush a lady's toes."

Lorelei grimaced.

"Oh, don't fret, Lorelei. I shall simply have to wear better shoes."

Lorelei and Lady Howell spent the next hour or so chatting excitedly about the possible guests and what the event could achieve for the orphanage. Lorelei didn't think she had ever seen the lady quite so animated and vivacious over anything. It was indeed lovely to witness.

Climbing back into the carriage, Lorelei felt warm and content inside, yet every time her mind slipped to Maximilian Lazenby, her stomach would do a little flip. She couldn't decide whether it was excitement or just apprehension at the thought of seeing him again. Excitement perhaps as she remembered how flirtatious he had been at their last encounter, yet apprehension, for she knew his blonde-haired daughter did not like her in the least.

Lorelei mindlessly chewed at the inside of her cheek. It seemed fruitless to look upon a gentleman such as Max with such fondness when it was evident she would not be welcomed by at least one of his daughters. It was a conundrum, to be sure—one that she was not sure she wished to entertain. After all, it was not as though she had not grown used to the idea of spending her life as an independent lady. And yes, Lorelei had indeed decided to relinquish the dreadful title of spinster, for she did not feel it portrayed her nor any other lady in a very elegant light. However, despite her acceptance of what she believed to be her only future, she was rather baffled by her silly little heart, for at the somewhat inconvenient age of nine and twenty, it appeared to have awoken from its lazy slumber and begun to do funny things inside her chest whenever Max Lazenby was near or whenever he popped into her brain.

Lorelei groaned, then quickly diverted her attention to the new clothes in the boxes and bags, promising herself that she would try not to think about Max Lazenby until the charity ball. Besides, he may very well be a dreadful rakish lord and turn his attention to another, *younger* lady, and if that was indeed to be the case, then she would not set herself up for disappointment.

"Good evening, Mama." Lorelei kissed her mother on the cheek, then made her way around to the other side of the dining table and sat down in the seat she had always claimed as a child.

"So, you finally found some time for your mama, did you? Off out with your fancy friends, no doubt," Lady Whitworth muttered bitterly.

"Mama, I did tell you that I was meeting Lady Howell for luncheon today," Lorelei replied in a rather serious tone. "I had to visit the modiste too."

"No one has to visit the modiste, Lorelei," Lady Whitworth snapped.

"Well, on this occasion, I am afraid you are wrong, Mama, for I had an appointment with Evangeline."

Lady Whitworth pursed her lips, unable to protest yet still visibly seething. "Be that as it may, Lorelei, it is seven in the evening. You cannot tell me that you could not have visited me before now."

Lorelei sighed dramatically. It really was no use arguing with her mother when she was in such a terrible mood, so she refrained from responding. There was not a single word or sentence she could say that Lady

Whitworth would not have refuted. It was tiresome, and all Lorelei wanted to do was spend a little time with her mother and eventually go home and finally rest. She understood that her mother was lonely. If she hadn't, she would not have felt the need to visit every day, but there were times when she wished her mother did not feel the need to tweak and tug at her heartstrings with her tales of woe. The truth was that Lady Whitworth was surrounded by many servants, and she often visited or was visited by her friends, but despite that, she had the strange need to always keep Lorelei tied to her like she was still a little girl. Most mothers, Lorelei considered, were perhaps guilty of treating their young adult children like babies, but she was sure it was for an entirely different reason than that of her mother. Lady Whitworth treated Lorelei like a small child, not because she was worried about her daughter's welfare but because she did not want her daughter to have a life apart from her. Lorelei had spent her adult years constantly entwined in a dreadful state of guilt for not being the daughter she thought her mother wanted her to be. It was exhausting.

Lorelei ignored her mother and decided to change the topic of conversation. "I have been invited to a ball, Mama," she breathed, still feeling rather thrilled at the news. "Isn't that exciting?"

Lady Whitworth sniffed. "I suppose I won't see you that day either," she grumbled, shifting back on her seat as she began to cut her steak.

Lorelei was slowly losing her appetite, so she pushed her meal slightly away from her.

"It is a charity ball for Lady Howell's Orphanage, where I volunteer," she added, trying to lift the spirit of the conversation.

"Volunteer!" Lady Whitworth scoffed. "No wonder you are a spinster. A lady should not lower herself to do something so menial."

A bubble of fury burned in Lorelei's chest as it scraped against her breastbone. "Mama, volunteering for a worthy cause is not menial. It is an extremely worthwhile job. The children are wonderful, and it makes me happy to see them happy."

"You should have gotten yourself a husband. Perhaps I overfed you."

Lorelei stared at her mother in shock. "I beg your pardon, Mama?"

"Hard of hearing as well, I see," Lady Whitworth snapped.

Lorelei pushed the chair backwards with the back of her legs as she stood. "I am suddenly quite tired, Mama. If you will excuse me, I shall take my leave."

Lorelei did not know what she could possibly have said to her mother that would have satisfied the anger in her heart and mind without making her reel from guilt of her words later that evening once she had calmed down. She knew it would be better to simply make her excuses and leave. Lady Whitworth could be quite spiteful, but she hadn't always been that way. It was born out of grief for her father and for the years that had passed, lost to time. In some ways, she felt only sympathy for her mother, but that did not mean that she should have to endure such unkindness.

"Are you coming back tomorrow?" Lady Whitworth asked, a note of panic in her still bitter voice.

"Of course, Mama." Lorelei sighed as she placed a kiss on her mother's cheek.

Lady Whitworth nodded. She looked frail, Lorelei mused as a gentle ache pressed her heart. If her heart had its way, she would have stayed, but she was quite aware that she knew better than her heart on matters like this, for in the long run, she had to cut the conversation short before it spiralled out of control with words that may have cut deeper than what her mother had already pierced her with.

"Get some rest, Mama. I will see you tomorrow."

Lorelei took her leave, leaving only silence in her wake and a nod of understanding from the butler.

"You will send for me if my mother should need me, won't you, Jenkins?" Lorelei enquired beseechingly.

"Of course, m'lady, but, and I hope you do not mind me saying it, but your mother is stronger than she allows you to see, m'lady." Jenkins smiled apologetically.

Lorelei gently patted the gentleman's arm. "I do not mind you saying, Jenkins, for it is a relief to hear it. Thank you."

The butler nodded, stepping aside as Lorelei exited

her childhood home.

Chapter Eight

The blissful silence of the hallway as Lorelei stepped through the door of her home was as wonderfully soothing to her mind as a warm bath was to her body at the end of an exhausting day. The journey from her mother's house had been short but made rather noisy by the sounds of city life clamouring around her as well as her thoughts battling within her head. By the time she had reached the front door, she had become considerably resigned to the ways of her mother and simply pushed away any hurt she was feeling—her strength bolstered by the lies she disguised as excuses for her mother's unkindness. It was so much easier for Lorelei if she convinced herself that her mother merely lashed out at her because the lady was frightened of losing her daughter. After all, when Lady Whitworth had accused herself of feeding Lorelei too much, hinting at a fault with Lorelei's body shape and size, then the lady would have been insulting herself as well, for they were very similar in that respect. Surely it meant that she could not have meant it. None of it made sense to Lorelei, but then again, her mother rarely did, and she, herself, could not imagine ever treating her daughter the way Lady Whitworth apparently believed she could treat her. "Stop it," Lorelei whispered to herself as she began to lose her train of thought and thus her grip on everything that was beginning to make her feel a little better.

"Evening, m'lady," Florence whispered. "Is everything alright?"

"Good evening, Florence. Yes, thank you. I was simply woolgathering, nothing to fret about. Spending time with one's occasionally cruel mother seems to occupy one's mind even when one is not with her." Lorelei offered a tight-lipped smile as the maid gave her a look of sympathy. That look alone would have been enough to make a lady crumble into tears, she thought, as she swallowed an ache in her throat. But Lorelei was determined to divert her mind away from the very subject that, she deduced, dwelling upon did not benefit her in the slightest, and she was not about to defy herself of the little sense she possessed where Lady Whitworth was concerned.

"Would you mind terribly if I asked you to prepare a bath for me, please, Florence? I know it is later than usual, but I doubt I will be able to sleep if I do not try to relax somehow." Lorelei pulled at the fingers of her gloves, removing them from her person, then placed them in the palm of her left hand.

"I shall do that now for you, m'lady."

"Thank you, Florence. You are a rare diamond," Lorelei crooned softly as the maid hurried off to prepare

Lorelei's bath.

"I've put some lavender in, m'lady," Florence informed Lorelei as she poured in the last of the hot water. "My mother always says it helps a lady to relax, so I thought it might help you too."

"I can smell it, Florence. It smells wonderful. Thank you. Would you mind just unfastening me at the back, and then I shall leave you to your evening?" Lorelei turned her back to Florence so the maid could set about releasing her from her dress.

"There you are, m'lady. All done," Florence announced, stepping backward. "Is there anything else you need?"

"No, thank you, Florence."

As the door clicked shut, Lorelei dropped her gown to the floor, removed her undergarments, and then stepped into the bath. She sighed with pleasure as the warm water lapped her skin. The heady scent of lavender rose in whispers of steam, dampening her hair and kissing her skin with tiny fragranced droplets. She hadn't realised how much she had needed something so simple. It was wonderful, she mused, allowing the water to cradle her body.

Her mind slipped dreamily to the charity ball and her new gowns. She and her maid had mulled over her options as Florence helped her in and out of each one so that she could, as Florence had put it, give Lorelei her honest opinion. Despite the gowns all being rather splendid indeed, they both agreed she should wear the plum velvet one, and both were indeed a little in love with Evangeline's artistic talents.

Of course, her mind did not simply linger on the gown, for it carried her from her house to the very event where she would be wearing it as she pictured herself walking in amongst the guests. There would be people she most probably had not seen for a few years at such a prestigious event, and perhaps some she may have never met at all, but there was one gentleman in particular—one who most certainly would not be a guest but indeed the host of the ball. He kept rising in vivid images in her mind as she imagined him struck with awe at the very sight of her. It was fanciful and ridiculous, she admonished herself, and quite frankly, she thought, smiling gleefully at the memory of him, she should still be quite snippy towards the man for leaving her covered in filthy rainwater. Lorelei sighed. Who was she trying to fool? It had only taken a few minutes for him to win her over. She had told herself that it was because she could never manage to hold a grudge, but really, had it been anyone else, she knew she could have lasted at least another half an hour. The gentleman had the ability to crush any ill-feelings she may have had towards him simply with a glance from those pleasingly blue eyes of his and a word spoken with that rumbling voice she adored.

Lorelei lowered her body further into the bath, allowing the water to lift her hair and fan it out around her head. She was grumbling at the perilous future she was allowing her heart and hopes to lead her towards. She had already told herself that he would look for a younger bride, not one of her age. No gentleman wanted a spinster. It was an unsaid rule of the ton, and she was well aware of it, so then why was she even considering Maximilian Lazenby as anything more than a friend at most? It was her heart that beat faster for him, it was her stomach that fluttered when he so much as looked at her, and yet she did not have a single answer—well, at least one that was not quite so dangerous.

"You are still attending tonight, aren't you, Lorelei?" Lady Howell questioned as Lorelei placed her hand on the doorknob of the orphanage office.

"I will be, Lady Howell," she replied gracefully.

"That is good. I have a feeling Lord Lazenby may be a little disappointed if you do not." Lady Howell pinched her lips together and gave Lorelei a stifled yet rather mischievous smile.

Lorelei could feel the heat of embarrassment crawl up the back of her neck. "Oh?"

"Yes, indeed. He keeps mentioning you. The strange thing is that I do not believe he even realises he is doing it." Lady Howell's eyes were twinkling as though she may have been plotting some maniacal scheme that Lorelei was very much the victim of.

"It is probably simply because he knows that I volunteer here," Lorelei responded, feeling quite satisfied with her reply.

"Perhaps," Lady Howell replied thoughtfully. "Although I can't say anybody else who knows you work here talks quite so often and animatedly about you." Lady Howell frowned. "Oh, heavens. That probably didn't sound quite how I meant it. What I meant was-"

Lorelei held up her hand. "Please do not fret; I am well aware in what way you meant it, and I have to object to the insinuation that he thinks so highly of me, for Lord Lazenby, I should imagine, is quite a powerful man and can have his choice of any unmarried lady of the ton. I hardly think he would settle for a spinster such as myself when there will be young ladies who would be more than willing to marry him."

"And, Lady Lorelei Whitworth," Lady Howell began, "if, for example, he did choose you, what then?"

"That is not even worth answering, Lady Howell, for it will never happen."

Lady Howell studied Lorelei's face. She had previously thought that the young lady may have liked Lord Lazenby, but now she was utterly positive. "Humour me, Lorelei, please," she requested kindly.

Lorelei looked down at her feet, wondering why the conversation was so terribly difficult. She thought that maybe if she stared at the floor for long enough, then the ground would open up and swallow her, but alas, it did not. However, she pondered, there was no shame in liking the man, even if he didn't think of her that way, nor was there any shame to even consider that one day she would have liked to have been Lady Lazenby, even though she knew that that idea was utterly inconceivable.

Lorelei inhaled, closing her eyes for fear that they would betray her by revealing just how shattered her confidence had become where matters of the heart were concerned. "If I were a debutante and Lord Lazenby wished to court me, then I would have considered myself very lucky indeed," she stated, letting out the breath she had been holding back with her fear.

Lorelei's admission of what her heart desired—despite her belief that the organ in her chest would be sorely disappointed—had thrown her somewhat off-guard, but then she realised it was because she had spent so much time resigning herself to a future alone that she had never even allowed herself to picture the possibility of a marriage in her future. She was answering the question that she had not even allowed herself to contemplate with anyone. When the seasons had come and gone, she knew she had to protect herself, to protect her heart, yet there she was at nine and twenty, forcing back the flood gates of possibility because of one single man... Max. She was terrified.

Lady Howell was frowning at her. "You do know that you are a very beautiful woman, don't you, Lorelei?" Lady Howell sighed. "Although, by the way in which you stand there, unable to even open your eyes, so that I may not see what lurks behind them, I do not believe you have heard those words very often, if at all."

Lorelei ground her teeth together as the ache in her throat magnified. She tried to stop it, but the tear welling in her eye seized its moment, breaking free and trickling down the side of her nose, following the contours of her face until it rested at the corner of her mouth. "I do not love him," she rasped. "But I cannot say that I do not think highly of him."

"Open your eyes, Lorelei," Lady Howell pleaded. "I shall fetch some tea, and perhaps we can talk."

Lorelei nodded, slowly opening her eyes, and walked back towards the desk, taking a seat in the chair opposite Lady Howell. "I do apologise, for I do not know what has come over me," she offered, a little embarrassed by her performance.

"You have no need to apologise, Lorelei," Lady Howell soothed, pouring them both a cup of tea. "If I had thought my asking you about Lord Lazenby would have upset you so, I would not have breathed a word, but I do want you to know that I was not lying, for Lord Lazenby appears quite enamoured with you."

The teacup and saucer rattled as she took it from Lady Howell's hands. "Thank you," she whispered, delighting at the proffered cup of tea. "Truth be told, it would not have taken much to have made me fall apart this morning."

"Would you like to talk about it, dear?"

"There really isn't much to tell other than my mother has quite a wicked tongue. It can wear one down over the years, especially when she is forever trying to convince me that I am on par with her and her friends." Lorelei did not mention her mother's comment about her body.

Lady Howell looked positively aghast at hearing the news of Lady Whitworth's suggestion that her daughter was considered a lady of a rather mature age. "If I am correct, I assume that your mother made the ludicrous suggestion that you would never be chosen for marriage?"

Lorelei nodded.

Lady Howell snorted. "Preposterous!" she trilled angrily. "You are to forget your mother ever even suggested such a thing because it was a lie and rather wicked one too."

Loyalty to her mother twisted in Lorelei's chest as she remembered the mother who she knew as a little girl. "She wasn't always like this," she said quietly. "I think she is scared that she will lose me now that she has lost my father."

Lady Howell sat back in her chair and lowered her teacup onto the desk in front of her. "Perhaps, but either way, Lorelei, it was not kind of her to say such a terrible thing to you... to her own daughter, no less. I am most likely overstepping by saying this about the older Lady Whitworth, but I cannot bear to see you so broken. Even if you and Lord Lazenby may not be suited, I am quite certain that there is a gentleman out there who would walk over burning coals to marry a lady as wonderful as you."

Lorelei was positively pink as she listened to the compliments pour from her friend's lips. "Thank you," she replied. "That is most kind."

"Do not take my words as anything less than truth, my dear Lorelei."

Both ladies sat quietly for what felt like a terribly long time, Lorelei thought, as she finished her tea.

"Would you like me to send a carriage for you this evening?" Lady Howell enquired, breaking the silence, for which Lorelei was extremely grateful.

"Oh, if you are sure, you do not mind, then that would be lovely. Thank you," Lorelei responded happily. Her shoulders felt lighter, and somehow, she felt freer after airing her previous thoughts to the lady opposite her.

"It would be my absolute pleasure, and, of course, it will mean that I can be certain of your attendance. Say eight o'clock?"

"That would be perfect. Thank you, Lady Howell."

"You, my dear girl, are most welcome indeed."

"M'lady!"

Florence knocked profusely on the door of Lorelei's bedchamber as Lorelei took one last glance at her reflection in the looking glass.

"Come in, Florence," Lorelei called.

"Oh, m'lady," the maid gasped as she looked at her through the reflection. "You look like a... a... I was going to say queen, but I don't think that would even be good enough. I'm in awe, m'lady."

Lorelei chuckled at her maid's reaction. "Thank you, Florence. Even without finding the words you were looking for, you have made me feel rather lovely indeed."

"The carriage is here, m'lady," Florence announced, remembering the reason she had ventured up to her mistress's room. "Shall I tell them you are ready?"

"Yes, please, Florence. If I am not ready now, I am not certain that I shall ever be."

The maid frowned, then quickly smiled. "I'll let them know, m'lady."

Lorelei chuckled to herself as she slipped her matching cloak over her shoulders and followed Florence down the stairs. Anyone would have thought it was her wedding day, what with the swarm of butterflies that appeared to have taken flight inside her stomach, she thought. *What a silly lady, you are Lorelei Whitworth*, she quietly chided herself.

Chapter Nine

Ava sauntered into the parlour to find Max leaning against the fireplace, his crisp white shirt taut over the muscles of his back, mimicking the tension within his body as he appeared to be quietly contemplating something whilst gazing into the hearth.

"Penny for them?" she enquired, quickly taking up a seat that would give her a good view of her brother, simply so she would not be able to miss even a fraction of a twitch on the man's face.

"My musings are worth far more than a penny, dear sister, and I do not believe you could afford them." He grinned. "Besides, why so interested?" he asked.

"Well, I wondered whether you had a certain Lady Lorelei on your mind as it is the ball this evening, is it not?" she retorted, feeling quite satisfied that she had not allowed her brother to make her stumble over her own words, as he so often seemed to rather enjoy.

"She had crossed my mind once or twice," he admitted. "Speaking of Lady Lorelei, has Cassandra mentioned anything of her and the somewhat painfully awkward situation of the utter contempt she has for the poor lady?"

"Well, she hasn't openly admitted it to me. I should imagine that jealousy is not something one cares to confess to."

"That is certainly true." Max walked over to the small table and popped the cork off a bottle of expensive champagne."

"Max," Ava exclaimed. "That is supposed to be for the ball, not now."

Max chuckled. "Oh, so you do not want any then?" he queried, holding the bottle briefly up in the air. "Oh, well. I suppose I shall have to drink it all by myself then," he crooned, feigning a terrible hardship at the prospect.

"I didn't say that," she grumbled playfully. Ava stood and grabbed two glasses from another table and handed them to Max. "If we are going to behave like naughty children, we may as well do it properly, so I believe we will need to dirty these two polished champagne flutes as well," she added, grinning mischievously.

"What a bad influence you are, dear sister."

The champagne bubbles popped on Maximilian's top lip as he took a sip. "I do hope she will attend," he remarked, returning to the matter of Lorelei. "I won't regret the event either way, of course, for it is for a very good cause, but the fact still remains that I would very much rather Lady Lorelei were here."

"What will you do if she is not?" Ava queried, keeping her eyes fixed on him. She couldn't help but hope her brother would not give up on the lady. From the moment he had said her name, and she had observed how his eyes sparkled at the memory of her, she knew this was different for Max. Even when he had married, it had never been for love, but that look he had when he had spoken of Lorelei had told her that her brother could very easily fall in love with the lady, and it would be a terrible shame if he allowed her to slip through his fingers.

"I suppose that I shall have to pay her a visit." Max inhaled deeply, placing the empty glass on the table. "But for now, I have a few more matters to tend to, then I shall get myself ready for the ball," he announced.

"Yes, I shall have to do the same," Ava declared happily. "And do not fret about Cassie. I will keep an eye on her. Hopefully, we will find a match for her tonight."

"Let us just pray that she can refrain from scowling," Max retorted. "It turns her whole demeanour quite sour." Max sighed with obvious exasperation and a touch of irritability.

"Hmm, that may be a bit tricky, but between Katie and I, we shall do our very best, dear brother."

"That is all I ask, Ava. It is all anyone can ask."

Max placed his large fingers over the top of his cravat and gave it a tug. The apprehension of the evening ahead had gripped him quite dramatically, making every item of clothing verging slightly on the side of uncomfortable, which was not helping his mood in the slightest. He did not think there was anything that could relieve him of the Cassandra-shaped, thunderous cloud over his head other than, of course, if the girl found some manners and decided to act upon them. Although he was quite sure that the sight of a raven-haired lady by the name of Lorelei could quite easily dispel the tension from his body.

"I need to get some air," he grumbled, ripping the cravat away from his throat. "I simply cannot be bothered with this wretched thing." Max had begun to realise that his temper flared not only from Cassandra's poor behaviour but a dread that he would not see Lorelei. He could not understand how he had gone from being unmoved by anyone at any time in his life to being utterly shaken to the core with desire and something quite indescribable for the lady. He had never expected such emotions to grab hold of him at any age, especially at forty-five. However, be that as it may, he could not deny them any more than he could be rid of them.

When Max had reached the age of two and twenty, he found himself quite detached from the possibility of a love match, hardened by the firm belief that he was not capable of such emotions as love for a wife. It seemed rather all too fanciful, and only that which existed within fairy tales rather than real life. Every lady he had met on the marriage mart never conjured any feeling anywhere near what he was experiencing in the present. Of course, it was not as though he did not look at the feminine form and admire its beauty, but it was always short-lived. The longest period of time that he believed he kept any attraction alive was with the late Lady Henrietta Lazenby, but he knew neither of them were joined in matrimony out of some incredible love for one another. It was all a little cold and uncaring, he thought, recollecting the business-like transaction of their marriage. He shuddered at the truth. *Why had he not seen it all those years ago?* Such thoughts led to a rather eye-opening conclusion as to why Henrietta had sought love in another.

Max recollected the years he had spent tasting the acidic burn of Henrietta's betrayal of their marriage, his memory forming a bubble of regret that he had not seen what he was now convinced had been the truth all along. He had not even considered that she may have had such feelings for the other gentleman as he was having now for Lorelei. *How could he have when he had not been aware that they had even existed?* Perhaps his late wife's spite was born out of his lack of understanding, he pondered heavily.

Max was never a cruel husband, but he could not deny that he was not the husband to Henrietta that she may have needed him to be, nor in the way she may have wished. He had failed her in matters of the heart and scolded her unjustly when she eventually found what she had been looking for. *"I'm so sorry, Henrietta,"* he whispered into the darkness, gradually pooling around him. *"I have understood you too late."*

Max continued walking as the air stroked his skin with its cool touch—thick, smooth ribbons of wind curling around him. It was wonderful, he thought, allowing himself to simply close his eyes and let the strong breeze ruffle the mop of black hair atop his head. It was uncanny how something so terribly simple could seem priceless when one took the time to pay attention to it, he mused.

He sighed as the air seemed to rush towards him, dragging away all that troubled him as it whipped by with thief-like hands. The heavy ache of regret lifted from his body, allowing him the time to contemplate whether to wait for Lady Lorelei on the steps of Hawthorne House or venture back inside. He supposed it would not do for the host of the event to lurk in the shadows like an intruder rather than greet his guests, he considered, running his hands through his hair, then swiftly turned on his heel and headed inside to attempt that dratted cravat of his and wait.

"Oh, Papa, everything looks absolutely splendid. I expect Lady Howell will be most pleased," Katie sang as she rushed past Max at a running speed, gliding in her satin slippers across the polished floor of the ballroom and began to spin.

"Do be careful, Katie," Ava implored. "You could slip and hurt yourself." Ava followed her niece as her eyes swept across the room in awe. "Oh, my," she gasped.

"Yes, they have decorated rather splendidly, haven't they?" Max remarked, following the trail of his sister's eyes with his own, stopping only when he realised that he had not seen Cassandra. "Where is my other daughter?" he enquired.

"I am here, Papa."

Cassie entered the hall with a fraction more poise than her sister, yet somehow it made her appear rather more prickly than prim. Max placed an arm over the shoulders of both his daughters and pulled them in towards him in a fatherly embrace. "You both look beautiful in your new gowns," he whispered, placing a single kiss on top of their heads successively.

Katie returned her father's affection with a smile and a quick squeeze as she tightened her arms around her father's waist. "Thank you, Papa," she beamed. "And you look rather dashing in your suit."

Max chortled as his youngest daughter's happiness filled him with merriment. "Why thank you, young lady," he replied with a gentle bow.

Cassie seemed to have frozen to the spot. She had been that way from the moment Max had curled his arm around her. He noted the way her lips were strained into a poor attempt at a smile and the anger glinting in her eye like the edge of a knife blade. Max did not know whether to enquire as to her well-being. In truth, he was a trifle afraid of the response she would have given him.

Instead, he looked to his sister for silent advice, which was a simple yet definite shake of her head, warning him that he should only ask if he had very little care for his own life. Max ground his teeth together as annoyance began to ball in his chest, growing with fervour as it began to spin.

Ava cleared her throat, snapping the tension in two and Max out of his downward spiralling mood. "And what about your favourite sister?" she hinted playfully. "Do I pass muster for your grand charity ball?"

Max smiled, relieved for his sister's wonderful wit, as he walked up to her, raised her hand up, lengthening her arm, and forced her to twirl beneath his whilst gazing at her attire with approval. "Radiant as ever, dear Ava."

"Why, thank you, my lord." Ava bobbed a quick curtsey, then gestured to the door. "I believe your guests await."

Lord and Lady Howell were the first to arrive, which was a surprising relief to Max. The sudden influx of guests had left him speechless and a little overwhelmed. Of course, he knew the guest list was considerably lengthy, but never did he expect them all to attend. He feared he may have underestimated the allure of a London ball. Lady Howell had always taken quite naturally to meeting and greeting whether she knew the person or not, but Max was perhaps a little more reserved when there was a crowd such as the one practically hurtling towards him. However, he had opted to be the host for this event, he reminded himself, and that meant that perhaps he should really pay more attention rather than scanning the faces of the *ton* for Lady Lorelei.

There was, of course, Max's rather clever idea that allowed him to do both. He was rather pleased with himself at conjuring such a fine plan. The entrance via the stairs had been a last-minute tweak to the ball arrangements, with Max excusing the sudden change as a simply wonderful addition that would make the event seem far more prestigious. But the truth was simple: Max wanted to know the very moment Lorelei arrived. He could not bear the idea that he could possibly miss her. He had even instructed the butler to announce the arrival of every guest as they began their descent down the marble stairs, adding to his instructions with determined specificity that the man did not forget the ladies.

Max absentmindedly straightened his jacket as he simply continued to watch.

"This is absolutely marvellous, Lord Lazenby," Lady Howell exclaimed as she stood at his side trying to gauge what the man was looking for. "Are you looking for anyone in particular?"

"Good evening, Lady Howell. No, nobody in particular. I am simply trying to keep a mental note of those who have arrived and those who have yet to arrive." Max rocked on the heels of his polished shoes, trying, quite unsuccessfully, to hide the discomfort of telling a lie.

"Not even Lady Lorelei?" she enquired, raising her eyebrows in a teasing accusation.

Max could feel the burn of her curiosity on the side of his face as she studied him, so he turned to look at her, hoping he could deny what she evidently could see. "I-I..."

"*Lady Lorelei Whitworth,*" a loud, booming voice announced, interrupting Max.

Max turned his face abruptly back towards the stairs. The rush of blood in his ears as he gazed at the raven-haired beauty sauntering down the stairs had diminished the chatter of the ton to nothing more than slight, inconsequential murmurings. The beat of his heart thumped over the flurry of gossip and greetings as his body ached to be near her.

Max thought she looked devastatingly enchanting as the light from the overhead chandeliers skimmed over her tresses. The ribbons of her obsidian hair were kissed with a delicate, shimmering red as her dusky pink lips curled into a smile. She wore small circular diamonds, twinkling like stars upon her ears, but it was her green eyes that truly sparkled, stealing his breath as they settled on his.

Max's tongue felt terribly dry as he took in her radiance, mustering a rather lovesick, lopsided grin that, if any fool had observed, would have informed them of how Max's stomach had suddenly tightened around the most strange but wonderful feeling he had ever known.

His eyes roved over her where his hands could not, drinking every inch of her in, yet even though it may have appeared somewhat inappropriate, he could not tear his eyes away from her. Lady Lorelei was dressed in an exquisite plum velvet gown with a neckline that settled just off her shoulders and plunged delicately at the centre of her breasts. It was rather elegantly done, he noted as his gaze caressed the peachy-white display of decolletage, his eyes whispering across her skin until they met the diamond teardrop pendant, resting teasingly above the sweet, kissable line that trailed beneath the fabric.

The velvet of her gown cinched in just so at her waist and flowed over her shapely hips in a waterfall of opulence. There were no other ways to describe the lady before him other than as a goddess. Lady Lorelei Whitworth was intoxicating and utterly divine.

"Are you quite sure, Lord Lazenby?"

Max had quite forgotten that there were other people in the room. "Pardon?"

Lady Howell laughed. "Go to her, Lord Lazenby. Do not leave her on her own, for she is quite the belle of the ball."

Max did not need to be encouraged. He simply nodded and walked determinedly through the crowd towards her.

Chapter Ten

Lorelei tried desperately to still the tremble in her legs as she inched toward the top of the stairs. She had been momentarily struck with fear when she had seen the way in which every member of the *ton* was required to make his or her entrance. Had it not been for her dedication to the orphanage and the unexplainable desire to lay eyes upon Maximilian Lazenby, she would have simply made her excuses and left.

As the butler announced her presence, Lorelei inhaled deeply, silently admonishing herself for being so nervous. She focused her eyes down toward the very centre of the room only to find that they fell directly upon Max. His piercing blue eyes were focused solely on her, inciting her heart to repeat the funny little dance it had participated in at the garden party. Maximilian Lazenby was incredibly handsome, she thought, sighing, feeling rather tingly all over as he slowly perused her entire being. It was positively scandalous how her body had instantaneously reacted to him, she thought, not daring to look around her in case it had been obvious to anyone else but her. *'Just keep moving, Lorelei,'* her mind encouraged.

The ambience of the ballroom was as rich and warm as golden honey, with the ethereal appearance of glittering chandeliers overhead. Plump, white roses filled tall and short vases and lay at the feet of candelabras, platters, and bowls. Max had brought the beauty of a garden in summer into his home, and although she could not quite tear her eyes away from the man who awaited her to pay the décor such meticulous attention—the attention she knew it deserved—Lorelei still thought it magical to behold.

Lorelei took a breath as she descended the final step of the grand staircase, giving herself a few moments to regain her composure. It had been rather daunting to be on display, she mused, but as she looked up, readying herself to move towards the gentleman who she knew was waiting for her, she did not have to move an inch, for he was right there in front of her.

"Lady Lorelei," Max's voice rumbled. "May I just say that you look utterly divine this evening."

"Thank you, Max, as do you. Handsome, I mean." Lorelei groaned at her sudden need to tell the godlike man that he looked handsome.

Max grinned and kissed the back of her hand tenderly.

"Papa, Lady Whitworth." Cassandra was practically pinned to her father's side, her gaze raking over Lorelei with considerable venom.

"Cassandra Lazenby." Max uttered the blonde young lady's name with considerable warning.

Cassandra smiled sweetly, then pinned her attention upon Lorelei as she pursed her lips. "I apologise for the interruption, Lady Whitworth," she hissed. "It is simply that I must introduce Papa to one of the most wonderful ladies I know. She is quite the belle of the ball."

Lorelei did not miss the narrowing of the young lady's eyes nor the way her grip tightened around her father's muscular arm.

"Cassandra, whomever it is you are referring to, they can wait, for I have just requested this dance with Lady Lorelei," Max drawled, an even glare fixed on his daughter.

"But Papa, she is the most beautiful lady here," Cassandra insisted, panic seeping into her voice.

"On that matter, Cassandra Lazenby, you are, without a doubt, utterly incorrect because I am about to dance with the most beautiful lady here. Please excuse us." Max grasped Lorelei's fingers and weaved her arm through his as he led her towards the dance floor. He was exceedingly gentle, Lorelei thought, despite his frustration at his daughter's unkind attitude that evidently tensed the muscles in his jaw as he bit down, locking the words he wanted to say behind the cage of his teeth.

Lorelei watched him as he closed his eyes and focused simply on breathing, pulling her in towards his body as the music began to play.

"Please forgive my eldest daughter, Lorelei," he

pleaded. "She has been rather difficult to deal with for quite some time."

There was an obvious anguish in his eyes that Lorelei longed to erase. "Oh, it is as I have said before, Max, she cannot be as bad as my mother," she offered.

Max opened his eyes, gazing down at her as she bit her bottom lip, trying to suppress a random giggle incited purely by the nerves she felt in his embrace.

"How do you do it?" Max asked.

She could feel the warmth of his large hand on her back and the comfort of his other curled around her dainty fingers. "What is it that I do?" she queried because she was feeling quite confused as to what it was that he was referring to.

"Smile even when it was extremely obvious that my daughter was unforgivably rude to you."

"Believe me, Max, when one has spent many years dealing with the wrath of the elder Lady Whitworth's tongue, your daughter is an utter darling," she sang.

Lorelei was far too content with being held in Max's arms to even worry about what his daughter was trying to do. Although, she considered, she had to wonder why she had become the young lady's target.

Lorelei missed her step. "Oops. Sorry," she offered, blushing. "It appears that I am out of practise." Thinking, she decided, was not a good idea whilst one was trying to dance.

After speaking with Lady Howell earlier in the day, she had quickly decided that she was not going to let her mother nor anyone else make her feel as terrible as they so obviously wished to, but, on reflection, she realised that she had not accounted for the words from Cassandra Lazenby's lips.

"What are you thinking about?" Max asked, ignoring the slight error in her footing.

"Just how lovely it is here," she lied. "It looks rather formidable."

"It complements your beauty, Lorelei." Max leaned forward, his forehead resting gently upon hers.

"I don't... I don't think..."

"Shhh," he whispered, secretly brushing his lips over hers. "You, Lorelei, are the belle of the ball despite what my daughter would try to have you think."

The burn of Lorelei's blush was quickly swept away by a pleasurable shiver that shimmered over her upper body. His touch had rendered her speechless.

"Perhaps this is not the place for one to be so forward," Max said, apologetically, "but I have been searching for you for quite some time, Lady Lorelei, and without any success, I might add."

Max smiled wolfishly, his eyes revealing his undeniable desire. Lorelei found herself wondering what it was that she revealed to him when he looked in her eyes. She hoped he would see that she felt safe with him, as though she would quite happily remain curled in his arms for eternity if he would permit it. The heat and strength of his body seemed to nurse her vulnerability into a state of non-existence, for he defied everything unkind anyone had ever said to her or made her feel.

Something cold splashed over Lorelei's bare shoulders, snatching her and Max away from the moment.

"Oh, terribly sorry, Lady Whitworth," Cassandra crooned. "I thought I would bring you some champagne because you both appeared to be finding this heat rather too much."

Max's body tensed as his arms remained around Lorelei, his burning glare fixed on Cassandra with considerable fury, yet despite this, Lorelei knew she had handled ladies like Cassandra before. She had seen firsthand their attempts to embarrass and ridicule one another as she had watched helplessly from the sidelines. "Oh, please don't worry," she offered sweetly, ignoring the intent of Cassandra's actions. "It is only a little splash, and it was very kind of you to think of us."

Lorelei brought Max's feelings to the forefront of her mind, allowing her to muster a genuine, warm smile at the young lady. She may not have been willing to play Cassandra's game, but she was quite willing to play her own. And there it was, the first sign of her success, for Cassandra was positively seething, gritting her teeth as she attempted a smile of her own. Lorelei could not understand why she was so intent on coming between her father and any possible future happiness. Although, she considered sadly, Cassandra had tried to introduce Max to another lady earlier, so perhaps she simply did not like Lorelei.

"I shall just go and clean up," Lorelei muttered, unfurling her body from the comfort of Max's arms as she left him standing alone on the dance floor with his eldest daughter.

The evening continued in a very similar pattern until Lorelei found herself avoiding Max altogether as she tucked herself away in the library, legs curled beneath her in a chair as she opened a book and settled down to read. She supposed she could quite easily have requested her carriage and taken her leave, but it was peace she required more than escaping the ball entirely, and she really didn't want to let Lady Howell down nor Max.

'Ah, Max,' she sighed to herself. The gentleman's daughter was a conundrum, to be sure. She wondered whether Cassandra had managed to convince him to dance with the lady she so obviously preferred for her father.

Lorelei rubbed the centre of her chest with her knuckles. The sudden onset of pinching caught her by surprise. She shook her head. Max was far too splendid a gentleman. She had to consider that perhaps Cassandra was correct by taking the upper hand in choosing a match for her father. Lorelei knew Max was too good for her. *Hadn't everyone always told her so? Hadn't they been reminding her of her worth or lack thereof?* Perhaps she was a fool to even hope for someone such as Max.

The image of his dark hair and blue eyes had etched itself firmly in her mind. The sea green silk cravat he was wearing looked dashing with his dark suit wrapped around his broad frame. Perhaps that image alone would have to suffice, she decided. After all, she did not want to be the one to drive a divide between a father and his daughter.

"Hello."

Standing at the door was a replica of Max's youngest daughter, Katie, but Lorelei knew it wasn't her because the woman must have been at least two decades older. "Hello," she replied meekly, quickly uncurling her body and legs to stand and greet the lady properly.

"Please do not stand on my account, Lady Lorelei. It is Lady Lorelei, isn't it?" she asked, walking further into the room.

Lorelei nodded. "Yes, but please, you may call me Lorelei or Lori, whichever you prefer."

"Thank you. My name is Ava. I am Max's sister. I believe you have met Max?" she queried.

Lorelei swallowed. She did not know what she would do if Max's sister had come to confirm Cassandra's sentiments. "It is a pleasure to meet you, Ava." Lorelei's voice had lost its even tone, replaced with a version that revealed the anxiety rippling through her blood. She could not even look at Ava.

"I watched you sneak out of the ball, and although Max is looking for you, I know when a lady requires some time alone, so I did not tell him where you were," Ava explained, walking closer and depositing herself in the seat opposite Lorelei.

Lorelei could feel the strength of Ava's gaze upon her, yet she did not have the courage to return it.

"I must tell you that I have never seen my brother taken with a lady as he is with you. Not even with the mother of his daughters."

Lorelei grimaced. "I'm sorry," she muttered. She didn't know why she was apologising. It seemed ludicrous to apologise for it.

Ava giggled.

She wasn't ridiculing her, Lorelei realised, as she found the strength to raise her head. The lady's face was filled with kindness and compassion.

"Please do not apologise for bringing a smile to my brother's face. Do you know how long I have waited to see that smile on his face?"

Lorelei shook her head.

"Forever, I tell you. I had started to believe that I may have had to haunt him from the grave merely to get a glimpse."

A giggle bubbled up from inside of Lorelei. She liked Ava a great deal. "Well, I am glad to have been of service, Ava," she replied playfully whilst grinning. "Although," she added, "I do not believe Cassandra is quite so thrilled."

"Indeed," Ava murmured. "She has become quite the handful since her first season. I do not think she would be happy if her father married anyone, so please do not take it to heart."

"But what about the lady she was trying to get him to dance with when I first arrived?" Lorelei questioned.

"There was no lady. In fact, she has been stepping between her father and any lady who steps even within a mile of him." Ava sighed and shook her head vigorously. "If she is the reason you are hiding in here, then may I suggest you return with me? I will make sure she is on her best behaviour, and I know a gentleman who will be thrilled to have your company."

Slowly gathering her thoughts, Lorelei conceded with a nod of her head. "If you are sure I will not cause any upset, I will return with you."

"Wonderful, and no, you will not cause any upset, Lorelei. Sadly, I believe Cassandra's issues do not lie with any particular person but more so that she requires a romance of her own. She hasn't admitted it, and I highly doubt she will, but she didn't have much success last season, and I believe she is rather afraid that she will never marry. Of course, it is not helping that she is witnessing her sister, Katie, embrace it with a splendid vigour."

"And her father."

"Well, that may be the case, but I would not ask Katie to put her happiness on hold, and so I certainly would not ask you or Max to. If Cassandra diverted her attention away from what others were doing, I believe she may realise that there has been a certain set of eyes upon her all evening. He looks positively smitten."

Lorelei raised her eyebrows. She suddenly had a desire to help this troubled young lady. She knew all too well what it was like to feel the intensity of the marriage mart and supposed it could very well make one bitter. "Perhaps we could help her?" she offered.

"I knew I liked you, Lady Lorelei. Just like your name, you are utterly splendid."

Chapter Eleven

Lorelei sauntered back into the ballroom, looking rather less flustered than she had been when he had last laid eyes upon her. She was obviously not a lady who spoke without thinking, Maximilian Lazenby mused, for if she had been, he knew that Cassandra would not have been looking quite as composed as she had when Lorelei made her hasty escape. Max growled silently, disgruntled at his eldest daughter's despicable behaviour. He had hoped that Ava would have been able to make the girl curb her tongue and her spiteful antics, yet it did not appear to be the case because she was making Lorelei's evening an absolute nightmare.

Giving his head a shake, Max pushed politely through the crowd to greet Lorelei. "We thought we had lost you, Lady Lorelei," he smiled, offering her his arm.

"No, I believe it was *you* who thought you had lost her," Ava interjected.

Max grinned, unable to contain the chuckle at the truth of his sister's words. "Indeed," he replied. Max observed the way in which Lorelei bit her bottom lip and blushed. Whatever he was feeling was evidently reciprocated, and it thrilled him to his core.

"Not at all," Lorelei replied. "I simply needed a little quiet, that was all. It is rather crowded in here, do you not think?"

Max nodded. From the corner of his eye, he noted the familiar figures of his daughters gliding towards them. "Would you like to take a turn about the ballroom?" he enquired, brushing a kiss over the back of Lorelei's bare hand. "I fear we may be crushed if we simply stand here."

"Yes, of course, Max. That would be splendid, but perhaps we may walk towards Katie and Cassandra, for I believe they are indeed walking towards us," Lorelei suggested kindly.

"After what my eldest daughter has put you through this evening, Lorelei, I am not entirely certain that I wish to speak with her right now," he replied with honesty, closing his eyes briefly in obvious regret and perhaps a little embarrassment of the situation.

"I do not think she means to be this way, Max," Lorelei soothed. "There is hurt in her eyes when she does it."

Lorelei's willingness to try to understand Cassandra hit Max pleasantly by surprise. It only added to the warmth she infused within his chest.

"Let us see if I cannot win her round, Max. I would hate to have to be your most hated friend."

Max wondered how she did not know that she was becoming far more than simply a friend to him. In fact, he recalled, he had never truly seen her as merely a friend. It was alarming in some respects, yet, unless she told him that she did not want him, he did not wish to change any of it. However, with Cassandra almost within talking distance, it really was not the time nor place to declare his intentions towards her.

"Lady Lorelei," Katie beamed. "I am so happy to see you again. I believe we met at the garden party." The young lady did not bother curtseying yet leaned in and embraced Lorelei in a warm and welcoming hug.

'At least one of my daughters is being kind to her,' Max thought, smiling in their direction.

"It is wonderful to see you again, Katie," Lorelei replied. "I trust you are enjoying the ball?"

"Oh, yes, thank you. My dance card is quite full." The youngest Lazenby daughter was grinning with sheer excitement whilst waving her dance card about for emphasis.

Max observed as Katie's excitement passed between the two ladies, watching the way in which Lorelei's broad smile lit up her face and made her eyes sparkle with genuine happiness for his youngest daughter.

Max curled his arm protectively and somewhat possessively around Lorelei's waist, pulling her a little closer and resting his warm hand upon her hip. Perhaps he should not have assumed he could, for he had not even requested to court her as yet, but they had, he admitted to himself, fallen into a comfortable, unspoken relationship. As if in response to his mental meanderings, Lorelei placed her hand over his. He felt the brush of her soft skin as her fingers glided between each of his. Their hands were like two parts of a whole, he thought, as he tightened his grasp in response, his body growing taut with his sudden hunger for her touch.

Max gave her hip a gentle squeeze in happy recognition. He had never known anything so natural as what it was that he was experiencing with the woman at his side. It was as though he had finally found the other half of him—the very half he hadn't even realised he had been searching for.

"Lady Lorelei." Cassandra stepped forward. Her eyes flicking from her father and Lorelei's entwined hands to Max and then to Lorelei. Her eyes narrowed as they paused on Lorelei's face, deepening into a scowl. "I thought you had gone home," she stated abruptly. A sickly smile strained the colour from her lips as she tried to cover her malice.

Lorelei smiled sweetly, tightening her grip on Max. "Not yet. Tell me, Cassandra, did you and Katie help your father arrange all of this?"

Cassandra's brows pinched into a v as she tried in vain to weigh up where Lorelei was leading the conversation. It was obvious she had expected a sour response that would set Lorelei in a bad light and was currently sorely disappointed or perhaps extremely confused. Max could almost see his daughter's mind struggling for a scathing response.

Lorelei evidently did not want to wait for the

young lady's words to burn her, so she simply continued with considerable hope etched on her face that she may enlighten Cassandra of the true intent of her words rather than give her ample time to make any dreadful assumptions. "I suppose you must have, for there is a wonderful feminine touch to the décor. It really is splendid, and the orphanage is very grateful, of that, I am sure."

Max bit his lip as Cassandra stood silent. Lorelei was a clever little minx, he thought proudly. He had never known anyone to leave his daughter speechless. Of course, he knew it wouldn't last very long. The colour was already rising on Cassandra's face. She was furious that the lady before her was so obviously kind—kind enough to not mention the wicked things she had said and done to her.

"What about the champagne on your gown?" Cassandra sniffed. "One would have thought a lady would want to look presentable at such an occasion, yet you have simply ignored it."

Max stiffened at Lorelei's side, ready to reprimand the spoilt child his daughter was behaving as, but he was stopped in a silent, reassuring stroke of Lorelei's thumb on the side of his hand.

"This?" she enquired, referring to the slightly dampened and darker patch on the fabric that touched her shoulder.

"Yes... *that*," Cassandra bit off. "It is most unbecoming."

'That's it,' Max thought, preparing himself to discreetly haul his daughter from the ball, or perhaps he would simply haul Lorelei away so they could be alone.

Lorelei was chuckling. He couldn't believe his eyes. "Oh, heavens. I do apologise, Cassandra," she said, her eyes twinkling. "I am not laughing at you, I promise. You see, I have simply lost count of the times I have had something spilled on me when volunteering at the orphanage. I can assure you that champagne is far the most pleasant of all."

Cassandra curled her lips into a smile, which, Max thought happily, appeared quite genuine. His heart lightened at the hope that his eldest daughter was softening towards Lorelei, but then the light in her face switched off, turning her expression sour.

"I could never work with children," Cassandra spat, even though she knew it was a dreadful lie. "I can't bear them, nor anyone who works with them!" Cassandra turned, her face paling at the sight of her father's glare and the shocked amusement on Lady Howell's face, then hastily pushed through the crowd until she had disappeared.

"I am so sorry, Max," Lorelei offered. "I feel I may be more trouble than I am worth. I simply wanted to…"

Max brushed his lips on the top of her head. "Come with me, sweet Lorelei." He had noted the tremble in her limbs. It had begun the very moment when Cassandra commenced with her scathing retort. It was apparent that Lorelei had simply been trying to smooth over whatever it was that Cassandra had been trying to create between them. Max was angry and ashamed of his eldest daughter, but he was also angry at himself for not better protecting the angel at his side. Of course, he loved his daughters, but he could not understand why Cassandra had sought Lorelei out with every intention of being rude and extremely unkind. He would not pave over his eldest daughter's flaws when she was so clearly in the wrong.

Max led Lorelei back to the library.

"It appears I am meant to be here this evening," Lorelei teased, untangling her hand from his and walking towards the lit hearth.

The flames kissed her hair with a rustic red glow as she turned her head to the side, staring across the room and out of the window. Max could not surmise what it was she was looking at, for the night sky had painted the view in an untarnished river of black.

"My eldest daughter has been unforgivably rude," Max began, a sharp, severe tone to his voice.

"You really do not need to say anything, Max," Lorelei protested. "As I explained before, she is hurting. Ava explained that it may very well be because of her lack of success last season, and now she is merely afraid. What with Katie having her first season, perhaps she feels as though she will be left alone, especially now that…"

"Yes?" Max knew she wanted to refer to what was going on between them, and he was so very tired of talking about Cassandra.

"Nothing," she smiled, turning her head to gaze back at the hearth.

Max found himself moving closer towards her until eventually his hard body was flush against her back. She smelled delightfully of lemons and orange blossoms, he thought, breathing her in as he lowered his lips to her bare shoulder.

Lorelei gasped, leaning her head slowly to the side in a silent invitation. "Were you referring to this?" he asked, drawling his words, allowing them to skim across her flesh, leaving a trail of goosebumps.

"Mmm-hmm."

"I am glad we are of the same mind, Lorelei, for you are quite the most wonderful lady I have ever known, and I would very much like to make you mine."

Max kissed her neck, listening to her sigh at his touch. She was utterly perfect. How his hands glided around her waist and caressed her abdomen was as though that was indeed what they were made for. "Of course, I shall not make you completely mine, here and now, Lorelei, but eventually I shall."

Lorelei nestled against him, twisting her body around to face him. The sensation of her breasts against his chest through the thin fabric of his attire was enough for him to throw caution to the wind, but, although he did not know her past as he would have liked to, he knew she deserved so much better.

She was looking at him; her eyes were two glittering pools of emerald green filled with a happy curiosity.

"I wish to court you, Lorelei," Max explained. "Do you know, I do not believe I have ever wished to court anyone before."

"But what about…"

"Nothing more than an arrangement between our parents," he replied. He did not need to hear the words to know the question. "There has never been any other who has ignited such emotions in me."

Max did not hear what she wanted to say, for he did not give her a chance to speak. She was radiant and pliant in his arms, and as his lips captured hers in a deep and rather hungry kiss, he promised he would never waste such a tender moment, not then nor in their future. He would not let anything come between them.

"Where is Cassandra?" Max enquired casually from behind the morning paper. He had risen almost an hour ago, and his rage was simmering at the memory of Cassandra's behaviour.

Ava sniffed. "I believe she is still abed, Max. I am quite sure she is rather reluctant to face either of us this morning."

"Quite," Max remarked, lowering and folding the paper. "Was anything discussed between the pair of you after the ball? I am afraid I was rather cowardly and retired before she had the misfortune of seeing me."

"I do not call that cowardly," Ava replied, correcting him, "but more of a wise form of restraint, dear brother. You forget that I know you, and even though you were indeed pleasant in the face of that girl's dreadful behaviour, it was obvious to Katie and I that you were livid with Cassandra. And, I might add, Cassandra is no fool either."

"Yes, well, I am just relieved that she has not scared Lorelei away. I shall call on the dear lady later this morning to apologise once again, and then, when I return, I shall be having a rather stiff word with her. I simply want to know why, Ava. None of this makes any sense, and it has to stop."

"I thought Lorelei was utterly splendid with the way she responded to her," his sister commented as she poured herself a cup of tea. "The lady is elegant in appearance and in character. I am not sure I could have held my tongue when dealing with such unkindness."

"Indeed, and that is why I do not intend to allow Cassie to interfere between us." Max brought his cup of tea to his lips, his brows pinched with an air of frustration with it all.

"I had spoken with her prior to the event as I had said I would," Ava mused aloud, "but it appears that Cassandra is not willing to see sense. I would suggest that I have another word, but perhaps this may be something that we will need to confer with Lorelei about. After all, it is she who Cassandra is victimising, is it not?"

"We cannot expect that Lorelei simply put up with her," Max exclaimed. "For all my sins, Cassandra is my problem. I could not possibly put this on Lorelei."

Ava pinched her lips, dragging them to one side as she narrowed her eyes thoughtfully. "I do not believe you would be putting anything on Lorelei."

"How so? Please tell me, Ava, for I do not see how I could possibly discuss my daughter's dislike for Lorelei with Lorelei without making her feel some kind of pressure." Max leaned forward, resting his elbows on the table whilst rubbing his eyes in anguish.

"Max, believe me, I do understand, but I do not see how it would benefit you by excluding her. Cassandra is evidently struggling with seeing her father with another lady." Ava held up her hand to halt the obvious protestation from her brother. "Yes, I am aware that it has been many years since their mother passed. However, one cannot know the workings of her mind in full. Although I do not believe the absence of Henrietta is the driving force behind her recent behaviour. I think she is jealous, Max."

Max's forehead wrinkled. "Lorelei did mention you had discussed such a reason. Perhaps if Cassandra paid less attention to her sister and who I am spending my time with, then she would have no need to be envious. She is, after all, a very beautiful young lady. A man would be a fool not to notice."

"And that, dear brother, is the reason we need to include Lorelei in our discussions. I believe, what with her obvious generous patience and kindness, she may be able to help us steer Cassandra in the right direction. I have already noticed one particular gentleman who keeps looking at her. Of course, Cassandra has not seen him, for, as like you say, she is too preoccupied with the actions of others."

Max was not certain that Cassandra would appreciate Lorelei's assistance, but then again, she did not appreciate Lorelei's anything it seemed, so he supposed that it could not hurt matters, providing, of course, that Lorelei did not run a mile at the very mention of it. "Alright, we shall seek the assistance of Lady Lorelei, but if at any moment it appears too much for her, then we stop. Is that clear?"

Ava nodded; a small, cunning smile curled her lips. "I do believe I am going to enjoy manipulating that little vixen of a niece," she crooned. "Let us pray that the young man who seems rather taken with her has not been put off by her recent behaviour."

Chapter Twelve

Lorelei was surprised to hear the announcement of Maximilian Lazenby's arrival the following day. Despite their level of intimacy at the ball, she had had to wonder whether his eldest daughter may have enlisted her arsenal of persuasive powers and ensured that Max would know that his desire to court Lorelei would lead to no end of trouble. She thought that perhaps he would see the effort of it all as too much trouble and her as not worth that effort. Yet there he was, standing in the entrance of her parlour with that magnificent air about him that sent shivers down her spine and made her want to leap from her chair simply to curl her body around his. However, despite the temptation, she greeted him as any respectable lady would by simply standing and offering a curtsey.

"Good morning, Max. To what do I owe this pleasure?"

Max stepped forward. "For you, Lorelei," he said, passing her the roses displayed in a radiant bouquet of rich red and dark green.

"Oh. Max. Thank you so much. These are beautiful," she replied, her eyes vibrant with genuine gratitude.

"Florence," she continued, turning to her maid. "Please could you put these in some water for me. I do not wish for them to wither. And perhaps you could bring us some tea, please?"

Florence nodded with a smile, relieving Lorelei of the roses and exiting the room.

"It is wonderful to see you, Max. Please have a seat." The clock on the wall ticked loudly as if emphasising that they were the only two people in the room.

"If I am honest, Lorelei, I was not certain that you would want to receive me," Max began as he settled back into the chair. "Of course, I am very glad that you did."

Lorelei gave him a confused smile. "I cannot think of a single reason as to why I would not wish to see you, Max. On the contrary, I had wondered whether you would want to see me. After all, it appears that my being around you may be more trouble than it is worth."

"Well, that is why I am here." Max inched forward in his seat as Lorelei's face paled at his words.

Lorelei felt her heart drop to her stomach with the sudden onset of dread. She had never felt anything like it. It was a helpless feeling, believing that the gentleman before her had come into her home to tell her that he did not want to see her again.

Before either could speak—not that Lorelei thought it was possible for her to do so—Florence entered with a fresh pot of tea, crockery, and a plate of biscuits. She eyed Lorelei with concerned curiosity, but Lorelei simply shook her head to assure her that she must not worry. "Thank you, Florence," she rasped.

Max's eyes were intent on Lorelei as she leaned forward to pour the tea. He reached out, gently placing his large hand over her trembling one. "I think you misunderstand me, Lorelei. It is my fault, for I am not wording this very well."

Lorelei placed the teapot on the table. She had only managed to fill Max's cup. Her mind was an explosion of thoughts that would not settle, and her heart did not know whether it should simply shatter or wait for Max to explain.

"Please, allow me," Max offered, picking up the teapot and filling her cup. "When I said that that is why I am here, I did not mean that I wish to end what we have between us."

"You don't?" Lorelei asked breathlessly, the surprise evident on her face.

"Good grief, no, Lorelei. Why would I throw away the lady that I cannot stop thinking about?"

Lorelei blushed profusely with joy at his words. To hear he had been thinking about her seemed to pour a liquid warmth into her heart, relieving the terrible ache as the fear stood down and allowed the knowledge of his feelings for her to seep into the very centre of her chest. "My heart and I are terribly relieved to hear it, Max."

Max's mouth softened into a boyish, lopsided grin. "Your words make me a happy man, Lorelei," he replied softly. "My eldest daughter is the only concern I have.

That does not mean, however, that I will adhere to her unspoken demands, but as her father, I would like to resolve whatever it is that has been making her behave in such a despicable way."

"Indeed," Lorelei agreed. "I do not like making her unhappy, Max. I know that look in her eyes. I believe I have worn the very same look."

"I cannot imagine you behaving the way in which Cassandra has," Max offered, a little surprised.

"No, perhaps I did not behave as she has, but the look I was referring to was that particular look of hurt. That is the one I recognise. She feels like she will never have anyone to love her in the way that she wishes to be loved—the way any young lady wishes to be loved." Lorelei sipped her tea. "It is a very difficult emotion to deal with, Max."

Max sat back silently in the rose-pink wingback chair, a frown set deep into his forehead as he waited for Lorelei to continue.

"I was always the wallflower, Max," she stated calmly. "From my very first season, I stood at the edge of the ballroom dancefloors and merely watched."

Max was speechless. How it was possible that she, Lorelei Whitworth, could have been placed in such a position was indeed confusing to him. She could see it in every line of his face.

Lorelei chuckled. "Don't be so surprised, Max. I am classed as a spinster now for that very reason."

"Not for much longer," Max mumbled under his

breath.

Lorelei caught his words. "Is that so?" she teased.

"Indeed."

Both grinning, Lorelei continued. "I have always been rather generously curvaceous…"

Max raised his eyebrows with a smirk of approval.

"Yes, well, perhaps you should have attended those balls, Max, for no other gentleman thought so highly of them. They preferred the slighter feline-esque figure of the other debutantes.

"As for Cassandra, she is not like me, for she has what these gentlemen prefer, however, she is terrified that she does not. This has made her somewhat ignorant to their glances and, I might add, a little unapproachable."

Max nodded. "Yes, Ava said as much," he agreed. "I wonder whether you would consider it a little presumptuous if one were to ask that you bear with me while we help her gain this lost confidence so that she may enjoy the season?"

"I would only find it presumptuous if you were to deny me the pleasure of helping you to help her. You will need to be gentle, Max," she reminded him. "One does not gain confidence simply because one is assured that they are good enough. We need to show Cassandra that that is the case."

Max stood and walked over towards Lorelei, his hand outstretched for her to take. Lorelei brushed her fingers over the skin of his palm as he closed his hand around them in a gentle embrace, pulling her to her feet and closer towards him. "Do you know how wonderful you are, I wonder," he mused, tucking a stray, glistening black curl of her hair behind her ear.

Lorelei softened against the firmness of his body, her breathing heavy with the intimacy of their proximity.

"I don't believe you do, Lorelei. To most, it is a shame that it has taken so very long for you to be told something so obvious, but for me, in a rather selfish sentiment, it is not, for I wonder whether I would have been so lucky to be standing here with you in this manner if they had. I am sure that you would have been married by now, and we would have never so much as spoken." Max brushed his lips over the tip of her nose. "It is rather strange to imagine never knowing you now that I have met you. I do not think I like it very much."

Lorelei surprised him by closing the distance between them, her arms snaked around his neck as her fingers fumbled through his hair. She was breathtaking in beauty and with every stroke of her touch, from her hands and lips to the press of her body against his. Max groaned as he pulled her even closer, feeling every inch of her that he was permitted. He did not think it had been possible to be this close to someone, but as she sighed with contentment, he felt it echo through his core.

"This," Max drawled, his breathing heavy with desire, "leads to only one place, Lady Lorelei, and as much as I wish to lead you to that particular room and ravish you, I promised you that I would court you. You deserve to be treated with respect and as the lady who you are. Especially," he added, quickly placing another kiss on her lips, "after you have expressed your wish to help my eldest daughter. My god woman, could you be any more perfect?"

"I..." Lorelei began in an effort to protest.

"No," Max interrupted. "It was merely rhetorical, for I already know the answer. Now, my lady, a carriage awaits."

Chapter Thirteen

Lorelei removed the bonnet from atop her head, passing it to the awaiting outstretched hands of her mother's butler and her lifelong friend, Jenkins.

"Good evening, my lady," he greeted her, smiling. "May I say that you look delightfully happy today?"

"Thank you, Jenkins. I feel delightfully happy. I have had the most splendid day."

"Lorelei, is that you?" Lady Whitworth bellowed from the drawing room. "What is taking you so long?"

Jenkins grimaced, then offered Lorelei an apologetic smile. "She has been a little anxious this afternoon, my lady," he offered kindly.

"Don't worry, Jenkins, for I shall brace myself," Lorelei chuckled, patting down the front of her indigo day dress. She supposed she should have changed her clothing after Max had returned her to her home, but she knew her mother would be worse than she was at present if she had been a minute more. Besides, she could still smell the rich, warm, and woody fragrance of cinnamon on the fabric of her gown, where Max had curled around her whenever he had had the chance. She did not want to be parted from him entirely.

It was strange, she mused as she slowly walked towards the sound of her mother's strong voice, as to how she and Max had formed their courtship with so few words. It was not that they did not converse but simply that it had felt so utterly natural. Lorelei had never heard of any relationship that had formed in such an easy manner. She had always assumed that it was a matter of formal discussions, and often, she noted, with rather extended bouts of painful silence between both parties. It had all seemed rather stiff and pompous, but what she and Max had was nothing of the sort, and she was rather relieved, for she was enjoying it immensely.

"There you are," Lady Whitworth snapped. "You are here later and later every day, Lorelei. I shan't have it, I tell you."

Lorelei simply gazed at her mother, her lips unmoving as she considered the woman's display of displeasure. Perhaps she should apologise, she considered, but then that seemed like a slight on Max's behalf, for she was not sorry at all that she had spent the majority of the day with him. She would like very much to spend every day with him if he were to ask. Lorelei shook her head. That was a hope she would pocket for another day. She knew he thought highly of her, but she did not know whether he was even considering marriage despite his teasing.

"What are you shaking your head at?" Lady Whitworth narrowed her eyes, addressing her daughter as though she was acting all too peculiar for her liking.

"I was just woolgathering, Mama. How have you been?" Lorelei enquired, taking her usual seat.

"On my own," her mother sniffed, "as you well know."

"You are never on your own, Mama. You have a household full of wonderful, caring staff and more friends now than I have ever had in my entire life."

Lady Whitworth pinched her lips together. "Yes, well, you are here now."

"Indeed, Mama." Lorelei kept her attention on her mother's face. She was not sure whether to wait for her to speak or say something herself, but as the air grew taut with an obvious tension, Lorelei decided she would have to be the one to fill the void. "I attended a charity ball yesterday evening, Mama," she began, watching for any signs of her mother softening. "I believe I mentioned it the last time I visited."

"Yes, you did."

Lorelei noted the acid in her mother's voice, but she would not allow it to detract her from the subject. She hoped that her mother, given time, would be happy for her, especially if she told her about Max.

"Lord Lazenby is the most remarkable gentleman. He went above and beyond with regards to the event for Lady Howell's Orphanage. It was indeed very generous of him."

Lady Whitworth turned her head towards her

daughter. Her eyebrows had risen with impatience, waiting for Lorelei to continue.

So, she did. "It is true, Mama. The ballroom décor was exquisite, as was the rest of his home. I believe you would have been rather in awe of it all."

"Did you meet Lady Lazenby?" Lady Whitworth enquired abruptly, her mind obviously solely on that particular detail.

Lorelei sighed. She wondered whether it would be wise to mention that there was no Lady Lazenby, but then she remembered that there were two. "I did, indeed. There are two, Mama," she smiled sweetly, enjoying the widening of her mother's eyes.

"Two?" her mother breathed. "Two Lady Lazenbys?"

"Indeed, Mama." Lorelei pinched her lips, stifling the laughter. If only her mother had reworded her question, she thought mischievously. Now if Lady Whitworth had asked whether Max had two wives using those descriptors, then she would have explained that the two Lady Lazenbys she had referred to were merely his daughters and nothing quite so scandalous. But Lorelei had decided she was having far too much fun to enlighten the woman. "There is Lady Katherine Lazenby —or Katie as she prefers to be called—and the other is Lady Cassandra Lazenby. I believe Lady Cassandra Lazenby prefers to be called Cassie, but we are not yet on very friendly terms."

"Oh?"

Lady Whitworth appeared utterly enthralled, Lorelei observed. No doubt her mother was collecting every snippet of the information to repeat them at a later date to her friends. Of course, Lorelei would not let it get that far, she promised Max silently, for she had every intention of revealing to her dear mama that she was referring to the gentleman's daughters. Not yet though, she thought.

"She was not best pleased when she noticed that Lord Lazenby was holding my hand, nor when we danced a waltz."

Lady Whitworth's mouth was gaping open.

"What is it, Mama?" Lorelei queried innocently.

"Lorelei Margaret Whitworth, your father and I did not raise you to cavort with another lady's husband!" Lady Whitworth exclaimed. "When people hear of your scandalous behaviour, we will be ruined."

"I do not understand, Mama. I am not cavorting with another lady's husband. Well, I suppose I am, but she is no longer with us, so it does not count as such." Lorelei feigned a look of confusion.

"You were holding the man's hand in front of his wife!" she all but bellowed at Lorelei.

Lorelei had never seen her mother quite so passionate about a matter. Her reaction had left her a little speechless, yet she knew she had to correct her mother before the matter went too far. "I did no such thing, Mama. Lady Cassandra and Lady Katherine are Lord Lazenby's daughters, not his wives. You did not ask me whether he was married, only whether there was a Lady

Lazenby, to which I replied with honesty."

"Lorelei Whitworth, you will be the death of me," Lady Whitworth grumbled. "I was quite enjoying the idea of a little gossip until I thought you were involved, and now I have none whatsoever, and I was quite excited to divulge the matter of the man having two wives to my friends. It would have been a delicious bit of scandal had it been true."

"See, Mama, you do have friends." Lorelei smiled smugly as the truth silenced her mother into a nod of surrender. The lady could not deny that she did not have a wide circle of friends around her.

"I am glad that you have so many, Mama," she added, not wanting her mother to believe her to be unkind, "for Lord Lazenby and I are courting now."

"But what will I do without you?" Lady Whitworth asked quietly.

"I do not know what you would do without me, Mama, but you will not have to find out because I will always visit you. Just because Lord Lazenby and I are courting, it does not mean that I will not have time for you."

"It appears I did not overfeed you then," Lady Whitworth stated, looking rather embarrassed.

"No indeed, Mama," Lorelei replied, sighing as she remembered her mother's unkind words. "I believe Max likes me as I am."

Lady Whitworth's eyes were filled with regret. "I feel I have been terribly unkind to you since your father passed, and I beg that you forgive me, Lorelei. It is no excuse, but your father's death has made me fear the loss of those I love with such an intensity that some days I do not know how it is that I breathe."

Lorelei moved her body to the seat adjacent to her mother, lifting the lady's hands into her own with such a gentleness that it brought tears to Lady Whitworth's eyes. "It is alright, Mama," Lorelei crooned kindly.

"It is not, Lorelei, but I thank you for saying so. In my efforts to keep you close, I could have easily pushed you away, yet here you are still by my side, promising me that I will never lose you, and I do not think I deserve your kindness."

Lorelei brought her mother's hands to the side of her face and leaned into them. "You forget that I know you, Mama. I know the lady you were before Papa passed and the lady you have become. I know when you changed and the reason why. I am only glad that we get to clear the air like this."

Lady Whitworth leaned forward and kissed her daughter's cheek. "As am I, Lorelei, and I am truly sorry for everything."

"It is the past now, Mama. I think we all lost our way a little bit after Papa died, and I think we can all be forgiven. Let us forget it all and return to how we once were. What say you?" Lorelei asked, her eyes glistening with tears of grief for her father and relief to be reunited with the mother she missed.

"Indeed, my darling," Lady Whitworth crooned.

"Indeed."

Lorelei felt considerably lighter as she lay upon her bed, recollecting the day. She allowed her mind to wander through her memories, diving into every detail simply to take a closer look, as her raven hair fanned over her pillow. Lorelei was glad of her silent ramblings, for she did not know the words to explain how everything was beginning to fall into place within her life. She hadn't even realised that it had been quite so jumbled. As far as Lorelei was concerned, there were rules to society, and she had taken up her designated position as a wallflower and then a spinster quite nicely. It wasn't ideal, she had thought on several occasions, but she accepted it with what she hoped was grace and had pushed everything else to the side. Yet there in her bedchamber she knew that her misconception of what life was supposed to be for a lady of her age had been exactly that—a lie. One did not cease being worthy of love at the age of nine and twenty. In truth, one did not have to consider oneself as a spinster at all, for one simply became available to the gentleman whom fate had always known was right for her. Had she not been a wallflower when attending every season, then Lorelei may never have had the good fortune to know Maximilian Lazenby, she realised. Of course, one could argue that she may still have met him that day, but that was simply impossible, for she would not have needed those new gowns from Evangeline because everyone knew that married ladies were always so very well-dressed, and even if she had met him, then she would have been married, therefore depressingly unavailable. Oh, heavens, the very thought of that prospect was rather unpalatable, for, although they had not known each other terribly long, he made her very happy indeed.

As for Lady Whitworth, the evening had gifted Lorelei with a wonderful surprise as she caught a glimpse of the mother she had missed so very dearly. She had often wondered whether she had lost her for good amongst the turbulence of grief that had swept the woman up after her father's passing, but indeed it appeared she was very much still there.

Lorelei nestled back into the pillow, feeling quite wonderfully free to be happy with regards to her heart, other than the small matter of Cassandra, of course. However, she had every intention of ensuring that she would help the young lady as much as she could. *'Perhaps she may never like me,'* Lorelei considered, *'but I shall not give up as yet.'* Max needed her patience, she decided, and so that was what she would give him.

A light knock on the door broke Lorelei from her musings. It was rather late for any of the servants to be up and about, she thought, trying to adjust her eyes to the dark. "Come in," she called quietly, pulling the coverlet up over her thin nightgown.

"So sorry, my lady," Florence breathed. "These are for you. They were delivered while you were visiting Lady Whitworth, but I have only recently been informed."

Lorelei sat up a little more and lit the candle on her bedside table. It was a tad too dark for her to decipher what it was that Florence held in her hands. After all, the candle wasn't exactly a beacon, but eventually it was indeed sufficient to make out a small square box and an envelope.

The maid placed the items in Lorelei's hands, curtseyed, and exited the room.

"Thank you," Lorelei whispered, paying no heed to the already closed door.

Confused by the items in her hand, she turned them over as if, by some miracle, it would explain everything. Lorelei scoffed at her bout of ridiculousness.

It was not her birthday, and she was quite sure it wasn't Christmas. Perhaps her mother had sent it and not mentioned it. Lorelei did not believe she had ever been quite so baffled over a box before. Yet, the small square box was most certainly a gift, but who would have delivered something so late and for what reason?

Without further ado, Lorelei swept back the coverlet and ambled over to the dresser, where she kept the letter knife. She really did not like such things, for they looked extremely dangerous and made her a little nervous when handling them. Slowly and carefully, she ran the blade through the top of the envelope, relieving it of the letter inside.

It was beautifully written, she thought, but most

definitely not her mother's penmanship, and the fragrance was, without a doubt, the very scent of one man in particular. Lorelei's heart pounded in her chest as her eyes skimmed the words he had so carefully scribed upon the parchment. They were gentle, considerate, and radiated a warmth she had never known a letter could contain. She brought the parchment to her nose to simply breathe him in. That alone, the warm and woody scent of cinnamon, caused her insides to shudder and tighten with pleasure. The man was practically edible, she thought, giggling to herself as she turned her attention to the neat package that almost fit in the palm of her hand.

The box was wrapped in simple brown paper. Each neat fold was kept perfectly in place by a beautiful, deep red ribbon tied into a perfect bow. Lorelei's fingers made light work of it as she watched the satin slide over the tips of her fingers, then simply allowed the ribbon to fall. Max's note had advised that she was to wear it at the upcoming dinner party on Friday evening at Hawthorne House. It all sounded rather exciting indeed.

A black leather, square box with a golden clasp sat in Lorelei's hand. It was exquisite to behold. Although Lorelei had never known a box so beautiful to hold anything else other than jewellery, she was not so presumptuous as to simply assume, nor so self-appreciative as to believe that she was deserving of such a gift, yet her heart still hammered within her chest.

    The hinged box creaked as she lifted the lid to reveal the most elegant emerald necklace Lorelei believed she had ever seen. It was delicate yet dazzling. Lorelei was astounded by the beauty of the piece and by Max's generosity. She had never owned an item of jewellery as extravagant as the one she held in her hands. She wondered how she could accept something so terribly expensive, yet she knew that her mother would have scolded her if she responded with anything other than gratitude. And indeed, she was so very grateful, she thought whilst sighing romantically to herself as she ran her fingers over the sparkling gemstone.

Chapter Fourteen

'Friday,' Max thought, sighing dramatically. 'There are far too many days until Friday.' Max was quite certain that he was utterly incapable of mustering the patience of waiting until then. He needed to be able to hold Lorelei much sooner, for it appeared that his sanity depended upon it. He was beginning to believe that he was slowly losing his grip on the very last morsel of what remained. Besides, he told himself whilst trying to bolster his conviction, he highly doubted that he would be able to do what he very much intended to quite so freely in front of his daughters anyway.

Max grinned wickedly at his private musings.

"Is everything set, Barrett?" Max enquired, climbing up into the carriage.

"Yes, m'lord."

"Excellent. Let us be on our way then, shall we?"

"Where first, m'lord?"

"Lady Howell's Orphanage, if you please."

Max sat back in the seat of the carriage. He could not have picked a more splendid day for an impromptu picnic, he thought happily, and there was no one he would wish to have that picnic with other than Lady

Lorelei.

In preparation of whisking the delectable Lorelei away from all that was demanded of her, Max had sent word to Lady Howell, hoping, yet not particularly caring, that she would not feel too aggrieved by his sudden demand for her best volunteer to spend the day with him. Although his missive was not quite as aggressive as it may sound, he knew she would not deny him. Max had plans for Lady Lorelei that simply could not wait.

Max's knee bounced up and down as nerves coursed through his veins. 'Perhaps it is too soon,' he pondered, yet it did not feel too soon. Lorelei was a constant vision in his mind, every minute of every day. And every night, for she filled every second of his dreams until he would wake up to a cold and lonely bed where he knew she should be. It was where she belonged. Max's constant need for her crept into his soul until he found that he could barely concentrate on anything but her. He was in love with Lorelei, he had realised, for how could one deny such intense feelings, knowing he had never so much as felt a fraction of such emotion for another in his entire life?

Max gazed out of the window, resting his head on the cold glass. "I cannot lose her," he whispered to the empty carriage, for where there was love, there came the most dreadful fear of loss.

The carriage began to slow as the driver entered through the orphanage gates, allowing Max a little time to compose himself as he straightened his grey coat and ran his large fingers through his hair.

A quick deep breath expanded his lungs as his feet hit the ground, but before he had time to take another breath or even think of what was to come, he was quickly escorted into the building and rapidly found himself tapping his foot anxiously, awaiting Lady Howell.

Bernadette Howell did not keep the man waiting long; she had been making her way back to her office as he had arrived. At her side was Lady Lorelei, and Max wondered whether someone had sucked the air out of the building, for he was finding it terribly difficult to breathe as he observed the radiant smile that curled Lorelei's dusky pink lips and the single onyx curl that hung loosely at the side of her face as it bobbed softly in time with her every step.

"Lord Lazenby, what a lovely surprise," Lady Howell exclaimed innocently. "To what do we owe this pleasure?" she added, looking from Max to Lorelei with affection.

Max turned his gaze swiftly to Lady Howell, a look of gratitude glimmering in his eyes. "Lady Howell, Lady Lorelei," he said, bowing before them as they came to a stop in front of him.

"I was just about to tell Lorelei that she could take the rest of the day off," Lady Howell remarked before Max could continue. "We are quite overstaffed today, and it is far too lovely for her to spend the day inside, don't you think?" Lady Howell announced with a smile of secrecy with regards to his missive.

"Indeed," he replied. "It must be a happy coincidence then, for I have come to whisk Lady Lorelei away." Max grinned, turning his attention back to Lorelei. "Would you like to spend the rest of the day with me, Lady Lorelei?"

"I would like that very much, Lord Lazenby." Lorelei blushed, placing her hand gently on his proffered arm. "Are you sure you will be alright though, Lady Howell?"

"Absolutely. Besides, what a terror I would be if I denied you both this splendid day. Now be off with you before I change my mind," Lady Howell replied jovially.

Max walked briskly, keen to steal Lorelei away and into the carriage where they could be alone.

"I have the distinct feeling that you are in a hurry, Maximilian," Lorelei stated, quickening her steps at his side. "Are you in a hurry, my lord?"

"I apologise, Lorelei. I have no excuse I'm afraid other than I am simply eager to have you all to myself. It seems like an age since I saw you last."

Lorelei giggled, then frowned with a somewhat generous serving of sarcasm.

She did it with a dangerously pretty little pout, Max noted, his body tightening.

"It has not even been a day yet, Max. Surely, you did not miss me that much?" Lorelei said, her eyes twinkling with a delightful humour.

"Do not be so sure about that, Lorelei," he breathed huskily in the arc of her neck as he lifted her into the carriage. "I cannot seem to think about anything else other than being with you."

Lorelei sat across from him, her hands in her lap. "I believe your feelings are reciprocated, my lord," she whispered coyly.

Leaning forward, Max brushed a kiss upon her plump lips and sighed as though his life had depended upon that one act of intimacy, although, he had to admit, he was unsure how long he would last before he would need the sweet tonic again. "I thought we could head out of the city to a lovely spot, I know. I had the cook prepare us a hamper so we may enjoy the afternoon without any interruptions," Max explained, watching the way Lorelei bit her bottom lip, then proceeded to slowly scrape her top teeth over it. It only served to heat his blood, for she was the very picture of perfection, he thought as he caressed every inch of her with his eyes and mind. Max could not help the growl that escaped the back of his throat as his fingers itched to follow the trail of where his eyes had been.

"Is everything alright, Max?"

"Absolutely. It is perfect. You are perfect."

A lake rippled in the distance; the melody of the subtle, tiny movements tickled their ears as the light of the sun prickled over the top of the water in perfect diamonds, adding an ethereal haze, gracefully mellowing the vibrancy of the picturesque scenery. It was a heady, intoxicating sight—one Lorelei believed she could, quite happily, envelope herself in for eternity. "It is rather beautiful here," she breathed, squeezing Max's hand as it trailed over her abdomen and rested just beneath her bust.

The heat of the side of Max's hand brushed beneath her breast, tightening the muscles at his core. It was a dangerous act to move so close, yet he did not want to merely stand at her side. She was warm, her body soft and delightful.

"Shall we find somewhere to relieve ourselves of this?" Lorelei tapped the basket in his other hand.

"Perhaps we should set it down over there under the tree," Max suggested, his body cooling as he uncurled it from hers.

The shade beneath the looming tree was ample to keep the glare of the sun from their eyes, Max thought as he watched Lorelei gaze longingly out over the expanse of water.

"Penny for them," he offered.

"I believe they are not worth that," Lorelei replied quietly, her eyes still drawn to the scenery. "I was simply admiring the wonderful view. It is quite spectacular here."

"I prefer the view I have from where I am sitting," Max replied, his eyes dancing with mischief. He could not help but smirk triumphantly at the blush he had summoned to the apples of her cheeks.

"Is that so, Lord Lazenby?" Lorelei retorted, her eyes unable to meet his.

"Indeed." Max shifted closer to her, carefully avoiding the fan of fabric surrounding her outstretched legs. "I believe," he drawled, "that my view is far more splendid."

Max placed his fingers beneath her chin, tilting her face towards him as a giggle softly blew from her lips. The warmth of her breath brushed his mouth as he moved closer, their proximity silencing her as laughter caught in her throat, punctuated by a sigh as his lips gently grazed hers. Something wonderful fizzed between them and poured over his skin, encouraging him to deepen their kiss.

"Lord Lazenby," she scolded breathlessly. "You shall ruin my impeccable reputation." She quieted as he leaned in to kiss her again, the thrill of his touch weakening any ounce of will she may have had to reject him for the sake of propriety.

"Then we shall have to marry, Lorelei," he whispered as he drew away slightly. Max gazed at her beseechingly, holding her still merely with his eyes.

Lorelei couldn't look away; the evidence of his sincerity blazed in the blue of his irises. He was breathtaking. "Max?" she queried, afraid to speak any further.

"I mean it, Lorelei." Max's voice had become quite husky, she noticed, as he picked up her hand, entwining his fingers with hers. "I would marry you if you would agree to it. I do not have to ruin your reputation to want you as my wife. I still very much wish to marry you with or without the scandal."

Max fumbled in the pocket of his breeches. As he pulled his hand out again, he produced a similar box to that of the necklace.

'*Oh, the necklace,*' Lorelei thought, yet she didn't say anything for fear of spoiling the moment. She quickly made a mental note to thank him as soon as she could.

"Lorelei," Max began. His hands were trembling, but he focused only on the warmth of her gaze. "I have been married before," he continued quietly, "yet I have never felt for any lady the way I feel for you. In all honesty, I did not believe that something so wonderful could ever exist for me until I met you. I am truly astounded at the power it holds over me, but I welcome it. I welcome you, Lorelei, for you have opened my eyes, and I cannot deny the love I carry in my heart for you every day."

Lorelei's eyes were glittering. The very image of her nestled with considerable warmth within his chest, spreading out into his rigid muscles as if giving him permission to relax as he kissed the inside of her delicate wrist.

"Do you think me somewhat forward, or perhaps a little hasty?" he enquired nervously.

Lorelei shook her head, unable to speak.

"Some may say that we have not known each other for very long," he continued, "but I must tell you that I know my own heart, Lorelei, and I am utterly in love with you."

Lorelei was smiling, her bottom lip trembling. She bit it gently, trying to silence the revelation of her emotions.

The seconds were stretching, dragging the silence painfully with it. Max knew he should just be quiet and let her speak, but he simply couldn't. He had to ask the question he had been meaning to ask her before he would lose this particular battle to his fear. "Lorelei, I would like very much to spend the rest of my life with you."

Lorelei gasped with glee, a grin spreading over her face and brightening her features.

Max chuckled, her response tickling him with unfettered relief. "Please, my love, will you do me the great honour of becoming my wife?"

Lorelei practically leapt from her position on the blanket, curling her arms around his strong neck as she pressed her mouth passionately to his.

Max grinned against the brush of her lips, his fingers sprawling around her waist and spreading up over her back.

"Oh, yes, Max," she beamed enthusiastically. "I will most definitely marry you."

Max's heart swelled in his chest to hear the words he had longed to hear from her lips. She was sweet, delicate, and pretty, yet also elegant, strong, and indeed a radiant force of nature. He did not know how one woman could possess so many desirous attributes all at once, but there she was before him as his betrothed.

"Oh, and by the way," Lorelei added, interrupting his silent meanderings, "I love you too."

"Well, that is most excellent news," Max remarked as he slowly and seductively slid the emerald ring onto her dainty finger.

"Oh, it is exquisite, Max," she sighed happily. "It will match the stunning necklace you gave me." Lorelei quickly tilted her head up so she could see him. "Thank you, by the way. I did want to thank you earlier, but you seemed terribly intent on asking me to marry you, and I did not want to put you off by interrupting."

"Anything for you, my sweet Lorelei. Absolutely anything."

Lorelei gazed down again at the ring on her finger, her concentration broken by the sensation of Max as he curled a loose strand of her hair behind her ear. His fingertip traced the line of her jaw as he angled her face upward, stealing another kiss.

Lorelei sighed as Max echoed her with a groan of desire that rumbled through his chest into hers as they leaned into each other.

"How did I get so lucky, Lorelei?" he whispered, his breath brushing over the sensitive skin on her neck.

"I believe you ruined my clothing," she retorted playfully, pulling his mouth back to hers as she scraped her teeth over his bottom lip.

Max growled. "Something I would very much like

to do now, but not in quite the same manner," he teased. Max kissed the natural rouge upon her cheeks. "I love you, Lorelei, but I will not make you mine here out in the open on the grass. You deserve much better than that."

There was a hunger in Lorelei's eyes, Max mused. It was a wonderful, heady feeling to see it there, for when the time was perfect everything would be that much sweeter.

Max and Lorelei sipped on champagne and devoured the prepared hamper of tiny sandwiches, fruit, and cake whilst whiling the hours of the afternoon away. Endless chatter filled the air as their conversation kept circling back to one person. The very person who could make things rather difficult for them, they'd agreed, but also the very person who needed their help—Cassandra.

Chapter Fifteen

Lorelei was rather glad when Max had insisted he would escort her to his home for the upcoming dinner party. He informed her that it was most probably for the best, which she had decided was rather astute of him, for if the way her stomach was roiling with anxiety, simply at the thought of coming face to face with Cassandra Lazenby, was any indicator of whether she would have been able to walk confidently into Hawethorne House, it would not have been looking very promising at all. And if those rather pesky little butterflies kept fluttering inside of her every time she thought of Max, she may even lower herself to request that he carry her up the front steps and over the threshold.

"Breathe, Lorelei," she whispered to herself, "just breathe. How hard could it really be?" Lorelei began to chew nervously on the inside of her cheek, desperately trying to remind herself that she and Max had already discussed his eldest daughter on several occasions. No matter how difficult, she was going to do all she could to make matters easier between her and Cassandra, thus making it easier for Max. "This is going to be positively disastrous," she groaned to herself as she pulled open the front door.

"Well, I don't think my company will be that bad," Max drawled sarcastically as he grinned at her; his eyebrow arched in amusement as he stood on the stone steps in front of her home.

"Oh, I apologise, Max. I certainly wasn't referring to you. Sadly, I have a terrible tendency of talking to myself." Her smile stretched into a playful grimace. "Perhaps I should have warned you earlier," she suggested, her eyes sparkling with humour.

Max threw back his head and laughed. "My dear Lorelei, can you keep a secret?"

Lorelei nodded, her eyes flitting over his face as she drank in the happiness it possessed.

"I too am prone to having the most informative of conversations with myself. The best part is, I do not argue."

Lorelei pinched her lips together yet could not hold back the giggle as Max wrapped his arms around her waist, lifted her off the floor, and quickly spun them both in a circle.

"I have missed you, my love," Max drawled as he lowered her to her feet and bent his head, his lips merely a hair's breadth from her ear.

The deep rumble of his voice skittered over Lorelei's skin; it washed over her body like an ocean wave that surged once more as his lips brushed against her cheek.

Lorelei sighed as she rested her head upon his shoulder. Her body was trembling as Cassandra crept into her mind; the thought of Max's daughter's temper stood hand in hand with the most terrible fear—the fear that she may end up losing the man who she now held so dear—because of it.

"I am terrified I shall make matters worse with Cassandra," Lorelei confessed, her words whispered against the fabric of his deep grey suit. He was the only gentleman she knew who could wear the colour so splendidly, she thought.

Max was surprised by the sudden change in Lorelei's mood, but his ability to understand was evident to her as he kissed the top of her head. "I will be with you, Lorelei," he said, soothingly. "You will not be on your own. Besides, Cassandra is my daughter; therefore, she is my problem. I do not expect anything from you other than for you to be yourself—the woman I am in love with," he added, pulling her closer to his side.

"Be that as it may, Max, I promise I shall try not to do anything that may upset her. I seem to be quite good at it," she rasped with a nervous laugh.

"We are all good at it, I can assure you. Although, I must say, I seem to excel at it far more than my sister and Katie," Max corrected with humour.

"I wonder whether you think it wise for us to announce our engagement tonight?" Lorelei queried, her mind still stubbornly pondering the dilemma. She had been thinking about asking Max before, but she did not know if there was a correct way to word such a question when it could be so easily misconstrued.

Max's eyes were sharp with shock.

Oh heavens! Definitely misconstrued, she thought.

"Oh, Max, please do not misunderstand me," Lorelei interjected before he could utter a word of protest. "If I could, I would tell the entire world about us and our wonderful news." She smiled. "I believe you know that though," she added softly, placing her hand over his heart. "I simply wonder," she continued, "what with your daughter being the way she is and the possible reasons for her behaving this way, whether our news may do more harm than good." Lorelei sighed, disappointed at the thought of having to keep such a happy occasion to herself.

"Lorelei, as much as I wish to make matters easier for my eldest daughter, you have to know that no matter what happens, you and I *will* marry, and she will need time to adjust to that knowledge," he replied with a hint of severity. "You are too good-hearted, my love," he continued, his voice softening, "but I will not allow her to spoil our moment when she will soon have her own. Of course," he added, clearing his throat, "there is also the matter of the announcement of our engagement in the morning paper. It has already gone to print, and I really do not wish to suffer a scolding from her when she finds out in the same way as the rest of London."

"Well, there is that, I suppose," she mused aloud. "However, should you change your mind, Max, please do not be afraid to tell me, for I will not object. As long as I get to become your wife in the end, I really do not mind."

"Have no fear of that, Lorelei. There will be no other Lady Lazenby except you."

The carriage wheels crackled over the loose stone chippings in the road as they sat, curled close to one another in companionable silence. The streets were far quieter in the evening than what she was used to in the daytime, Lorelei thought, as she watched the light of the sky begin to fade through the carriage window, gradually darkening into a spill of grey that bled into the cold, icy blue. The moon had risen from its slumber, attempting to shoo away the last remnants of the sun as the stars hid patiently in the pearl-white shadows of the ethereal sphere.

Max grazed his hand over the side of Lorelei's bodice as he rose slightly from his seat, reaching across her to loosen the ties of the damask curtains. They fell in thick, heavy swathes of black fabric, quickly shutting the world out as the light in the carriage intercepted the blanket of darkness. "Very soon I will have to share you, my love," he reminded her, his finger stroking the side of her jaw.

Lorelei turned her face towards him, her skin fearing the absence of his touch.

"But for now, I do not," he added, scorching the tail ends of his words onto her soft lips as she swallowed her response in a staggered breath of rapture. His hands explored her body through the layers of fabric, desperately wanting to roam beneath. He could feel the palms of her hands glide up his back as she pulled him against her, their body temperatures rising against the cold of the night air.

"My lord." A knock sounded on the carriage, interrupting their entanglement.

Max chortled, loving the way Lorelei remained in a molten state of deliciousness in his arms. Her eyes were glazed with the intoxication of his touch, and her lips were swollen in a darker shade of pink.

"What is so amusing?" she enquired, mystified by the way he was looking at her.

"I was just thinking how very lovely you are," Max replied, brightening the hue on Lorelei's cheeks.

Stepping down from the carriage, Max teased Lorelei with his hand as he quickly whisked it away, inviting her to fall into his arms. "Are you ready?" he whispered as he caught her and then lowered her to the ground.

"Ready as I shall ever be."

Max was not quite displaying his usual air of confidence, Lorelei noted, as he led her up the stone steps to the entrance of Hawethorne House. His mood seemed to linger between fretting, calm, and—rather oddly—some enthusiasm. However, Lorelei did not think she was exactly the picture of sanity either, for she was trying desperately to steady the dreadful sensation that was currently thrumming through her veins, travelling down her legs and up into her arms.

"Everything will be perfectly fine, Lorelei," Max soothed, patting her hands.

She had been focusing on the neatly pruned rosebushes placed carefully to the sides of the steps. The ivory hue of their petals seemed almost blue under the night sky, Lorelei mused with admiration.

"Ava and Katherine are sensible, so they already adore you," Max continued, "and given time, I believe Cassandra will come to her senses too. Of course, we both know she may take time." — Max was rambling. He was quite aware of it—"But she will, I assure you. Perhaps it will be once we have found her a match," he added, pulling back his shoulders.

Lorelei listened, taking her time as she took in his words. It felt a little underhand to allow Cassandra to shoulder all the blame. "It is not entirely Cassandra's feelings towards me that troubles me," she admitted quietly.

"How so, my love?" Max asked, feeling a knot of concern form below his ribcage.

"I am so used to blending into the background at events such as these and in everyday life as a rule, so I feel quite out of my depth," she replied truthfully.

The knot beneath Max's ribs unravelled. "I very much doubt that one as exquisite as yourself has ever simply blended into anything."

"That is indeed kind of you, Max, but nevertheless, you forget that I was once a wallflower," Lorelei chided kindly.

Max kissed the back of her hand. "Their loss is my gain, my darling. You are not a wallflower, for you are the most exquisite flower of them all," he assured her as they reached the doors, giving her one last look as he prepared himself to knock.

Lorelei felt his love for her sweep through the fabric of her burgundy gown as his eyes betrayed his thoughts. It penetrated her flesh, wrapping around her heart in the most wondrous feeling she had ever known.

"Let me be your confidence, Lorelei. I shall not leave your side, should you so wish it," Max declared, his free hand gathering the loose curl at the side of her face and tucking it tenderly behind her ear. Max pressed his lips into the palm of her hand, his mouth slowly trailing heat as it brushed along the inside of her wrist. He placed the side of his face where the kiss had begun, her hand curving delicately against his jaw as he leaned into her touch with affection.

There was a little roughness along Max's jawline, Lorelei considered as her fingertips begged to feel the handsome man beneath them. The contact sent tingles up her arm, heightening the intimacy of the moment. "You are a good man, Max," she breathed, "but if I cannot hold my ground alone, then I may make matters worse for you and your eldest daughter. The last thing Cassandra wants is to believe that you would choose me over her."

"But it is not as simple as that, Lorelei," Max protested. "If it were merely a matter of me being selfish and only thinking of my needs, and, of course, there was no love involved, I would perhaps understand her behaviour."

She really was quite dreadful at wording what she wanted to say, Lorelei grumbled inwardly at herself. She thought she rather resembled the verbal version of an overwrought bull in a… a… tearoom, simply knocking everything over in its path, for her words had made Max look as though she had just told him he was selfish, which could not be any further from the truth. He did not deserve to think that she thought so little of him.

"I know, Max. I did not mean for you to think that I think you are selfish, for I certainly do not," she assured him. "What I was trying to say in my rather clumsy manner is that it will be Cassandra's irrational way of thinking that would make her believe that you have chosen me over her. She does not see the recklessness and irrationality of her own behaviour. She will only view your gallantry towards me as an act of unkindness towards her." Lorelei gazed up at Max's thoughtful face. She was pleased to note that he was indeed listening, and that awful expression of hurt had disappeared. She did not like that expression one jot. "Therefore," she continued, "it is better that we do not give her any opportunity to misread our intentions and feelings towards her."

Max curled his arm around Lorelei's waist as he guided her towards a deep recess in the wall, hiding them both from prying eyes.

"Max," Lorelei chided, amusement twitching at the corners of her lips. "This behaviour will not help matters."

Max's hands were warm on her hips as his body pinned her against the cold stone of the house. "It may not help matters," he drawled, "but that does not mean I am a man capable of refraining. You, Lady Lorelei, do wicked things to me."

"So, I see," she replied wryly as he began to groan, teasing her bottom lip with a wave of tender kisses.

The abrupt click of the lock as the butler fumbled behind the door shattered the moment as they composed themselves and promptly returned to a more respectable position at the entrance.

"M'lord, Lady Whitworth," the butler announced in way of greeting as he eyed Max suspiciously.

Max grinned like a naughty schoolboy as he patted Lorelei's hand and led her inside his home.

Cassandra stood proudly by the fireplace. Her spine appeared rigid, and her neck elongated, giving her a regal stance as she pursed her lips. Her glare sucked any warmth from the room, sending a glacial chill deep into Lorelei's bones. The young lady would be hard to befriend, she thought gloomily.

"Lorelei!" Ava exclaimed. "How wonderful to see

you. Please come and join us. We were just talking about the ball next week. It is to be rather prestigious, or so I have heard."

"A ball?" Lorelei enquired as Ava prompted her to sit on a sage green striped settee.

"Yes, indeed," Max interjected. "I had hoped you would join me, Lorelei."

"Oh. I would love to, thank you," Lorelei replied, ignoring the obvious grunt of disapproval from Cassandra before she felt it necessary to turn her back on them. "If everyone is agreeable to my presence, of course?" Lorelei added awkwardly.

"Of course we are," Katie beamed, sweeping her skirts along the settee to sit closer to Lorelei simply to hold her hand in an act of silent assurance. "We would love for you to attend with us," she added. "Perhaps you could give me a little guidance on the marriage mart."

Ava cleared her throat.

"Of course, my aunt Ava is quite wonderful with regards to that particular matter, but surely it does not hurt to have more than one opinion," she said chidingly, glancing sideways at her aunt.

"Oh, well, I shall certainly try, Katie, if that is what you wish, but you must be warned that I was quite the wallflower when I was your age, so—"

"Who would have thought?" Cassie cut in snippily as her back remained the only view she would allow.

"If you wish to say something, Cassandra Lazenby," Max growled with displeasure, "perhaps you would have the decency of turning to face us when you speak. It is clear you have something you wish to say, so you either say it so we can all hear, or you do not say it all." Max's jaw was rigid as he held back his anger.

As unpleasant as it was to see how his daughter had upset him, Lorelei was remarkably impressed at his ability to contain his rage. There were not many men she knew of who were capable of such a feat or willing to even endeavour to do so. Max was like her father in that respect, she thought.

"I did not say anything, Papa." Cassandra's voice was strained with emotion. Lorelei could hear the edge of her voice sharpen with the tension in her throat.

"Why don't you sit with us here?" Lorelei encouraged. She could not allow this thing between them to grow, for it would become all too consuming and eventually irreparable. "I have seen a particular gentleman who is quite taken with you, Cassandra," Lorelei added, remembering the young gentleman Ava had shown her.

"I think you are mistaken," Cassandra spat. "And why you would think that I would need help or advice from a spinster, I cannot fathom."

"Oh, I...I..." Lorelei could feel her skin burning with embarrassment.

Cassandra's eyes flicked to her father, the vicious sharpness of her features straining as her eyes met his. Lorelei did not need to look at Max to know that he had burned her with a glare that would be more than ample to melt the skin off a person's bones.

Cassandra dropped her gaze to her feet and let out a long, exasperated sigh. "I do apologise, Lady Lorelei," she began, her voice flat and lifeless as though it had been rehearsed. "It appears I have forgotten my manners. I hope that you can forgive me."

"Of course I can, Cassandra, and there really is nothing to forgive. You are absolutely correct; it is quite ridiculous for a lady such as myself to offer such beautiful young ladies like you and Katie any advice on the marriage mart. Perhaps it is I who should apologise for overstepping."

"I, for one, would love your input," Katie kindly interrupted. "It takes quite an exceptional lady to win my father's heart. In truth, I have never seen him quite so enchanted."

Lorelei covered her left hand, discreetly twisting the ring so that the stone would sit within her palm. Max had not announced their betrothal, and she wasn't sure he was going to so soon now that he had witnessed the way in which his eldest daughter had reacted to her simply being there.

"That I am," Max crooned as he walked up to Lorelei, placing his warm hand upon her shoulder. His touch was one of solidarity, sending a bolt of strength up her spine.

"Well," she smiled, turning her head towards Cassandra, "it appears that I, a wallflower come spinster, have found myself rather lucky indeed. You know," she added, "some may think that if I, at my age, have been able to capture the heart of a wonderful man, then you and Katie will have no trouble at all."

Lorelei caught the glimmer of hope that flashed in Cassandra's eyes and the tiny involuntary smile the young lady battled to suppress. She was not so full of anger, after all, Lorelei mused, nor was she as spiteful as she had allowed many to believe. There was hope yet, Lorelei thought, smiling to herself. Perhaps she could win Cassandra over after all.

The dinner party was quite splendid; the conversation, amiable and easy. Lorelei had even managed to prise a few amicable words and a wonderful giggle out of Cassandra, and she was feeling rather hopeful indeed. Everything seemed to be progressing quite nicely as the courses were served one after the other. But then Lorelei always did get carried away in her wishful thinking, she had realised, and it appeared that the dinner party was not going to be any exception to the rather unpleasant rule.

Lorelei knew the exact moment the blade sliced through the rapport she had been building with Cassandra. It was her fault, she berated herself mentally, she should have kept it hidden. Lorelei had forgotten about the ring on her finger.

Chapter Sixteen

Max watched as Cassandra's gaze fixed itself upon the emerald ring on Lorelei's finger. The colour of her face was crimsoning rapidly, albeit the pale line that outlined her pursed lips. His daughter was simmering with evident rage. Max sighed and rolled his eyes, knowing his announcement could wait no longer. He could feel his own jaw tensing, displeased at being forced to dull the magic of what he had hoped would have been a romantic moment—one where he had intended to declare his love and intention towards Lorelei with a bottle of expensive champagne. Yet Cassandra had left him no choice; he would have to speak before she did, for Lorelei deserved better than their upcoming marriage to be announced in a scathing scream of humiliation delivered by Cassandra Lazenby.

"Ladies, may I please have your attention for one moment." Max rose to his feet; the gentle scrape of his chair cut through the quiet as he pushed it backwards with his knees. "By tomorrow morning, the rest of London will be informed of our news, but I, or rather I should say we," Max's eyes rested upon Lorelei with a look of adoration, "would like you, Cassandra," he continued with a subtle yet effective warning tone, "Katie, and Ava to be the first to know."

"Oooh, I think I know what it is," Katie squealed quietly with obvious exhilaration.

Lorelei offered a restrained happy chuckle at Katie's excitement, which Max knew may have been more had Cassandra not been piercing her with her venomous glare.

"May I?" Max laughed, smiling warmly at his youngest daughter.

"Sorry, Papa. Do continue. I shall be as quiet as a mouse," she said, smiling serenely.

"Lorelei and I are getting married. I have asked for her hand, and she has bestowed upon me the greatest honour by saying yes." Max broadened his shoulders with obvious pride, although if one were to ask him what else he may have been feeling, he would have told them that he was tremendously relieved that Cassandra had managed to keep her spiteful tongue to herself.

Ava stood, walked around the table, and planted a kiss on top of Lorelei's head. "This is wonderful news. We will be sisters," she beamed as Lorelei rose to stand beside her fiancé. "May I see the ring?" Ava pleaded enthusiastically.

Lorelei held out her hand, the delicate cut of the emerald catching the light. Katie and Ava gasped in unison. "Oh, Papa, you have exquisite taste," Katie breathed. "I am so happy for you both."

In the throes of celebration, Max had almost forgotten Cassandra until he raised his head, and their eyes met. He had never seen her eyes quite so dark, he thought sadly. They held a bitter contempt for him and a heated yet bridled fury, both of which dimmed the light of her golden tresses. One would assume that one would have had to have done something dastardly to have conjured such an incredibly nasty look from another, yet he did not know what any of them in the room could possibly have done to deserve it. He held her glare with a gaze of disappointment in her. It was not possible for him, as her father, to match her formidably piercing glare, for he had no hatred for his children, only disappointment, it seemed, in Cassandra's behaviour and a longing to understand why.

Cassandra blinked, and then blinked again. He knew then he had reached her, for she was losing her grip, mentally cowering beneath him. Without another word, she turned her back on every person in the room and took her leave.

Lorelei observed the silent exchange between father and daughter. The hurt and disappointment in Max's eyes were hard to look upon as a sense of guilt writhed beneath her skin. She believed that if she had not been there, perhaps the exchange between Lazenby family members would have been amiable, enjoyable, and certainly not fraught with such raw emotions. Lorelei was convinced she had become the bane of their lives.

"May I have a word?" Ava linked her arm with

Lorelei and led her away from Max and Katie, who were happily chatting about the wedding. It seemed that Katie was bursting with ideas, and Lorelei knew she would hear of them soon.

"Of course." Lorelei walked side by side with Ava, the lady putting a distance between them and her brother.

"It is not your fault; I hope you know that." Ava squeezed her arm affectionately. "You do not have to speak, for your face cannot lie. You and Max are very similar in that regard."

"Yes, so my mother tells me," Lorelei chuckled uncomfortably. She did indeed want to believe Ava, but it appeared that the dreadful friction between Max and Cassandra was new—she could not understand how it could not be her fault.

"I believe such a quality is a good thing, especially for those who meet you, for it merely makes it easier for us to trust you," Ava assured her. "It is also why I know that you do not believe me when I tell you it is not your fault.

"I promise you, Lorelei, that it is no lie. Cassie has always been a girl of a somewhat fiery nature. Certainly, she has never been particularly easy to be around, especially when she feels it is her life's purpose to keep up with what she looks upon as a competition—life itself to Cassie is a competition. Do not get me wrong, for we all love her dearly, but we cannot deny nor defend her in moments like these. She has been this way her entire life. Why, not so long ago, she was in a panic that Max would buy Katie new dresses and not her, which is something Max would never do, but nonetheless, she had to make certain that she would not go without, thus making quite the commotion." Ava shook her head. "In Cassie's mind, any female, even her sister, is a competitor. As I believe I have mentioned previously, her envious streak has become rather more unruly this season after she had a difficult time of it on her first. She is a beast to her sister now that Katie has made her debut. She believes that somehow Katie is a threat to her future happiness. Ironically, however, even if anyone is too kind to say it, Cassandra Lazenby is the only one who is a threat to her happiness."

Lorelei listened. It certainly made sense, for there were many ladies she had seen with the same or similar envious streak. It all seemed rather sad now, especially as she was jealous of her own sister. "What would you suggest I do?" Lorelei asked beseechingly.

"Apart from continuing to make my brother happy as you so obviously do, I suggest you continue to be the lovely Lorelei we know. Cassie will come round eventually. Although we may enlist your help along the way with that certain gentleman. In all honesty, I am hoping he will be the key to remedying all of this."

"Consider my help all yours whenever you need it." Lorelei was grateful for the talk. It did not quite get rid of the pang of guilt in her chest, but it had informed her that there was still time to make everything right for

Cassandra. "Perhaps I may be able to speak with her now?"

"I am not certain whether you are brave or foolish, Lorelei, to offer such a thing," Ava wondered aloud.

"I would like to try, if you would permit it... for Max's sake."

Ava nodded. "Very well, I wish you luck, Lorelei."

Lorelei could hear the quiet mumbling of Ava and Max as she straightened her dress and hair, preparing herself for the version of Cassandra who stood beyond the door. She was fumbling and tugging at her skirts, so much so that one would have been forgiven for suspecting that the lady was waiting to be announced to the queen. Lorelei chuckled softly and rather nervously, for Cassandra seemed to be quite on par with the queen, she thought, or at least as frightening to confront. Although knowing of Cassandra's importance to Max and that she was an extension of him, Lorelei had swiftly reached the conclusion that his daughter was even more important. Lorelei knew with the utmost certainty that she loved Max, and so whatever was important to him was indeed important to her.

By the tones of their rather rushed discussion below, Lorelei felt the heat of Max's concern seep into her bones. It was all rather detrimental to her mindset, she groaned inwardly whilst shaking her head, and most certainly to the cause. She didn't know what she would have to do to make everything as it should be, but she knew she had to at least try.

When she heard the tail ends of Ava's soothing and assuring voice rein in Max's panic, she let out a quiet breath of relief and knocked.

"Who is it?" Cassandra had lost the sharp, strong-willed edge to her voice.

Lorelei thought she sounded young, but more than that, she sounded lost. "May I come in?" she queried softly through the wood.

"What do you want?" Cassandra's voice sounded strangled. Lorelei did not have to see her to know she had been crying, or at least on the verge of tears.

Without uttering another word, Lorelei turned the cold brass knob on the door and let herself into Cassandra's bedchamber.

Cassandra's room was a beautifully designed little haven that represented the young lady—well, at least that of her hidden softer side anyway, Lorelei mused. "Your bedchamber is delightful, Cassandra," Lorelei offered, breaking the silence between them. "I should have known it would be, for your gowns are equally as exquisite."

Cassandra sniffed daintily and wiped her eyes. They were tinged with red. She had indeed been crying, but Lorelei could not decide yet whether she was stepping into dangerous territory, for the young woman did not speak.

Lorelei peeked at her through her long lashes as she feigned an interest in the carpet beneath her slippered feet. Cassandra's eyes had softened to merely a curious stare, heartbreak embroidered within the fabric of her gaze. Lorelei believed her to have looked the very picture of sadness.

"Why are you in my bedchamber, Lorelei? Surely you have not come here merely to comment on the décor?" Cassandra enquired, her voice hoarse and broken as she tried, verbally, to push Lorelei from the room.

"I thought we may get a chance to speak with one another." Lorelei kept her tone even.

"Ha!" Cassandra scoffed. "You want to tell me to behave and to remind me that you are more important to my father than I am because of some ridiculously silly ring, is that it?" Cassandra was seething, her anger simmering beneath sadness. Her knuckles were white as her fists curled around and scrunched her thin coverlet. The muscles of her arms grew taut as though she was absorbing her strength from the fabric beneath her as the colour rose on her face.

Lorelei calmly sat down in front of her. "No, that is most definitely not the case, Cassandra," she said softly. "A good woman would never expect to become more important to a gentleman than his own children, nor would she wish it to be so. I do not believe I could love a man who would dismiss his children for a lady."

"Then why?" Cassandra choked out, swallowing back her resentment.

"I would like for us to try to become friends, or, at

least, amiable," Lorelei began. She kept her eyes on Cassandra so she would not doubt her words. "I do not believe for one second that you are an unkind person, or that you dislike me as much as you try to portray. However, I do believe you hide behind that particular façade as a form of protection."

"Oh, you do, do you?" Cassandra spat, folding her arms across her chest and furrowing her brow.

Lorelei ignored the question and continued. "I believe you are disguising how you truly feel and whatever it is you are going through. You do not need to go through anything alone, Cassandra." Lorelei shifted awkwardly on the bed. Her own façade of confidence was beginning to crumble.

"Don't profess to know me, Lorelei," Cassandra scolded, spitefully. She was glaring again. "Have you ever thought that perhaps you are simply not that likeable?" Cassandra sneered, the corner of her mouth curling with satisfaction. "After all, you were left at the outer edges of a ballroom for a reason, and it wasn't only one person's opinion; it was the opinion of many. It is the very reason you are a spinster." Cassandra flicked her eyes to Lorelei's ring in disgust, then tilted her head to stick her nose haughtily in the air.

That invisible wall she kept building had to come down, Lorelei thought adamantly. "Oh, I profess no such thing. I am merely trying to understand rather than assume you to be the lady that you wish me to think you are. You mention my past, and you are correct, but did you ever think that it is because of my past that I can see you are hiding something? I spent every occasion with a barrier just as high as yours around me, warding off any possibility that I may be rejected yet again. Of course, I would never wish to be presumptuous of a person's character, but it is a very rare case indeed that one would be so terribly angry simply because one did not like a person."

"You were a wallflower; I am not. We are different," Cassandra objected.

Lorelei smiled. "Indeed, I was, and in many ways, we are. My wallflower status was merely because I was deemed a woman with far too generous curves," Lorelei replied, watching the young lady carefully.

Cassandra scrunched her face in disapproval.

"Of course, that is not the case for you, Cassandra. But," she added, "that does not mean that you may not be afraid of such a fate."

Cassandra's eyes conceded briefly as they flashed with the truth of Lorelei's words.

Lorelei was careful not to show she had seen and carried on. "I spent my evenings watching from the sidelines rather than being swept up in gentlemen's arms and waltzed across ballroom floors. I did not know that such wretched emotions existed until then, and I could not bring myself to confess them to anyone, so instead, I created an invisible barrier between myself and anyone I met or knew. I learned how to push people away. I was convinced it would be better that way, easier somehow, for I could always tell myself that I was the one that had rejected them rather than the other way around."

Cassandra's eyes had left the view of her lap and were now focused intently on Lorelei, seemingly enthralled with what she had to say. Lorelei did not want to lose her, so she pushed on with her story. "I did it to everyone and anyone, including my own mother and father," she lied. The pang of guilt in her chest made Lorelei wonder whether it had been a step too far as she offered her mother and father a silent, heartfelt apology. However, she quickly consoled herself, for it was the truth that she had indeed felt the sting of rejection, thus causing her to be a tad standoffish, even if it hadn't been to quite the extent that Cassandra had exhibited. She decided that it was not necessarily a lie but more of an exaggeration.

"It really is not the same for me," Cassandra protested as Lorelei watched her grapple for control over the situation, yet her eyes betrayed her with the wildness of fear. "I have had plenty of gentleman callers."

"Oh, I do not doubt that in the slightest, for you are beautiful. A gentleman would have to be devoid of sight not to notice. But one can be admired by many yet still be afraid of being alone," Lorelei replied kindly.

Cassandra met her eyes. She looked like a lost little girl, Lorelei thought. "Do not let your concern and fears for the future blind you to your present, Cassandra," Lorelei whispered kindly, "for there is at least one gentleman who I know is desperate for you to look his way."

"Was there really a gentleman admiring me?" Cassandra queried, her longing for it to be true leaking from her as she willed Lorelei to expand on the matter.

"I would not lie to you about something so important, Cassandra. A heart is not to be played with. It is a very cruel deed to mislead a person's heart, and I would never partake in such unkindness." Lorelei truly believed that a person had to be the most despicable of beings to play recklessly with another's emotions. "Perhaps I can help at the next ball, so that you may get the chance to meet him or perhaps dance with him?"

Lorelei waited patiently, giving Cassandra sufficient time to mull over the idea. She knew if she pushed Cassandra, she would only push back.

"Yes, I think I would like that," the young lady replied sheepishly.

Lorelei stood. "Then I shall look forward to it, Cassandra," she said, smiling fondly at her, "and maybe eventually I will prove to you that I only wish to be your friend."

Cassie nodded meekly.

"Shall I tell your father that you have a headache, or would you like to return with me?" Lorelei offered, for she thought that if it were her in the state the poor young lady appeared to be, she would have preferred some time alone.

"A headache, if you please."

"As you wish, Cassandra."

"Cassie," Cassandra rasped. "You can call me Cassie."

"Very well, Cassie." Lorelei smiled again. "I will see you soon."

Chapter Seventeen

Lorelei held the indigo velvet against her body as she inspected the contrast of the hue against the tone of her skin and the deep black of her hair. Somehow, her hair seemed even more black against the blue, she mused, but she realised it was rather fortuitous, for it only served to brighten the green of her eyes like that of emeralds caught by the light and to soften the blush of her cheeks against the peach-pink of her skin.

She had considered wearing the luxurious, rich-toned plum gown once more, for it was indeed her favourite, but Lorelei was all too aware of the tittering that would ensue at the mere thought that a lady would even dare to wear the same gown twice in such a short period of time. According to the ton, it was a scandalous thing to do, which Lorelei wholeheartedly disagreed with, for she believed their attitudes were quite preposterous. However, everything was so fragile at present with Lady Cassandra that she did not need the ton adding their two penn'orth into the mix.

Perhaps she would visit Evangeline again, Lorelei considered; after all, she was going to pay her a visit with regards to her wedding gown, was she not? Lorelei bit her lower lip and smiled, for she had never thought that she, Lorelei Whitworth, would require a wedding gown, especially not under such happy circumstances. Her heart and stomach fluttered in unison.

Lorelei gave her head a little shake; she was already rather anxious as it was and did not need all the nerves of the upcoming wedding to wheedle their way in amongst it all. If she allowed such a disastrous concoction of emotions, she feared she may never be able to leave her house. Instead, she allowed her mind to ponder the prospect of visiting the modiste. Lorelei had never thought that she would ever consider visiting so soon after the last time, nor would she have believed she would ever have required so much new clothing as she appeared to do now. Her life had once been simple and, it had to be said, depressingly quiet with a lingering yet slightly suppressed feeling that she was missing something, or, as it so happens to have been proven, someone. She smiled to herself as an image of Max washed over her. An overwhelming sense of need to wear attire that made her feel beautiful clung to her like a second skin, and, although she knew Max loved her as she was, she wanted to prove herself worthy of him.

Lorelei took a last glance over the dress, then nodded. It was perfect—new, demure, and elegant. She had no desire to attract any eyes other than those that were a piercing blue and belonged to Maximilian Lazenby.

Those eyes do not lie, she thought, smiling to herself, as

they caressed the length of her body. There was an obvious appreciation in his penetrating gaze that made her tingle from head to toe. Max pulled her to his side possessively, leading her into a slow walk, his body bathing her in his shadow as they took a turn around the ballroom.

"I have not seen your daughters yet tonight," Lorelei offered, enjoying the warmth of his masculine form at her side. "Are they here?"

"They are, but Cassandra has promised me that she will not bother you." Max spun her to face him as he neared a darkened corner.

"Oh, but I have promised Cassandra that I would help her," she breathed, staring up at him. Max's eyes had darkened with desire. He looked positively menacing, but Lorelei was not entirely convinced that she minded in the least. The look sent a shiver cascading down her spine in a rivulet of pleasure. The man was breathtaking.

"Have you now?" he drawled.

Lorelei placed her hand on his chest. "I have indeed, Lord Lazenby, so perhaps I should—"

Max silenced her words as he placed his lips over hers, their entwined bodies hidden in the darkness of a recess.

"Oh," Lorelei squeaked. "I suppose it could wait a few more minutes when you put it like that."

"My sentiments exactly, my love," Max chuckled. "Of course, we cannot remain here the entire evening, as much as I would very much like to." He kissed the top of her nose. "People will talk," he said, smirking with mischief. "Perhaps you would allow me the honour of this dance. It is a waltz, I believe."

Lorelei did not need to answer, for Max simply knew she would follow him anywhere.

As the music commenced, Max pulled her close to him—possibly a little too close than was considered proper, Lorelei mused, feeling thoroughly delighted.

"So, what have you planned with my rather fiery daughter?" Max enquired with an arc of his brow.

"Did she not tell you?"

"I am the most hellish of beasts in my household at present. I am the man who dishes out scoldings for what is deemed inappropriate behaviour. She would not tell me even if I had asked." Max spun Lorelei around, lifting her feet slightly off the ground. She giggled, inciting a lopsided grin on his handsome face.

"Perhaps she was too upset to have gotten the words out, Max."

Max arced his eyebrow again at Lorelei.

"I am not a parent, so I certainly do not criticise, for you forget that I have seen Cassandra's ways, but as a lady, I cannot help but have sympathy for her, Max." Lorelei looked thoughtful. "When I spoke with her in her bedchamber during the dinner party, she had been crying. I believe that she does not think she is worthy of another gentleman's love."

Max smiled warmly at her. She could see an air of

wonder in his eyes that told her he was considering her words.

"I do not like to see anyone upset, Max," she continued. "I only hope you will allow me to try to help her."

Lorelei found herself briefly at the ballroom exit. Having been so intent on the conversation, she hadn't noticed that Max had led them both there. Without further ado, he twirled her into the garden.

"You do not need my permission, Lorelei, but I am certainly going to show you a little gratitude." Max's eyes were wild with a warm wickedness that made her tremble.

"There really is no need," she giggled as he pressed her body against the wall.

"I..."

Max kissed her neck.

"Beg..."

He trailed his soft lips along the delicate line of her collarbone.

"To..."

He bit the fabric trim along the neckline of her gown.

"Differ," he groaned, finishing his sentence as he kissed her mouth in teasing, sensual caresses carried out in devastating strokes with his lips and tongue.

Lorelei was speechless as the air from her lungs emanated in short gasps. His hands were cupping her breasts, and her legs were devoid of bones. Perhaps they were even devoid of muscle, her puddle for a brain mused. All her thoughts had melted in the heat of their passion, rapidly dripping to her core in a flood of desire. "Max," she whispered. "What are you doing?"

"Simply saying thank you," he replied huskily. "I'm nearly at the end of my sentence." He smiled wickedly, his lips curling against her skin as she let out a moan.

"Oh, that's good, I think," she rasped, "for I believe it is only possible to help if I am inside the ballroom and my brain is intact, which, I might add, it is not, for you are positively turning it to mush."

Max let out a hearty laugh, leaning his head on her shoulder. "Well, we can't have that, can we, Lady Lorelei?" Max's kiss on her cheek was stronger this time, with a hint of finality to their garden visit. "You are so utterly brilliant and devastatingly beautiful in every way, Lorelei. Even though Cassie has treated you so horribly, you are still willing to try to help her. You amaze me, my love, and that wicked tongue of yours only makes this," he continued, gesturing to the two of them, "so wonderful, and I know I could not ask for a better wife."

Lorelei returned to the ballroom vibrant with happiness and a newfound confidence instilled within her. Being in love was intoxicating, she thought dreamily as she scanned the sea of people for the familiar gleam of golden hair.

"There she is," Max drawled at her side. "Would

you like me to accompany you?" he offered.

"For me, yes, yet I do not think it will be appreciated by Cassie. She may feel like we are treating her like a child," Lorelei explained. "You do understand, don't you?"

"I trust you, Lorelei, and if you believe you can help her, then I am more than happy to abide by your rules. I shall miss you, of course," he added.

"I do not think that this will take me very long, for all your eldest daughter needs is a gentle nudge in the right direction."

Cassandra and Lorelei were not the best of friends, and the young Lady Lazenby was still weaving in and out of a tapestry of snippy comments, but now, Lorelei noticed, each one was being followed by a mumbled apology or perhaps a guilt-ridden sideway glance from the young lady. Lorelei found herself taking deep breaths to fortify her strength simply to proceed. She was not so easily swayed by mismanaged emotions from another.

It hadn't taken very long for Lorelei to see that Cassandra was struggling, as she would often close her eyes and sigh with a considerable amount of disappointment in herself. She should be proud of herself, thought Lorelei, for she had shown a self-awareness that many did not ever care to possess. The girl was obviously not overly stubborn, and Lorelei was indeed glad of it.

"Oh, there he is," Lorelei whispered discreetly in Cassie's ear. "He is very dashing."

Cassandra turned her head slowly, settling her gaze softly on the gentleman in question.

Cassie's cheeks were flushed with a natural crimson rouge—a clear indication of her approval. Lorelei could not blame the young woman, for the gentleman had thick chestnut brown hair and deep brown eyes with rather long lashes that seemed worthy of worshipping, for they outlined his eyes beautifully in a deep, inky black in such a way that would have made any lady envious. His jaw was brushed with fine hairs in a neatly trimmed beard. A style, Lorelei did not think she had ever seen. It was indeed a fine-looking beard, for gentlemen usually wore those that usually ranged from ones that were wild and fluffy to others that were sorely at the point of being ridiculously elaborate, but his could only be described as nothing other than perfection.

Cassie seemed to have curled in on herself. She was no longer the somewhat snippy chit that Lorelei had witnessed but an evidently and rather extremely shy young woman. The visual revelation stunned Lorelei. She could not quite comprehend the sudden change in Max's daughter.

Glancing behind her, she caught Katie and Ava, who had promised to allow Lorelei the time she would need to try and work her magic on their sister and niece. Their faces and the shrugs they offered revealed that perhaps it was the first time they had seen Cassandra behave in such a way. Lorelei's heart fractured at the sight of the young woman. Cassandra was not unkind; she was merely trying to mask how painfully shy she was around gentlemen. Her success on the marriage mart so far had been destroyed by her desperation to hide her true self.

"Shall we get some lemonade?" Lorelei suggested quietly. "Perhaps we may introduce ourselves to him as he is standing directly in front of the table."

"Oh, we mustn't do that," Cassie exclaimed. "We would need someone who knows him to introduce us." Her eyes were a little wide with panic, resembling the bewilderment of a small girl.

"Oh pfft," Lorelei practically snorted, trying to ease the tension rising in Cassie. "I shall just pretend that I thought he was somebody else, and then he will have to introduce himself and vice versa." Lorelei smiled mischievously at Cassie. "Oh, don't look like that, dear Cassie, for I have no qualms embarrassing myself if it will bring you happiness. Now, come along."

Cassandra's mouth hung slightly open as she stared at Lorelei, unable to ascertain how she should respond.

"I wouldn't look like that, Cassie, for I have known a person or two who have consumed a fly in very similar circumstances." Lorelei pulled a funny, grimacing face, delighting in the giggle it pulled from the young lady at her side as she quickly closed her mouth. "That's better," she crooned. "We shall be able to meet your future husband now."

Cassandra followed obediently through the crowds, deciding that perhaps she liked Lady Lorelei very much.

"Well, I never," Katie remarked, moving up closer behind Lorelei and peering over her shoulder.

"Look at that smile on her face. She is positively beaming," Ava added, standing to the other side of Lorelei.

"You are next, Katie," Lorelei grinned cheekily, turning her head to the side so she may see her from the corner of her eye.

Katie moved around her until they were side by side. "I thank you, Lorelei, but there is no need," she said, waving her evidently full dance card.

Ava giggled. "Katie has never been terribly shy, Lorelei. I hadn't thought Cassie was either until now. She was always a talkative child, but I suppose it is rather different when there is no pressure of expectation placed on one's shoulders. One can be carefree."

"It surprised me too," Lorelei replied thoughtfully.

"You have an excuse," Ava sighed, "whereas I have not. It makes perfect sense though, for her bad moods began to increase slightly towards the end of last season, then became worse this season. I am assuming that she felt more pressure this year because she believed herself in competition with her sister."

"Oh, but I—" Katie interjected, worry etched on

her face.

"It is not your fault," Ava declared before Katie misunderstood. "Sometimes we think and react in terrible ways, simply believing things that are just not true, and I suppose that is what Cassie had done. She was so consumed by how the gentlemen responded to you, Katie, that she forgot who she is and what she is worth. I am sad to say that it had begun to make her bitter."

"I am afraid I have to agree," Lorelei breathed, "but she did not do it on purpose. She was insecure, and insecurities creep up on people, sometimes manifesting themselves in words one might never have dreamed of saying before. My mother was the same when my father died because she was terrified of losing me as well."

"Oh, that is sad," Katie replied, squeezing Lorelei's hand softly. "I hope it is not like that now."

"Actually, it was only recently that she confessed how she felt. I must say it was a relief."

"I can imagine," Ava said, taking her other hand. "I believe you are a most wonderful addition to our family, Lorelei."

"I agree." Katie nudged Lorelei's shoulder gently.

"Thank you, ladies. Now," she continued, "I rather think that he may be a rather lovely addition too."

Ava and Katie's eyes followed Lorelei's line of sight to where Cassie blossomed beneath the affectionate gaze of the dashing Benjamin Sinclair.

"Yes," Ava sighed happily. "I believe you are quite

correct."

Chapter Eighteen

Maximilian Lazenby strode into the dining room, his shoulders back, feeling exquisitely carefree as contentment washed over him in pleasantly uplifting waves. Lorelei Whitworth was not only the most beautiful lady in all of England, for it appeared that she was indeed the most thoughtful and caring lady too.

"Good morning, m'lord," the maid mumbled, offering a small curtsey.

"Good morning." Max was grinning profusely. "It is a wonderful morning, is it not?"

"Indeed, m'lord," she mumbled. Her cheeks crimsoned as she scurried from the room, muttering something about tea.

"What on earth did you say to her?" Ava gasped, her mouth tilting up at the side in amusement. "She looked very hot and bothered, I must say. Do you know, I do believe we could have lit a candle with her face."

Max closed his eyes, his shoulders bobbing up and down with mirth as he pinched the bridge of his nose in a futile attempt to cease his laughter. "You are terrible, Ava," he responded, sighing happily. "As far as

I am aware, I did not say anything other than offering a morning greeting and commenting on the weather. I thought I was being rather polite."

"Must be that smile you are wearing, Max. Even I, as your sister, can see that you are terribly handsome, and even more so when you smile." Ava settled in a seat at the table and proceeded to pour the tea.

"Your Lorelei is an absolute miracle worker, Max," she remarked, changing the subject. "Cassandra was positively beaming all night. I am hoping your daughter realises how lucky she is that Lorelei even wanted to help her."

"Indeed," Max responded. "It has been quite a while since I have seen Cassandra that happy, and it was a wonderful sight. I am hoping, of course, that the young gentleman who seems to have captured her attention will be calling this morning, or I am afraid she will only return to how she was."

"Yes, I had considered that," Ava replied thoughtfully. "Still, we must remain positive. The man would be a fool not to call."

"I quite agree." Max's voice dropped to a low murmur as his eyes flitted in the direction of the door. He gave Ava a quick and familiar glance as a gentle warning that someone was approaching. He did not want either of them to say anything further on the matter until they were in private again and it was safe to do so.

"Good morning, Aunt Ava. Good morning, Papa,"

Cassandra sang sweetly. She was dressed in a powder blue day dress that looked rather elegant against the honey-gold blonde of her glossy curls. Her eyes were glittering beneath her lashes as though someone had turned on the light behind them. It was wonderful to witness, Max thought.

Katie teetered on the tips of her toes close behind her, her nose stuck in a book as her eyes devoured the words on the page.

"You will have an accident if you do not look where you are walking, Katherine Anne Lazenby," Max warned gently.

The use of her full name pulled Katie from the grasp of literature to face her father. "Sorry, Papa. I could not help myself, for it is indeed a very good book."

"You are forgiven. Won't you both have some breakfast with us?" Max gestured to the table and the rather elaborate spread of food.

"Ooh, this looks wonderful. Is it a special day?" Katie asked, tucking her skirts beneath her as she lowered herself into a chair.

"It was such a wonderful evening last night that it seemed a pity for everything to go back to normal so soon, so I requested a bit of a banquet for breakfast," Max replied, looking rather pleased with himself.

"A bit?" Ava snorted. "You could feed the British army with this Max."

"Well, perhaps I didn't mention that it was only for us four, but nonetheless, they did do as I had asked, so it would be wrong of me to moan. Perhaps I should let the staff know that there will be plenty left over should they wish to have some." Max looked a tad regretful that he had not thought to mention they would not need quite as much. It was, after all, a terrible waste of good food.

"Do not worry, Max. I do not believe that they would let it go to waste. If they do not eat it, then I am quite sure they will hand it out to those who will," Ava assured him.

Max raised his eyebrows, questioning whether she knew something he did not.

"Max," she responded, sighing gently. "You cannot expect the servants not to think of making use of the food we so easily waste. I would hope that they would. They know difficult times where we do not."

"Yes, you are quite correct, Ava. It would be a terrible pity to let it go to waste." Max turned to Cassandra. "Are you not hungry, my dear?" he enquired.

"I feel rather too anxious to eat, Papa," she explained. Cassie was sitting rather primly in her seat, making a meal of the inside of her cheek as she insisted on biting it repetitively.

"What are you nervous about, Cassie?" Max asked.

"No reason," she whispered.

"Are you worried that Mr Sinclair will not call on you?" Ava reached out and patted her hand.

"Perhaps a little," she admitted coyly.

"A gentleman would have to be without sight and mind to not want to call on you, Cassie," Katie piped up, planting a kiss on her sister's cheek.

Cassandra's eyes rounded as she stared at her sister; the obvious amazement of Katie's quick and kind response lit up her face. "Thank you, Katie. That is a very kind thing to say to me."

Katie shrugged, tearing off a bite of toast, making Max sigh at her lack of manners at the breakfast table. "It's merely the truth, Cassie."

"She's right, you know," Max interrupted, making Cassandra blush.

"You have to say that because you are my father."

"I may be your father, but I am also a gentleman, and I would not lie to you about something so important as matters of the heart," Max retorted with a smile.

"You sound like Lorelei," Cassandra remarked.

"Must be the tight breeches." Max grinned, watching the words register in the ladies' minds.

"Papa, you are naughty," Katie giggled. "You know Cassie did not mean it like that."

Laughter rolled around the table. Humour was a wonderful thing, Max thought, watching his daughters and sister giggle naughtily. He wished he could bottle it and save it for later.

"Of course I did," he said, his blue eyes twinkling with affection for his family. "Lorelei is a wonderful woman; we will be very lucky to have her as part of our family."

Cassie nodded. "I would like to get to know her better, Papa, if you will permit it? Perhaps Katie, Aunt Ava, and I can take her shopping?"

"Oh, yes," Katie exclaimed. "Lorelei's dresses are divine; I must ask her who her modiste is."

"I think she would be rather thrilled to be invited." A sudden rush of pride slammed into Max's chest.

'This Sinclair fellow better not spoil it all,' he thought, observing Cassandra as she forgot her worries and began to eat. Such a feisty young lady in appearance, yet the vulnerability of a little girl. Max's heart clenched as it registered his thoughts. *'Sinclair had better not break her heart,'* he seethed inwardly.

"I will send her a missive after breakfast," Ava said, smiling approvingly. "Shall we say Thursday if she is in agreement?"

Katie and Cassie nodded simultaneously.

"Excellent."

Benjamin Sinclair called every day for two weeks, armed with fresh, vibrant bouquets of flowers and small gifts with Cassandra in mind. The gentleman's name trickled off the young woman's tongue in almost, if not every, sentence. Hawthorne House had not been so thoroughly pleasant for two years. In fact, Max wondered whether his home had ever been quite so calm. Katie was having a wonderful time on the marriage mart; Ava was excitedly counting down the days until her husband, Jake, would arrive; Cassandra was in the throes of romance; and Max was growing deeper in love with Lorelei with every single beat of his heart.

"I have a meeting with Mr Sinclair this afternoon," Max declared as Lorelei rested her head lightly upon his chest.

"Oh, that is very promising indeed," she replied. "Although I am not surprised, for I have never seen a gentleman quite so enamoured with a young lady as Benjamin is with Cassie."

Max cleared his throat suggestively.

"Well, yes, I do believe you may be on par with Mr Sinclair with regards to us, but you are more sophisticated and debonair; therefore, it is rather different."

Max frowned in playful confusion. "I am not quite sure how one can be deemed sophisticated and debonair in matters of the heart, Lorelei," he quipped.

"Hmmm, yes, well, perhaps I do not have the correct words, but what I mean is that you—"

Max leaned over Lorelei as she lay on the blanket beneath them, her expression tormented as she gazed beyond him, pondering in quite some depth as to how it was best to explain the difference between the love between a lady and gentleman—such as themselves—and the love between a younger couple—such as Cassandra and Mr Sinclair. Yet as Max nuzzled into the arc of her neck, his breath hot and heavy rushing across her décolletage and over her breasts beneath the satin of her gown (the scoundrel was doing it on purpose, she mused), she knew that to even try would simply be futile. The man was incorrigible. "I was trying to think, Max," she grumbled half-heartedly.

"I've heard that thinking is terribly bad for you, darling," he drawled as he nipped her ear.

Lorelei chuckled, yet refused to relent. "Do you think Mr Sinclair will ask for your permission to marry Cassie this afternoon?" Lorelei queried, her sentence leaving her body in broken fragments, cracked and splintered by the onslaught of desire seeping into her brain.

"It is no good, my love," Max exclaimed with exasperation as he rolled onto his back beside her. "I simply cannot ravish you whilst there is talk of Mr Sinclair with my daughter. It is rather off-putting."

"Does that mean you will tell me more about it?" Lorelei asked with far more enthusiasm than Max would have liked.

"Your wish is my command, my darling," Max sighed, pulling her in towards him. He may not have been able to ravish her as he had wished to, but he would take what he could as he savoured her familiar fragrance and the heat of her body against his. "What else do you wish to know?"

"There is much I would like to know, yet I believe I am merely eager to receive some sort of guarantee that this Mr Sinclair will not break Cassandra's heart."

Although Max was not able to offer the woman he'd held in his arms such a guarantee where his daughter's heart had been concerned, the meeting with Mr Sinclair brought much hope as he, as Max and Lorelei had suspected, was indeed seeking Max's permission for Cassandra's hand in marriage. Max thought he seemed a decent man, and one did not need to be a genius to note the way his face lit up at the mere mention of Cassie.

Max always believed that to give permission to a gentleman to marry either one of his daughters would be simple, but amongst the ease of accepting Mr Sinclair into their family, he felt something slip from his grasp, a gentle ache nestling at the centre of his chest that resembled that of loss. It was only when the sparkle in Cassandra's eyes outshone that of the elaborate engagement ring did Maximilian Lazenby feel any relief.

"That is wonderful news," Lorelei gasped, reaching up and wrapping her arms around Max as he towered over her the following day. "Perhaps when we return to the modiste, Cassie might wish to discuss her wedding gown with her. That is, of course, unless she has another modiste in mind."

"From what I have heard, you all had a lovely time. It makes me very happy to hear. All my girls together," he said, pulling her up so that they were face to face.

Lorelei leaned in towards him. "If you are happy, then indeed I am happy, Max," she said, dropping a quick kiss on his lips.

Max growled. "You say the most devilish things," he breathed, placing his hands beneath her bottom as he guided her legs around his waist.

Lorelei gave him a playful, withering glare. "I do not comprehend how one saying 'If you are happy, then I am happy' can be considered devilish, Max."

"Everything you say is devilish to me, darling."

"I have decided that your mind is permanently—"

Lorelei gasped as Max spread his hands over her bottom and squeezed.

"Maximilian Lazenby, you have quite evidently proven my point. Please put me down."

"Over here on the settee? It looks rather comfortable."

"Max," she warned, a smile creeping over her face.

"Upstairs in your bedchamber? You have not shown me that as yet."

"Certainly not. You shall not see that until we are married, and even then, we shall be at Hawethorne House, so perhaps never," she retorted. Lorelei began to wiggle, trying to release herself from his grasp.

Max laughed as her stubborn streak flashed across her face, yet he was immensely proud of her for standing her ground. Slowly, he lifted her away from his body and settled her onto her feet, planting a kiss on the tip of her nose. "You know I only tease because you look even more delicious when you are vexed. I am merely weak in the face of beauty, my sweet Lorelei."

Lorelei curled against him as he placed his chin on top of her head. "I want to thank you for what you have done for Cassie. I do not believe we would be here now without you—"

"Of course you would," Lorelei cut in, dreading the awkwardness that always seemed to follow.

Max placed a finger on her lips. "You are too modest, my love. You have done for Cassandra in one night what I have not been able to do for her in two years. I need you to know that—even though I did not think it was possible to love you more—I love you so much more for it."

"I love you too, Max," she rasped, hiding her face against his chest and beneath the black curls that bounced over her face in a pretty curtain.

"I believe it is time that we start to plan our wedding, Lorelei. I do not know how much longer I can bear to be apart from you."

Chapter Nineteen

Lorelei pressed the palms of her hands against Max's chest as she nudged a little distance between their bodies, bewilderment gripping her thoughts. She couldn't believe her own wedding preparations had slipped her mind. How does one forget one's own wedding? she pondered, berating herself for being such a nincompoop. She could be forgiven, she supposed, for Cassie's happiness had seemed to have taken up rather a lot of her musings, and in the remaining time she'd had, she had been swept away in the precious moments with Max. Although one would have thought that spending time with the gentleman one was to marry would have been a rather obvious reminder. One had to wonder whether one thought the wedding would magically manifest all of its own accord. Lorelei snorted in self-mockery.

Max grinned. "Did you just snort, Lady Lorelei?"

"What if I did?" She blushed, then giggled.

Max shrugged his shoulders.

"Do you know, I have been so caught up with the matter of Cassie and Mr Sinclair, I had not even thought of planning our wedding. I think it would be lovely to start doing just that, even if merely a little. However," she continued, "I do not think it would be wise for us to marry before Cassie does." Lorelei kept her eyes focused on Max so that she might gauge his reaction. The last thing she wanted to do was hurt or offend the wonderful man.

"How so, my love?" Max did not look perplexed or insulted; he looked interested. He trusted her opinion, she realised. It was invigorating and rather rare to be looked upon with such respect by a gentleman, she thought, adding another delightful trait to Max's list of many.

"She needs to feel as though this is her moment with Mr Sinclair and not one that will be shared with her father and his wife-to-be." Max remained quite happily intrigued, so Lorelei continued. "I know that I would be happy to share my moments, but Cassie needs this, Max," she implored.

"Come," Max breathed. "Let us sit."

Max took Lorelei's hand and led her to the settee, curling his arm around her as they sat side by side whilst he pondered over how he was to respond to such a selfless request. Lorelei had quite honestly left him rather speechless. Max had never thought such a feat had been possible, and yet she seemed to be quite a dab hand at it.

Lorelei shuffled forward toward the edge of the settee, her relaxed demeanour beginning to tighten and tense in the silence. "Have I upset you?" she asked, running her hands over the sage green and tiny embroidered flowers of her skirts. "You are very quiet."

"How could I possibly be upset with you, Lorelei? I was just mulling over how long it would be." Max frowned. "It is two weeks, I believe."

"Two weeks?" Lorelei queried.

"Yes, that is when Cassandra and Mr Sinclair will marry, which means, my darling, if I have you correct, that we shall marry soon after?"

"Oh, yes, Max, that sounds perfect. I shall have time to see to those preparations too."

"I hope you realise that I may expire within that time from the sheer torture of having to wait," Max said, clutching his heart as he feigned a terrible ache in his chest. "However, I believe I shall manage it," he added with a chortle as he pulled Lorelei towards him, nestling them both lazily against the soft back of the settee.

"Lady Lorelei Lazenby," Lorelei whispered, smiling as she let the name linger in the air. "Yes, that sounds rather lovely. A little more than two weeks it shall be."

The following week was a whirlwind of preparations for Cassandra and Mr Sinclair's wedding, with seven days gloriously filled with the brightest of smiles and the merriest of laughter from the bride-to-be. Lorelei was thrilled to be part of it all and could not help but feel the utmost relief that it all appeared to be working out quite splendidly. Of course, she did not want to step on the young lady's toes, so-to-speak, so she took a backseat in the proceedings, erring on the side of caution by only helping when requested.

The match between Cassandra and Mr Sinclair could not have been more perfect, Lorelei had mused, for every time she saw them together, they seemed very much in love. It was almost poetic as it should be, she thought, feeling quite honoured to bear witness to Cassandra's happiness as it unfolded.

Content and as happy as she was, she could not help but think so very often of Max. She missed him. It was not as though she did not see him as much, but they never seemed to have a moment alone together, and she longed for the warmth of his arms whilst they would simply talk of everything and nothing all at once. Still, she sighed to herself, there was only one more week and they would be able to finalise their own plans.

Lorelei nestled her body in the velvet-padded chair. It felt rather wonderful against her back and beneath her bottom, she thought, as she bathed in the calm of Hawethorne House all the while sipping rather hot tea from a delicate porcelain cup as her eyes rested upon the women opposite her. Katie was in the throes of regaling a story of one of her gentleman callers. Observing the way in which she lit up like a flame as she dove deeper into the tales of the ballroom, Lorelei could not help but note that Max's youngest daughter was a strong, confident young lady. She watched as Katie's eyes dazzled brilliantly with elation, noting the depth of their blue; the highlights of her hair as it caught the light; and the confidence the young lady portrayed—all of which so very much reminded Lorelei of Max.

Ava twisted her head towards the grandfather clock. "She is a little later than we expected," she breathed, her brow pinching into a v at the centre of her forehead. "I do hope she is—"

The front door to the house slammed shut, crashing through Ava's words and everyone's thoughts, followed by a rapid succession of footsteps on the cold, hard flooring, the clacking of heels softening as the person's feet ascended onto the carpeted stairs.

Lorelei's eyes widened with question.

"Oh, dear," Ava sighed defeatedly. "I believe Cassie may have just arrived." Ava rose from her chair. All humour had been wiped from her expression, replaced with another that, Lorelei was quite convinced, looked rather similar to her own.

"Is there anything I can do?" she offered, not certain what else she could say or do yet wanting to be of some help, at least.

Her stomach was roiling with a horrid feeling that everything they had hoped for for Cassie was beginning to unravel into a horrid mess. She wished terribly that Max was there to guide her. Katie, on the other hand, looked somewhat startled. The twinkle in her eyes had become a sharp-edged blade of light, revealing her concern. All three ladies who had been waiting patiently for Cassandra to return from her curricle ride with Mr Sinclair had reacted on impulse, with one of them hurrying from the room to chase her. The bellow of Cassandra's voice confirmed her identity as it ascended into the volume and pitch of a healthy yet tormented scream.

Katie gulped. "That does not sound good," she stated.

This was terrible, Lorelei fussed inwardly. They could not afford all the drama and dilly-dallying so close to the wedding, for there was too much to do. She did not want to even consider that the wedding would not proceed. *I need to try to fix this*, she thought.

Ava returned to the parlour looking quite flushed. "That girl," she seethed. "There is no talking to her."

"Whatever happened?" Lorelei enquired, desperate to know yet dreading the answer. However, she was quite aware that for one to fix something, one must know what it is one needs to fix. And Lorelei was adamant that she must find a way to remedy this apparent disaster.

"All I could get out of her is that he will not marry her yet because they do not have anywhere to live." Ava flomped down into a seat, exasperation oozing from every inch of her as she pressed her thumb to the middle of her brow. "I don't know what to do," she groaned.

"Oh, Aunty Ava, you know what Cassie can be like. Perhaps she is overreacting because she is afraid," Katie offered kindly, sitting on the arm of Ava's chair and rubbing her back in a soothing manner.

"Might I try and speak with her?"

Katie and Ava shot matching bewildered expressions in Lorelei's direction. "You wish to approach Cassandra whilst she is in this mood?" Ava asked incredulously. "You are more than welcome to try, Lorelei, but I am not quite sure whether you are brave or merely verging on the brink of insanity."

"Most likely the latter, but I cannot bear to see all this effort we have put towards making Cassie happy go to waste. I would like to know what exactly Mr Sinclair has said to her." Lorelei inhaled as she got to her feet, then quickly exhaled as though she were a soldier heading into battle—she certainly thought she felt as though she were heading into war, or perhaps it could be more likened to plunging headfirst off the nearest cliff. Nobody could quite forget Cassandra's temper, even if they had only suffered her wrath a few times.

"Yes, I have to admit that with all the bellowing, she wasn't making much sense, only that he doesn't want to marry her yet." Ava had begun nibbling nervously on a biscuit. "You will have to excuse me, as I tend to eat when I am nervous," she explained.

"Save one for me, for I have a feeling I may need it," Lorelei remarked with a nervous grin, then headed in the direction of Max's eldest daughter.

As Lorelei made her way out of the parlour towards the stairs, she debated with herself as to how she would approach the subject, or perhaps just Cassie in general. It was not as though her being upset was a secret, she thought, yet she did not want to make the young lady flare up again into another rage. By the time she reached Cassandra's bedchamber, she had decided that there was no correct way to begin the conversation she was about to have with her—well, at least none that would make everything better again. She had thought Cassie and Mr Sinclair were deeply in love, but of course love can be a turbulent affair, and it seemed as though Cassie's mood was a rather dark cloud in this particular storm.

"Go away!" Cassandra called from beyond the door. "I do not wish to see nor speak with anyone."

The bitterness of Cassandra's voice forced its way through the gaps between the door frame and the door, meeting Lorelei's ears in an unwanted warning of the change in the young lady. Lorelei closed her eyes, leaning her forehead against the wood as she let out a breath whilst steadying herself for the impending barrage of venom she knew Cassandra was indeed capable of. "Will you not at least tell me what has happened?" she asked. "Perhaps I may be able to help you."

"Pah!" Cassandra barked. "If it wasn't for you, none of this would be happening!"

Believing she could be, quite literally, basking in the sea of insanity by what she was about to do, Lorelei pushed the door to Cassandra's bedchamber open.

Cassandra was sitting on her bed with her knees

bent in front of her, her arms wrapped around her legs pulling the fabric of her skirts close to her body. Her eyes were red-rimmed where she had been crying, yet her irises appeared almost black as the anger within her defied the sadness that evidently thrummed harshly beneath her ribcage. Lorelei did not say anything but merely stepped inside.

"I *said* go away!" Cassandra yelled, emphasising her words as she let her face settle into a scowl, her line of sight pointing directly towards Lorelei.

She seemed wild, Lorelei thought. If Cassandra were an animal with claws and fangs, she doubted very much that she would even dare to approach, but all Max's eldest daughter had were words. Lorelei could handle those, for she had had plenty of practice rebuffing the tittering unkindness of the ladies of the ton. "I can't, Cassie," she soothed, "for I do not like to think of you so sad like you are. I would like very much to help."

Cassandra's face was crimsoning with what Lorelei could only assume was a mountain of rage as her eyes glittered with indignation. *"I would like to help very much,"* she mocked. "Do you know, Lorelei, we were happy before you came here with your perfect hair and big green eyes, offering your help? I was perfectly happy to —"

Lorelei sat on the bed with an air of nonchalance. If Cassandra wanted to use her to rid her body of her anger, then she was perfectly happy to let the young lady rage on. Of course, she knew Cassandra had not been happy before, for she had even confessed to it amongst several conversations. Even without Cassandra's confessions, one would have had to have been a fool to ever have thought that she had been happy before simply by the way she appeared when she first met Mr Sinclair. The difference in her since their initial encounter had been astounding.

"Why are you sitting on my bed?"

"I am simply listening," Lorelei answered calmly. "Do carry on."

Cassandra's mouth hung open. The fight in her eyes was flickering on and off. Sadly, it was more on than off, but Lorelei had fractured her tirade, and it was indeed satisfying to see.

"You were saying that you were quite happy to…"

Cassandra gritted her teeth as she screamed from the back of her throat. "If you hadn't forced me to meet Benjamin, then we would never have been betrothed, and then he wouldn't have told me he couldn't marry me yet," she seethed, pushing back hot, angry tears. "This is all your fault, Lorelei, and I wish you would leave."

Lorelei stood up and moved further from the blonde, feminine bundle of rage. She may have been used to harsh words, but from Cassie they stung. "Cassie," she sighed, "I had no intention of seeing you so upset. I introduced you to Mr Sinclair because he obviously likes you. If you truly believe that I would be so callous, then, I am afraid, you do not know me nor have taken the time to."

"Whether you meant to or not," Cassandra screeched, "you did!"

Lorelei wondered whether it would be wise to ask further questions, but the expression on Cassandra's face warned her that any more discussion on the matter would have to wait. If it had been merely her she had had to consider, she may have probed into what happened, but she had Max to think of. The thought of losing him perhaps made her understand Cassandra a little more than one would expect. She did not know what she would do if Max walked out of her life. Although, truth be told, it did not sound as though Cassandra had lost Mr Sinclair at all; it was more so that the young woman had blown whatever reason he had given for the delay in the wedding all out of proportion simply from the disappointment she was reeling from.

"I shall leave you alone, Cassie. I apologise if you believe this is my fault, but I hope in time you will realise that I would never do anything intentionally to hurt you."

"Yes, we wouldn't want to upset Papa now, would we?" Cassandra sneered. "Heaven forbid that the prim and perfect Lorelei would upset Lord Maximilian Lazenby. You'd become a spinster again, Lorelei, for nobody is quite as foolish as my father. Although what he sees in a frump like you, one can only guess."

Lorelei held her tongue; she refused to rise to the

bait. Cassandra was playing a game for little girls, in which she was not willing to partake.

With a click of the door, Lorelei left any ill-feeling for Cassandra in the young lady's bedchamber, taking only the concern and mystery of the conversation with her. She had to speak with Max, for there had to be something she could do to fix this for his eldest daughter and for him.

Chapter Twenty

"Did Lorelei leave?" Max enquired, stepping into the parlour. The faces of his youngest daughter and sister were a tad paler than what he was used to, he noted with suspicion as an unwanted fizzle of panic bolted up his spine.

They shook their heads in unison.

"Then where is she?" Max's concern bled from his body as aggravation simmered in his blood. Katie and Ava were merely looking at him quite wordlessly—deep contemplation as to how they were to break the news to him, playing over their faces in illegible scripts. Max wanted to know what was going on. He couldn't deal with their strange glances, and why couldn't they bloody well just spit it out?

"She is in the library," Ava declared softly.

"She said she needed time to think," Katie added, cutting in. The young lady was tightly clasping her hands in front of her bodice, one finger bending and stretching repetitively.

"I need to know what exactly has happened." Max exhaled, broadening his shoulders as he stood to his full height.

Katie looked at her aunt and then turned back to her father. "Well, I would say that you should ask Cassandra, Papa, but I do not think you will get any information that will be terribly helpful from her."

"You'd better sit down, Max," Ava suggested, settling herself into a seat. "Perhaps we all should."

"I need to see Lorelei, Ava. I do not want any of this dancing around the truth." Max had not meant to sound quite so irritated or, indeed, irritated at all. He prided himself on stifling his anger, yet the thought that something had upset Lorelei, specifically his eldest daughter, sent ferocious bolts of burning fury through his veins. He did not know how long he would be able to suppress the full extent of it.

"She is in the library because Cassandra came home upset and blames Lorelei for it," Katie rambled quickly, then looked down.

"But why was Cassie upset?"

"We think Mr Sinclair doesn't want to marry her anymore," Katie replied. She was now twisting her hands, one over the other.

"And are you sure of this?" Max asked, astounded.

"No, we are not," Ava interrupted, eyeing Katie. "We merely assume, although we did hear her blame Lorelei for it all."

Max stood still, wondering which lady he should seek out first. Was he to console a heartbroken Cassandra or a faultless Lorelei who was undoubtedly taking on Cassandra's words with the full force of their weight and feeling utterly terrible?

"I heard Cassie tell Lorelei that she was a frump," Katie rasped.

Max's eyes darkened, his jaw muscles rigid with anger. "If Cassandra attempts to leave the house," he barked, "do not let her. I will be in the library trying to mend the damage she has done."

Both ladies nodded to Max's back as he stormed out of the room.

Max pulled back his shoulders and closed his eyes as he caged his anger and hid it from sight. He did not know what damage Cassandra had caused, and so he did not want to do anything that might make it worse. Slowly, he pushed the door to the library open. There was nothing but silence and the soft sound of gentle breaths. Lorelei lay upon the chaise longue, her delicate hands tucked in a prayer-like pose beneath her head. Her glossy black hair had tumbled out of its pins, tucking itself along the line of her jaw and draping over the feminine curves of her bosom. Max's gaze softened with sadness at the sight of the slight swelling of her lips and the kiss of pink on her nose. It appeared as though she had been crying. No doubt she had hidden it from his daughters and sister, but he knew the damage Cassandra was capable of, and it hurt him to think that perhaps Lorelei had believed anything of what Cassandra had thrown at her.

Max crouched in front of her. She was divine in so many ways, he mused, tucking her hair gently behind her ear and away from her face. She moaned, sending a bolt of adoration for her to his chest as he leaned over and kissed her dusky pink lips.

"Max," she breathed. Her eyelids hung heavy as she tried to open them; her lashes darkened by the spill of tears. Even as she was waking, the remainder of her emotions tumbled from the corners of her eyes.

Perhaps crying had exhausted her, Max wondered. "How are you?" he asked, rising up and settling beside her as she made room for him.

"Just tired, is all," she replied, not daring to look him in the eyes.

Max could see the moment reality set in. She flinched as though somebody had struck her. "Ava and Katie told me some of what happened," Max said, pulling her against him. Just the feeling of her at his side heightened the misplaced guilt he felt as a result of Cassandra's actions. "I'm so sorry Cassandra has been so horrid to you."

"Perhaps she has a right to," Lorelei offered. "After all, if I had not encouraged her with Mr Sinclair, then she would not be feeling like this. There is a reason I have been a spinster for so long, Max. I only wonder why you cannot see it."

"If you hadn't encouraged her, I am without a doubt that Ava and Katie would have. If I remember correctly, it was Ava who mentioned Mr Sinclair in the first place."

Lorelei sighed. "Perhaps, yet I did, and now look at her." Lorelei shook her head. "I just want to make her happy again, Max, but she did not tell me what Mr Sinclair actually said other than he didn't want to marry her *yet*."

"Hmm, I am assuming that by all the tears and tantrums, my daughter has made a few simple words into a debacle as though the man has broken off the engagement?"

Lorelei nodded. "I do not really understand what has happened. Indeed, I was surprised by the way she was acting that it was a simple postponement rather than a refusal. Perhaps I have misunderstood."

"My daughter has a rather nasty flare for the dramatics. Did she say anything else?"

Lorelei answered with a kiss, trying desperately to avoid having to answer.

"Are you trying to distract me, Lady Whitworth?" Max teased. His hand caressed over her curves as he pulled her against him. "You," he growled, "are not a frump, no matter what my eldest daughter may have tried to convince you of."

"You already knew," she gasped, playfully pushing at him, then leaning in as their kiss grew deeper.

Max lowered her onto her back as she wrapped her legs around his waist. Her hair fanned over the golden and beige-striped fabric of the cushions. She was a goddess, Max mused, drinking in the sight of her beneath him with admiration. He was at a loss at how she had been unmarried for so long. It was as if she was meant only for him, and fate had simply taken her time.

Max glided the palms of his hand up her outer thigh, bunching the fabric of her skirts beneath his palm, layers of fabric forming a barrier between the explosion of sensitivity caused only by the sensual touch of skin to skin. There was no way that he would allow Sinclair to postpone the wedding. He needed Lorelei, and he could not wait until the man sorted himself out. They would have to fix it.

Max groaned as his hands cupped her bottom. "I think we should distract ourselves by deciding what needs to be done to get their wedding back on track," he drawled reluctantly.

"Yes, I think that would be wise, darling," Lorelei crooned with a whisper of seduction.

"Minx," he growled, giving her one last kiss before he adjusted his breeches and returned to a composed position at her side.

Lorelei gathered up her hair, arranging it into a loose chignon with several pins she had retrieved from around her. "Before I fell asleep," she said, quickly taking a peek at her reflection in the looking glass, "I was thinking that perhaps we should speak to the gentleman directly." Lorelei looked at Max to watch for any hints of objection to her plan, but there were none. "I believe we may get more sense from him than I have been able to from Cassie."

"It sounds like an intelligent plan, Lorelei," he replied thoughtfully. "At least we will be able to ascertain as to whether he still wishes to marry her. Cassandra is not the most level-headed of young ladies. Although I fear I do not need to inform you of that, for she has wholeheartedly proved it by the way she has spoken to you today."

"She is merely hurting, Max. Mama always says that one feels more free to be such a way with those they care for." Lorelei laughed. "I think she may have said that because of how terrible she had spoken to me."

"Yes, but be that as it may, it is not right."

"No, indeed, but now that you are here, I feel much better." She smiled. "It appears that you are a tonic to me, Max."

"I am hoping you mean a pleasant one and not one of those ghastly concoctions my mother used to force upon me, Lorelei, or I believe I may have to reconsider things." He chuckled, amused as he watched her roll her eyes at him in jest.

"Maximilian Lazenby, you do not escape from me that easily."

Max leaned in to kiss her.

"Oh, no, you don't," Lorelei reprimanded. "Cassandra and Mr Sinclair need whatever this is between them remedied, then you can continue with that thought."

Max grinned, imagining the moment in particular

detail. "I shall take that as a promise, Lady Lorelei. Now where do we start?"

Max refrained from visiting Cassandra in her bedchamber. If Ava and Katie could not conjure civility from her, he knew for certain that he would not be able to either, nor would he be able to keep a civil tongue if she burst into a tirade about Lorelei. It was better that they both had time to cool down and think about what they would say. Instead, Lorelei and he had sought Mr Sinclair's address, bundled into the Lazenby carriage, and travelled across town. They were currently sitting outside the gentleman's place of residence in the hope that he may be able to shed some light on what was really going on between he and Cassandra.

Mr Sinclair lived in dwellings that were the usual associated with a young man of his age and lack of title —not that Max was concerned with all of that, for he merely wished for loving husbands for his daughters— but he could not deny that they were indeed not the kind of dwellings that were fit for a marriage, Max thought.

"Are you going to ring the bell, Max, or shall I?" Lorelei enquired teasingly. The people on this street are going to think we are very strange if we do not make ourselves known soon."

"Yes, you are quite right. I was just admiring his home."

"Maximilian Lazenby, is that an air of snobbery, I

detect?"

"She is my daughter," Max warned, a little peeved that his concern had been scrutinised.

"Yes, of course," Lorelei mumbled. "I was simply trying to lighten the moment."

Max had never seen Lorelei's light dim quite so quickly. He felt terrible that he had been the one responsible for it. It was not surprising after everything Cassandra had put her through, he grumbled inwardly at himself, wondering whether she thought them to be a rather rude and ungrateful family. "I apologise, Lorelei. I did not mean to behave so rudely. None of this is your doing, yet you seem to be taking the brunt of it all. It is extremely unfair of us." Max slipped his hand into hers and squeezed.

"It is a rather stressful time, Max. Let us speak with Mr Sinclair to see whether we can get this wedding underway for the sake of Cassandra's happiness, then you will not have to fret so much." Lorelei gave Max a tight-lipped smile, making him feel like the ogre he had briefly behaved as.

He kissed the back of her hand as he gazed up at her, his eyes offering her yet another apology.

"Come, Max, you are merely a man," Lorelei teased. "If you think I am able to bear the wrath of Cassandra but will crumble because you grumbled at me, well…" Lorelei chuckled, rolling her eyes in jest.

"I do not deserve you," Max whispered, dropping a kiss onto the top of her head. "Thank you for understanding."

Before Lorelei could answer, a tall man dressed in livery opened the door. "Yes," he drawled, peering down his nose at them.

"Lord Lazenby and Lady Whitworth to see Mr Sinclair," Max replied curtly.

"Very good, m'lord, won't you step inside."

Lorelei and Max stepped into Mr Sinclair's home. The outward appearance did not even whisper of the décor inside. Mr Sinclair, it seemed, prided himself on a rather exquisite home with a bright, clean interior etched in gold, silver, ivory, and cream. It magnified the size of the dwellings. Max was impressed, and his fear caused by his assumption that the man did not care for a nice home dissipated.

"If you would like to wait in here, m'lord, m'lady, I will inform the master that you are here." The butler led Lorelei and Max into the parlour. The décor matched that of the hallway, and Lorelei could not draw her eyes away from the details.

"The man surprises me," Max remarked quietly, clasping his hands behind his back as he took his protective fatherly stance.

"In a good way, I assume?" Lorelei enquired.

"Very much so. I am sad to say that you were correct because I was being a snob when I laid my eyes upon this house from outside. It is rather different on the inside. It's almost magical."

Mr Sinclair stepped into the parlour. He looked

older than the last time either of them had seen him. Lack of sleep and incessant worry, Max thought.

"We apologise for disturbing you, Benjamin," Max began, "but we thought it best that we visit to get the entirety of the story. Unfortunately, Cassandra has got herself in a state, and we cannot get any sense out of her."

"Of course, of course. Please, won't you have a seat?" Benjamin Sinclair gestured to the settee behind them. "Brookes," he called to the butler. "Please fetch some tea for us."

The butler bent at the waist, then turned and exited the room.

"I do hope you like tea," Mr Sinclair said as he lowered himself into the seat opposite them. "After this morning, I feel it will be the best medicine. It has given me a frightful headache."

Max frowned.

"Perhaps you could explain, in your own words, Mr Sinclair," Lorelei said, straightening her skirts as she moved forward to perch on the edge of the seat. "Lord Lazenby and I are quite confused as to what has happened and believe that Cassie may be upset for no reason."

"She *is* upset for no reason," Benjamin Sinclair retorted with an exasperated sigh. "When I told Cassie that we may have to wait another month to marry, so that I may find us somewhere suitable to live, she started crying, saying that I couldn't cancel the wedding."

Sinclair ran his hands through his hair. "I love Cassie, and I have no intention of refusing to marry her. I simply want to do everything perfectly. I want to give her a good life." Benjamin Sinclair looked at Max. "I really did not mean to hurt her, m'lord."

Max did not need for the young man to try and convince him of that; it was obvious in the ruffled hair on his head, in the lost look in his eyes, and in the air of confusion as he spoke whilst still trying to figure out how everything had blown up in his face. "I believe you, Benjamin," Max replied, giving him a warm smile. "The wedding will still go ahead, whether it be on the day originally planned or a month later. I am afraid that because my daughter has very strong feelings for you, she panicked, assuming the worst instead of actually listening."

"Thank you, m'lord." Sinclair greeted the butler as he entered with the tea tray. He began to pour, looking for something to do with his hands rather than sit idly in front of his future father-in-law. "I only hope she will listen."

"She will listen, Benjamin. My daughter can be rather feisty, as you have come to learn, but you will also learn that she requires a little space, and then she will come to the right conclusion. My fiancée here, Lady Whitworth, has crossed paths with Cassandra and is still learning, haven't you, darling?"

"Indeed." Lorelei smiled kindly. "I am afraid I have

gotten caught up in this particular storm, but I believe she is worth battling it for, Mr Sinclair, as I hope you do."

"Absolutely, Lady Whitworth," Benjamin replied. "She is everything to me."

Max smiled proudly. "That information, Mr Sinclair, warms a father's heart."

Chapter Twenty-One

"Where is Cassandra?" Max enquired rather loudly upon entering Hawethorne House. He wasn't quite sure whether he was a little angry or utterly seething. If his eldest daughter had simply listened to what her fiancée had said rather than overreacting, then perhaps Lorelei wouldn't have been dragged into something so unnecessary nor treated so abominably. Although, he pondered quite bitterly, Cassandra had no right to be that way with his fiancée, whether she had interpreted Mr Sinclair's words correctly or not. The young lady needed to mend her ways before she pushed everyone away.

"She has gone for a walk across the grounds, m'lord," the butler drawled. "I am sure she will not be very long."

It was rather unwise, Max thought, that she not be waiting for him as he returned. She had inadvertently given him time to seethe further, and he was indeed seething now.

The latch on the front door clicked as the butler informed Cassandra of Max's request to speak with her. He had been waiting patiently in his study, trying, yet failing miraculously, to keep busy. Her footsteps were hesitant, he thought as he leaned back in his chair expectantly.

"Papa, you wished to see me?" Cassandra queried meekly. Her eyes were red-rimmed, yet they still held the familiar fire he knew all too well that she possessed.

"Sit down, please, Cassandra." Max gestured to the seat in front of his desk. The study was quite a large room with forest green velvet and deep mahogany wood décor. It was rich and sophisticated, every detail revealing something of the gentleman who sat at the desk.

"I'm not feeling too well, Papa. Could we talk about this another time?"

"We cannot," Max retorted. He could feel the anger burning in his eyes and wondered whether he should close them for fear of making matters worse, but she had crossed the line, and she needed to understand what had happened and what could have happened if Lorelei had not insisted that they help her once again.

Cassandra slowly ambled towards the seat. The earthy, rich brown of her gown with the ivory trim mimicked the blonde of her hair against the brown of her eyes. As she sat, Max could almost see her defensive armour rise around her in a barrier. Cassandra's spine was rigid and straight, her eyes had lost the whisper of vulnerability she had had on entry, and her lips were pursed as though she were ready to spit poison.

"I predict that by your sudden change in demeanour that you are quite aware of why you are here, Cassandra?"

"As you refer to me with my full Christian name rather than Cassie, I assume you are not pleased with me, Papa."

"You would assume correct," Max retorted. "Go on. Anything else?"

"If you have been listening to Lorelei, then there is no doubt that she has done all she can to ensure that you believe me to be a monster. The lady doesn't like me, Papa."

Max gave her a withering stare. "I would not blame her if she didn't. You have been nothing but rude to her since I introduced her to the family, except, of course, on the occasions when everything is going as you wish it to."

"That is not—"

"Do not interrupt me, Cassandra Lazenby," Max warned with a piercing glare. "And do not assume that I am defending her because I am in love with her. I love you both, and I will not be manipulated."

"You are not in love with her, Papa. It is merely—"

The crash of a wood against stone filled their ears as Max stood abruptly, sending his chair tumbling back into the wall. "Do not ever believe you have the right to tell me how I feel, Cassandra." Max had managed to lower his tone to a hiss as he leaned across the desk with the heel of his hands pressed against the wood. "Whether you like Lady Whitworth or not is not of concern to me. I will not punish myself or her because you blame her for everything, despite none of it being her fault."

"If she hadn't introduced me to Benjamin, then I may never have had to suffer this awful rejection. It is humiliating." Cassandra sniffed, pressing a handkerchief delicately beneath her nose for effect. Her father's stance had not even caused her to flinch.

Max did not like to see his daughter upset, but he could not pander to her when Lorelei was to be part of their family, as was Mr Sinclair if the young lady did not destroy her chance with him. "Your aunt Ava was the one who noticed Mr Sinclair's admiration for you. Lorelei was the one who helped you when you feared approaching him. I fail to see how your upset is anyone's doing other than your own." Max's jaw clenched as he tried to release the tension from his body. His brain began to thud against the inside of his skull.

"How is this my fault?" Cassandra practically screeched.

"If you had listened rather than assumed what Mr Sinclair was saying, then you would have known that he has not rejected you." Max waited as he watched his daughter curl backward in the chair as though the string that had held her body taut with anguish had been cut loose.

"H-he told me that he could not marry me," she whispered. "I do not see how else I can interpret those words."

"If you had listened, you probably would have heard the word '*yet*'," Max snapped, "but once again, you heard what you wanted to and blundered into a bleak version of your future. You, Cassandra Lazenby, are dangerous to your own happiness. You need to absorb the words so that you may not only hear what others are saying but actually listen and understand."

Cassandra held her hands together on her lap, her face paler than when she had entered the study. "I've ruined everything, haven't I?" she whispered, her voice altered by an obvious clenching in her throat.

"You could have, but thanks to Lorelei, who kindly suggested we try and fix things for you, we paid Mr Sinclair an impromptu visit this afternoon," Max began.

"Lorelei suggested it?"

"She did indeed," Max drawled, arcing his eyebrow at her. "Thankfully, Mr Sinclair has advised that he has never wished to break off the engagement. If he had, what with your behaviour, I would not have sued him for breach of promise."

"But I thought—"

"You did not think, Cassandra, you assumed. However, Mr Sinclair has advised that he simply needs a little more time so that he may arrange a more suitable place for you both to reside. Sadly, the dowry is insufficient, and because he is a gentleman and would like you to have somewhere better than he is staying now, he wishes for more time to be able to offer that to you."

"Oh," Cassandra breathed, concentrating on the twisting and turning of her hands in her lap.

"Oh, indeed, young lady. I believe you owe Lorelei an apology, wouldn't you say?" Max's temper had mellowed. There was no need to vent any more anger, he noted as he observed the way in which Cassandra's cheeks flushed crimson. It was ample to assure him that she had genuinely listened.

"I shall visit her tomorrow morning, Papa. Perhaps I shall take some flowers, so she knows that I mean it."

"Although that is indeed very kind of you, Cassie, I think Lorelei will simply be relieved to make things right between you both." Max walked toward the door. "For now, though, may I suggest you do whatever it is you ladies do before meals because I have invited Mr Sinclair."

Cassie's eyes sparkled at her father. "You have?"

"Yes, Cassie. We don't want to be late."

Cassandra wrapped her arms around Max. "Thank you, Papa."

"That thank you belongs to Lorelei, Cassie. Perhaps you may give that to her along with your apology tomorrow instead of the flowers?"

"I think I shall give her an apology, a thank you, and some flowers, Papa."

"Very well. Now, do not forget what I have said,

for we do not want any more misunderstandings."

Lorelei had no plans to venture out after yesterday's debacle. She was thoroughly exhausted from the whirlwind and storm of emotions that she had been dragged into. A quiet day in the comfort of her own home was exactly what she needed, she thought as she stretched her arms lazily out across the bed, willing her body to follow suit. The light rippled through the gap in the curtains and lightened the thin fabric as it glittered beyond. Lorelei loved how it did that. It was the very reason she had chosen those particular curtains, for as the day broke, they let in the light gradually, coaxing her out of her slumber. She preferred the gently increasing nudge of light—a hint, as it were, of the morning's presence—rather than a short, sharp shock, as one's maid would breeze into one's room and whip open a thicker sort of fabric in a rather heavy-handed attempt at a wake-up call.

Lorelei wriggled down under the coverlet and snuggled into the soft mattress and pillows. Just a few more minutes, she thought blissfully.

"Good morning, m'lady," Florence crooned softly. "I know you didn't want to be disturbed, but there are some ladies who are waiting to see you in the drawing room."

Lorelei sat up abruptly. "I have visitors? I never have visitors, Florence."

The maid chuckled. "Looks like things are changing, m'lady. Are you ready?" Florence added, hands on the curtains.

Lorelei closed her eyes and nodded. "Tell me when you have done it."

"Curtains are open, m'lady. You can open your eyes now, if you like."

Lorelei slowly opened her eyes, adjusting to the additional light with ease. "Do you know who they are?"

"Didn't say, m'lady. They seem pleasant enough though."

"Perhaps it is Lady Howell," Lorelei mumbled quietly.

"Definitely not her ladyship, m'lady. I'd know her," Florence replied kindly. She was gathering Lorelei's soap and water for her toilette.

"Yes, of course you would. How silly of me. Oh, well, I am sure I shall soon find out."

Lorelei completed her toilette, requesting Florence arrange her hair in a simple braid—it was more comfortable like that, or, if one was feeling rather peeved at what others expected of her and thinking all hell to them, she preferred it loose about her shoulders—then made her way down the stairs to the drawing room.

She was pleased that Florence had thought of placing her guests in that room, for it was the most elegant, Lorelei considered. It was indeed her favourite—a little pocket of sunshine with a stream of natural light and the softest of yellow décor.

"Please could you fetch some tea, Florence," Lorelei whispered as she curled her fingers around the knob of the door. Without waiting for an answer, she tightened her grip, twisted it, and pushed the door open.

To Lorelei's surprise, Ava, Katie, and Cassie were sitting in her drawing room, chatting merrily. She couldn't understand why they had come to visit, but as her eyes fell on Cassie, Lorelei could not help but feel a little apprehensive. "Is Max alright?" she enquired, her voice filled with nerves.

"Oh, yes, yes," Ava crooned. "I am so sorry we have descended upon you like this. We certainly did not mean to make you think that something had happened to my brother. On the contrary, he is quite aware we are here, and everything is just hunky-dory, isn't it ladies?" she asked, turning to Katie and Cassie.

Lorelei couldn't help but notice how her eyes settled on Cassandra a little more fiercely than they did on Katie.

Cassie offered a brief nod, then stepped forward. "I am the reason we are here," she rasped. "I behaved terribly towards you yesterday and on several occasions prior, and I wanted to apologise."

"There is no-" Lorelei began, not knowing what else she should say.

"If you say that there is no need, then I shall have to disagree," Cassie interrupted kindly. "I overreact to almost everything, Lorelei. I seem to have a talent for pushing away the best people in my life, and I consider you one of them."

"In that case, I accept your apology." Lorelei smiled, wrapping her hands gently around Cassie's. "And I, too, must apologise for perhaps interfering where I shouldn't have."

"Oh, but you mustn't. I do not think that you interfered. You were simply trying to help me, and I threw it in your face because I needed to lash out at somebody, at anybody." Cassie exhaled, her regret evident upon her face.

"Shall we sit?" Lorelei suggested. She could not believe the latest version of Cassie standing in front of her. She did not think Ava or Katie could either, as their eyes were filled with a sense of happy surprise. Florence entered quietly and placed the refreshments on the small table.

"How are you feeling now?" Lorelei enquired, still unsure whether her words would cause further distress. She was beginning to feel like her words were fire, no matter what she wanted to say, and Cassie was covered in traces of gunpowder, ready to explode at any moment.

"Everything is wonderful, and once again, I believe I have you to thank for that. As you know, I did not listen to what Benjamin was trying to tell me. I flared up at him in the same way that I did at you. In truth, I have made an absolute fool of myself," Cassie replied.

"We are all allowed to have our moments, Cassie," Lorelei soothed. "It is whether we learn from them that matters. Now, tell me: Did Mr Sinclair visit yesterday evening as was planned?"

The three ladies nodded simultaneously, each one beaming but not quite as brightly as Cassie. "We are still betrothed," she said, grinning.

"That is wonderful news. Although you had me very worried when you were so upset." Lorelei poured tea for each lady and settled back into her seat. "What have you ladies planned for your day?" she enquired, savouring the heat as the tea warmed her from within.

"We hadn't really planned anything, had we ladies?" Katie offered. "It was rather nice to be able to come here.

"Your home is exquisite, by the way," she remarked kindly. "Is it yours?"

Lorelei sat forward, putting her teacup on the table as she brushed the fabric of her dress, trying to prevent it from rumpling. "Thank you, and yes. My aunt bequeathed some money to me in her will, so I bought it. I think she thought I would always be a spinster and wanted me to be financially independent." She observed the ladies' faces, each one thoughtful as to how they may have reacted if it had been them. She giggled. "When one gets to my age and is deemed a spinster, I can assure you I was not offended by my aunt's kindness. She knew that I did not have much luck on the marriage mart and so I believe she was rather shrewd in her forward thinking."

"Surely she would have thought you would marry, Lorelei?" Ava exclaimed breathily. "You are rather beautiful, after all."

Lorelei blushed profusely. "Sadly, that was not the impression I was given on my first, second, or third season. After that, I simply stopped paying attention and started to think of life on my own."

"Oh, that is terribly sad," Cassie whispered. She sounded raspy with emotion.

"I would have agreed with you at your age, but if the marriage mart taught me one thing, it was that I needed to find strength in my independence." Lorelei shifted in her seat. It was rather daunting to be so fully on display in one's own drawing room. Delightful as it was, she had never had quite so many eyes on her.

"But then you met, Papa," Katie interjected. "I do not believe I have ever seen him quite so happy."

"Not even with Mama," Cassie added.

"I am a very lucky lady," Lorelei replied.

"Yes, indeed," Cassie offered. "A man that loves you and this beautiful home."

"I am glad you like it." Lorelei brightened with the ease of conversation.

"It's exquisite. When Mr Sinclair and I marry, I do not wish for a large home with many servants, just somewhere ample and oozing with elegance, like here with a few servants. Yes, that would make me very happy indeed."

"I am sure that would take a lot of worry off of Mr Sinclair's shoulders," Lorelei said thoughtfully. A thought was pecking at the back of her brain, expanding with each moment as Cassie pointed out all the things she liked about Lorelei's home and exclaimed at how perfect it was. Lorelei even heard the young lady ask for her help designing and decorating her home when she had one. Lorelei had nodded, but her thoughts were multiplying and continuing to grow until suddenly they flashed in the most wonderful light in her mind. Lorelei believed she had had a most splendid idea.

Chapter Twenty-Two

Max had not seen Lorelei for several days. He had called on her on as many occasions, and yet each time, he had been informed that she was not at home. When he did receive word, it was in the form of a brief missive advising that he should not worry for her and that she would explain things to him at the Beckwith's ball. Of course, he had replied with the usual pleasantries, telling Lorelei that he missed her terribly —which was indeed true—and could not wait until he would see her again, but Max had transformed into a rather unapproachable beast, so much so that even Cassie had kept her distance.

"What on earth is the matter with you?" Ava admonished the evening before the ball. "I blamed your late wife for Cassandra's feisty nature, but now I am not so sure she is entirely responsible. You are like a bear with an extremely sore head."

"Did you have anything useful to tell me, Ava, or have you simply joined me so that you can heighten my exasperation?" Max enquired. Even he noticed how his dismal mood was affecting the entire house.

"It is because you have not seen Lorelei for a few

days, isn't it?" Ava enquired, ignoring his condescending tone. "I am correct in thinking you have not been able to see her, am I not?"

Max exhaled. He was being an absolute arse, and he was extremely aware of it, yet the tightness of irritability would not release him. "I know I am being priggish, Ava. I promise you I am trying not to be, but with all that happened with Cassandra and how she was towards Lorelei, I cannot help but wonder whether Lorelei has changed her mind about me."

Ava pressed her hand to her lips. "As I live and breathe, my brother is in love," she sang.

"Not helping, Ava," Max ground out. "Did she say anything about us when you and my daughters paid her a visit?"

"Only every other sentence. And before you ask, it was all good things. The lady is in love with you, and now that I have borne witness to you in your current state, I can assure you your feelings are entirely reciprocated."

Max sank down into his chair and closed his eyes. Ava's words seemed to loosen one of the knots forming in his chest created by the ebb and flow of anxiety that had haunted him since the day of Cassandra's hissy fit. "Thank you, Ava," he sighed. "I miss her terribly. They tell you that love is wonderful, yet I have come to understand that it can be made up of wonderful moments, and then there are the moments that leave you feeling as vulnerable and as lacking in control as a child. I will be happier when she is with me all the time."

"Have you set a date for the wedding yet, Max? With all the talk of Cassandra and Mr Sinclair, I am ashamed to say that I had not so much as considered it. What a terrible sister I am." Ava walked further into the room and poured whisky into two glasses. "Don't tell my husband, Max," she quipped, "for I shall never hear the end of it." Ava held the half-filled crystal-cut glass to her brother. "That should steady your nerves."

"Thank you."

"So, is there a reason you do not wish to set a date yet, my dear brother?" Ava asked, bringing the glass to her lips. "Oh, this is good," she whispered, enjoying the heat of the whisky on her tongue.

"Believe me when I tell you that Lorelei would have been my wife by now if I had had my way, but she insists that Cassandra has her day without having to share it."

"That sounds very much like your fiancée, Max. Selfless to a fault. Well, let us do something for her, then, shall we? I think it might be time for her to feel what it is like to be put first." Ava smiled, the mischief twinkling in her eyes.

"What do you suggest, dear sister, for I will do anything to make that woman happy?" Max frowned in a silent question. The look on Ava's face told him that she had planned everything within the few minutes in which she had merely suggested it.

"You wish to marry Lorelei as soon as you can, correct?"

Max nodded. "That is correct."

"She does not want to take away the attention from Cassandra, correct?"

Max nodded again. "Where is this going, Ava? You are starting to make me nervous."

"All you need to do is acquire a special licence and make sure that you invite the vicar to the after-wedding celebrations, and I will do the rest."

"Ava, I will need a little more than that from you if I am to be included in your shenanigans. It does involve my future wife, after all." Max gave her his best demanding stare, the one he had always used on his daughters when he knew they were up to no good.

"You have no need to look at me like that, Max. I am quite happy to share my plan with you."

"Go on," Max crooned, encouragingly, "I'm waiting."

Ava took a deep breath. "Lorelei is concerned that she will be deemed in a bad light if she plans her wedding while Cassie is planning hers, but what if she does not have to plan anything? In fact, she will not even know that her wedding is in the throes of being planned."

Max narrowed his eyes. "I thought all ladies loved that part of the wedding."

"Maximilian Lazenby. Tsk, tsk, tsk," Ava teased. "What we ladies love far more than planning are romantic gestures, or in this case, a romantic surprise because she will be the only one who doesn't know anything about it until the last minute."

"I have a feeling I know where this is going," Max remarked. The dark cloud that had hung above his head for several days had begun to clear. His eyes looked brighter, the element of happiness and optimism glinting in his gaze.

"We will not ignore Lorelei's wish to be married *after* Cassandra has married Mr Sinclair, but she will not have to wait as long as she thinks, for I will arrange for the wedding to come to you both in this very house."

Max opened his mouth to speak, but Ava held her hand up so that she may continue.

"I will make sure that the room will be exquisite. You will believe that it is far better than anything either of you could have planned, and as for the dress, I had every intention of probing the lady for the details of her perfect gown. I will organise everything, Max, if you will allow it?" Ava placed her glass to her lips and tipped back her head, draining the last dregs of whisky, then positioned her hands neatly in her lap and stared at her brother.

"You can do all of that?"

Ava nodded. "Indeed, I can, Max."

"And you do not think that it will upset Lorelei?"

"No."

"If it does, then I shall blame you." Max grinned. He was liking his sister's idea more and more with every second. "If I could get Mr Sinclair to marry Cassandra in a week's time—"

Ava held her hand up to interject. "Two weeks, Max. I am indeed a miracle worker, but even I need more than a week," she chided playfully.

"Two weeks. You plan the wedding; I shall get the licence and make sure the vicar will be here. Oh, and I shall see to my own attire, Ava," he drawled, arcing his eyebrow. "One does not want to look like a peacock on their wedding day."

"Wonderful, Max," she beamed. "But remember that you and I are the only ones who are allowed to be privy to this plan." Ava sighed. "Even though I do not like to admit it, I believe Lorelei may be right; Cassandra would not be best pleased to have to share her wedding preparations with another."

Max placed a finger on his lips in a silent promise of discretion.

Lorelei was glad of the list of things she would have to do. A list of places to visit and questions to ask had been flitting about in her mind for days—the exact amount of days it had been since she had last seen Max. Brief missives had been sent, assuring him that her absence was not that of avoidance yet couldn't be avoided, for she had a few matters to tend to—ones that would most likely consume the majority of the daylight hours. However, when Max's replies arrived with expeditious timing, they were pleasant on the surface with subtle traces of annoyance at her absence and perhaps misery, she mused, both of which were laced within his cursive penmanship. Lorelei felt terrible; waves of guilt would wash over her as she read each one, her mind then wandering to the simple pleasure of a warm embrace from him. It would have put the world to right, she thought, climbing into her bed—perhaps not the place to let one's mind wander in the direction of a gentleman, but she rarely had any other time. Her plan seemed to consume her thoughts throughout the waking hours, but as soon as the world quietened, and when one could hear nothing but one's own breath, Max would creep into her mind and fill her dreams. "One more day should be ample," Lorelei whispered into the dark. "Then I shall have to confess what I have done."

The following morning, Lorelei donned her deep plum day dress with matching gloves. She was thrilled with her new reticule in a simple deep earthy brown with gold trim. It seemed to match every item of clothing, she thought, smiling approvingly to herself.

"I will be going out now, Florence," she called as she approached the door. "I am not sure what time I shall be home as I may visit the orphanage."

Florence trotted up the hallway, a little out of breath. "Sorry, m'lady," she panted. "I didn't know you would be leaving so soon."

"Not to worry, Florence. I did not think I would be going so soon either, but I wanted to get a few more errands completed in the time I have, so I thought it would be better this way." Lorelei pulled at the fingers of her gloves. "Wish me luck, Florence, for I think I shall need it."

"Good luck, m'lady," Florence offered, looking terribly confused.

"Oh, before I leave, Florence," Lorelei added, "I wanted to ask you whether you wish to remain here when I am married or would like to live with me as my lady's maid at Hawethorne House. Before you answer, I need you to know that my only wish is for you to be happy, so please base your answer on that rather than what you believe I would like you to say."

"Your lady's maid, if you please, m'lady," Florence beamed, not even sparing a moment of thought.

"Wonderful!" Lorelei grinned. "We both have our wish then."

Florence blushed with happiness at Lorelei's words.

"Now I better be off, sweet Florence, or I have a terrible feeling that this day will bleed into the next, and I really do want this to be over with."

"Of course, m'lady." Florence bobbed in a curtsey. "We shall see you later."

"Is it done?" Lorelei queried. Her eyes were bright with hope as she awaited the man's response.

"Indeed, m'lady. Here are the deeds as requested with the change of name—"

"Names," Lorelei corrected.

"Yes, of course. Forgive me, Lady Whitworth, it was merely a force of habit, for it is quite a rare request to apply both the husband and wife's names to a property deed, but there are indeed the two names printed upon it."

"Excellent. Thank you, Mr Arbuthnot, but please remember that you must not breathe a word of this until after I have informed you of the marriage. Not even a visit," Lorelei added, somewhat sternly. She did not trust easily, but she really did not have a choice.

"As irregular as this is—"

"Yes, so you keep mentioning," Lorelei interrupted, somewhat peeved by the man's inability to accept her particular requests.

"As irregular as this is," he repeated, "I will not stray from a client's wishes, and you, Lady Whitworth, are my client."

Lorelei tucked the deed neatly inside her reticule, offered the man a farewell, and headed out of the stiflingly stuffy solicitors' office and on to the street, feeling rather thrillingly victorious.

The weather had changed dramatically. It was as though she had stepped from one world into the solicitors' office an hour before and then stepped out of it into another. She had assumed by the bright skies and the honey hue of the morning sun that the day would be wonderful. A perfect morning for a walk, she had hoped, yet the London before her looked rather bleak. The blue skies were a moody grey with clouds that were fit to burst and spill an abundance of raindrops over the dull cobblestones. As if on cue, a plump raindrop dripped down onto her skin, splashing beneath her eye and falling in an unwelcome tear down her cheek.

"Blast it," she cursed, remembering her foolish reluctance to wear more than a shawl.

Lorelei chewed the inside of her cheek whilst she contemplated the skies and her next course of action. She had intended to visit Lady Howell, but no plans had been made. She supposed she could hail a hackney—to her mother's horror—but it all seemed like rather a lot of trouble. She had wanted to discuss her wedding gown with Evangeline, she considered, and the modiste was not terribly far. The temptation was rather fierce, for simply thinking of the possibility had turned her body in the direction of all that wonderful fabric and designs, and her feet had begun to move in her usual ladylike steps.

Lorelei smiled to herself, ignoring the rain as it started to beat eagerly against her body. She was going to be thoroughly soaked by the time she entered the dressmakers, but, she thought mischievously, she could remedy it as she had done so last time with a new dress. Evangeline always had gowns that were samples, which she would happily alter quickly. Indeed, Lorelei believed that Evangeline made them in her exact size on occasion.

She was almost at the door when an exquisite carriage drew up beside her. The footman jumped down and greeted her. "Good morning, Lady Whitworth. The Lordship wondered whether you would care to join him?"

Lorelei gazed at the modiste, a mere two doors away, then back at the carriage. The door was open, and Max's large physique was sitting at the edge of the seat with his hand proffered. Her heart skipped a beat, dislodging the modiste and any gown she may have been dreaming about from her brain as her need to be with the man she loved screamed in every part of her body. "I would be honoured, sir," she replied, smiling broadly.

Before the footman could lay a hand on her, Max had pulled her into the carriage and onto his lap.

Lorelei squealed. "I am wet, Max," she gasped in a panic.

Max growled hungrily.

There had to have been an accidental inuendo there, she pondered briefly, dismissing it as she returned to the matter at hand. "I shall ruin your clothes."

Max scooped her up, closed the carriage door abruptly, then sat back further into the seat, taking her with him. Despite the soggy fabric of Lorelei's dress, he would not relinquish his hold on her.

"Where have you been, my darling?" he drawled, silencing her as he brushed his lips over hers. "It is a dangerous thing to leave a man without what he craves for so long." His lips had left her mouth and were travelling along her jawline towards her ear.

"I told—" Lorelei breathed. She was having trouble forming words on her tongue. Every kiss he placed upon her skin seemed to break the thread of her thoughts.

"You told?" he enquired, masking the laughter bubbling up inside him. He loved how she seemed to melt at his touch.

"I had—"

"Hmm?" Max ran his finger along the neckline of her dress, gently tugging it as he blew a breath over her skin.

"Max," she gasped as his hands cupped her breast.

"I can feel everything." His voice rumbled, vibrating from his body into hers, sending a shiver down her spine.

Reluctantly, Lorelei placed her hand on his chest and pushed him, creating a distance between them, severing the hold he had over her thoughts. "I do not know whether you will wish to do that when I tell you what I have done."

Perhaps she should not have worded it in such a way, for panic flashed across his face.

"I do not think it is that bad," she quickly added, "but I am afraid that you might. Shall I sit over there?" she asked, unable to read what he was thinking.

Max shook his head. "No, stay where you are. I will not allow you to leave me for so long again."

"Shall I tell you what I have been doing all this time?" Lorelei enquired sheepishly.

"Yes. Please go on, Lorelei."

Chapter Twenty-Three

"I do not know why I did not think of it before," Lorelei began. "When we spoke to Mr Sinclair, it never even occurred to me."

Max was growing a little fidgety beneath her.

"Let me move over to the other seat, Max. You cannot be comfortable with me on your lap in this drenched dress," Lorelei offered.

Max grunted and tightened his grip on her. "No, I do not permit you to move." He grinned wolfishly.

Lorelei laughed. "As you wish, my lord, but do not say I did not warn you.

"Now, where was I? Oh, yes," she exclaimed. "Mr Sinclair and his dilemma of a home for he and Cassandra. Well, as you know, Cassandra, Katie, and Ava paid me a visit, and whilst they were there…"

"Mmm-hmm," Max mumbled.

His eyes had the look that Lorelei knew all too well. He was gazing at her lips, and she was losing his attention. "Maximilian Lazenby, are you listening to your fiancée?" she scolded weakly, finding intense pleasure in the way he was looking at her. A lady could not help but feel a certain way when a gentleman looked at her like *that*.

"Always," he murmured, attempting to keep his eyes on hers.

Lorelei sighed with exasperation. "I think I should make this short and sweet," she remarked.

"Just like you, my love," he drawled, his mouth relaxing into a lopsided grin.

His expression was predatorial and delicious, Lorelei mused. The carriage suddenly felt rather hot. "I have transferred the deeds of my home over to Cassie and Mr Sinclair," she blurted out.

Max snapped to attention. "I beg your pardon? Could you please repeat that?"

Lorelei swallowed. She had a terrible feeling that she had overstepped. "I have signed the deeds to my house over to Cassie and Mr Sinclair for when they are married. Before you say anything, I will have no need for it when I marry you." Lorelei went silent. It had dawned on her that Max may change his mind now that he had heard what she had been up to. "If you still wish to marry me, that is?" she queried.

Max was silent for what felt like a lifetime. His gaze was set on her, never moving from her eyes. With every second, their colour and intensity seemed to soften until he closed the gap between them and kissed her tenderly. His fingers tickled as he caressed them over her cheeks, his eyes studying every inch of her face as though he were discovering her for the first time.

"Max?" she rasped.

"Never in my life did I ever believe a woman like you existed," he began, brushing his thumb over her bottom lip.

Lorelei loved the way he referred to her as a woman rather than a lady; it made her feel powerful and sensual.

"You are truly a gift," Max added.

"You are not angry with me?" she questioned, watching him as he watched her.

"Angry? No, Lorelei. In love? More than words can describe."

Max wrapped his muscular arms around her. One large hand spanned across her back and the other cupping her face. They were nose to nose as he closed his eyes, cherishing the close proximity.

Lorelei bit her lip as she observed the tenderness in his touch and even in the way his breath brushed her skin. She knew there would never be another man other than him for her. "There is one more thing, Max. Well, perhaps two, I suppose."

"What is it, my love?"

"I do not want anyone to know that I have signed the house over to them before the wedding. They must not even know. We will tell them that they may stay there for free whilst they gather the funds for a place of their own."

Max was teasing her lips, leaning in as though he would kiss her, and then pulling away, painfully heightening the longing that simmered between them.

"They?" he rasped, catching on to Lorelei's use of the term.

"Yes, that is the other thing…"

Max kissed her, sending her mind into a whirl of rather improper thoughts as it began to melt, drip by drip. She pulled away.

"The other thing, Max, is that I have put Cassandra's name on the deed as well as Mr Sinclair's. Too many women are left with nothing, and I will not have that for her."

Max noted the flash of stubbornness in Lorelei's green eyes. His lips fell into the warmest smile Lorelei had ever seen. "You really have thought of everything, haven't you?" he said.

"Yes, indeed," she replied, grinning. "I have even told my mother I will be staying with her whilst we arrange our wedding after Cassandra's."

"My clever girl," he drawled. "And as for your question earlier as to whether I still wish to marry you, Lorelei, I can assure you I have never wanted to marry you more than I do now."

Max dressed for the ball, feeling lighter and the happiest he had ever been. Without knowing, Lorelei had not only solved a problem for Cassandra and Mr Sinclair, but she had inadvertently given Max exactly what he had needed to be able to order Sinclair to marry his daughter in the two weeks he had agreed with Ava.

Perhaps he and Lorelei could broach the subject with the couple at the ball, he pondered. "The sooner the better," he mumbled as his valet rearranged his cravat.

"Beg your pardon, m'lord, did you say something?" the valet enquired. Max smirked; the man's tongue was poking out of his tightly pinched lips as though it aided his concentration.

"Nothing you should worry about, Henry."

"Very good, m'lord. There, all done. You look rather splendid this evening, I must say. The garnet red is delightful. Perhaps Lady Whitworth will wear her gown of a similar colour." Henry smiled.

"She may have mentioned it, my good fellow," Max replied, his eyes glittering with good fortune.

"Papa," Katie called from beyond the door to his bedchamber. "You are positively worse than a lady, for us ladies are waiting for you downstairs."

Max chuckled as he opened the door to witness his daughter mustering her best withering look. "Perfection takes time," he teased as her expression intensified, inciting a bark of laughter from the back of his throat. "Come now, Katherine, you have a dance card to fill, and I have a lady to woo."

The footman was to escort Katie, Ava, and Cassandra in one carriage, whilst Max insisted on taking one separately. He wanted to ensure Lorelei was by his side at all times, as well as the fact he absolutely dreaded the thought of being cramped in a carriage that contained five people.

"Are you meeting Lorelei first?" Cassie asked as her father placed his hand on the door, preparing to close it.

"Indeed. We shan't be far behind you." Max smiled as he closed the door, then banged against the side of the carriage, informing the driver they should leave.

Max may not have wanted to dress like a peacock on the day of his wedding—or any other day for that matter—but he was certainly strutting like one as he entered Beckwith House with Lorelei at his side. She looked like a queen in a stunning deep red velvet gown. The shade intensified the depth of her glossy black hair that was arranged in the most sensual style: black ribbons of silky hair were pinned in a small bun atop her head, while the remainder cascaded down her back in a waterfall of delicious curls. The green of her eyes had deepened to that of emeralds, matching her ring, and the red of her lips only served to taunt him with the most improper thoughts.

"Can you see Cassie and Mr Sinclair?" she asked, searching the crowd.

Max's eyes gazed over the sea of guests. There were some perks to being a little over the average height. "I can certainly see Cassie. I am not certain whether Mr Sinclair is there with her, but we can stand with them if you wish?"

Lorelei nodded, allowing Max to guide her through the throng of people.

"Finally," she gasped as they reached the other side of the ballroom. "It is rather a tight squeeze. I will be glad of that talk with Cassie and Mr Sinclair simply so we may go to a less crowded room."

Max placed a kiss on top of her head. It may have been frowned upon by the *ton*, but he really did not care for their opinion where Lorelei was concerned. There was not a chance that he could simply stand next to her and not show her some form of affection. He was also keen to get her into a much less crowded room—some might even refer to it as an empty one—but not with his daughter and Mr Sinclair, though. Max's lips twitched at the very thought.

"Max," Lorelei ground out. "What are you thinking?"

"Ah, there is Sinclair now," he exclaimed, turning the attention away from the smirk he had been trying to suppress.

"I shall get Cassie's attention."

As Lorelei waved in the direction of his daughter, Max pulled Sinclair to his side. "Might we have a word?" he queried rather seriously.

Benjamin looked a little taken aback by the fierceness in Max's eyes. "Of course, my lord," he replied. He narrowed his eyes questioningly. "Is there anything amiss?"

"On the contrary, Sinclair, for I believe you will welcome what Lorelei and I have to say. Cassandra will wish to hear this as well." Max turned, smiling at his wife-to-be, who was holding his eldest daughter's hand, both awaiting his word for their temporary departure from the ballroom.

"If you would all like to follow me," he beckoned.

The room to which he had lured them was Lord Beckwith's study. The man had offered the use of it to Max when he had requested a room in which he could have a discreet word with his soon-to-be son-in-law. No doubt the man thought Sinclair was going to get a grilling, but Max did not elaborate further, for he had promised Lorelei that she and he would be the only ones who would have the full details.

Cassandra released Lorelei's hand and sidestepped towards her fiancé. "What is going on?" she bit out nervously.

"There is no need for that, Cassandra," her father warned. "Have we not discussed your quick tongue before?"

Cassie pressed her lips together.

Max could see she was set to explode if he did not put her at ease. "There is nothing to worry about," he soothed. "In truth, we have something that may make things rather better for you both."

Cassandra's lips softened into an o as her eyes took on a curious glimmer.

"I believe this should come from Lorelei," Max continued. "It was her idea, and I am extremely grateful for her kindness, as I am sure you will be."

Lorelei stepped forward. "I do not require your gratitude," she said softly. "I simply want to offer you both the use of my home once you are married."

Mr Sinclair opened his mouth to speak, but Max cut in before he could say anything. "This is not something you should reject if you wish to marry my daughter, Sinclair. It will mean you will be able to marry in less than two weeks."

Benjamin closed his mouth.

"Very wise, my boy," Max remarked sardonically. Cassandra's eyes were bright and hopeful; he would not bear witness to the light going out in them again where her wedding was concerned.

"I do not wish to step on anyone's toes," Lorelei continued, "but I fear that you will leave Cassie waiting for you for perhaps years with what you wish to achieve. If you accept the offer of my house to stay in for as long as you wish, please know that there will be nothing for you to pay. This will leave you both free to save as much as you can for the home you both dream of." *Or you could just sell it and use the money*, she thought, knowing she could not reveal that until the two of them were married and had the deeds in their hands.

Cassandra looked at Sinclair beseechingly. "Lorelei's home is absolutely beautiful, Benjamin. Please say we can live there." Cassandra gasped. "Where will you live, Lorelei? I mean before you marry Papa. You could stay with us," she added kindly.

Lorelei chuckled, "I shall not impose on newlyweds, but I thank you for your kindness. I shall simply stay with my mother until then."

Cassandra's brow knitted as she appeared as

though she had been struck by a rather significant thought. "You have not even set a date yet, have you?"

Max shook his head. "Lorelei did not want to impose on your preparations, so we decided to wait until you are married, and then we shall plan our own."

Cassie lurched forward and wrapped her arms around Lorelei. "I can't believe that I failed to see how wonderful you are. I know I have already apologised to you, but I need you to know how deeply sorry I am. I was so caught up in my insecurities that I treated you abominably. I hope that you can forgive me, Lorelei."

Lorelei curled her arms around the young woman, allowing her body to send her a message that she genuinely cared and would not ever wish to hurt her. "You are forgiven, Cassie," she whispered, then turned to Sinclair. "Well, Mr Sinclair, I do not believe you would ever wish to upset Cassie by refusing our offer, now, would you?"

Benjamin Sinclair smiled. "Lady Whitworth, Lord Lazenby, we would be truly honoured to accept your offer. Thank you."

Cassie squealed with excitement, punctuating the sound as she kissed her fiancé's cheek. "Thank you, Benjamin. Thank you, thank you, thank you."

Max cleared his throat.

"Oh, yes," Cassie squeaked, still grinning profusely. "Thank you, Lorelei."

Max strode up to Lorelei and draped his arm around her shoulders. "Just when I think it is not possible to love you more than I do, there you are proving me wrong."

Lorelei swayed as she stretched up on her toes and kissed Max on his cheek. "The feeling is mutual, my future husband," she whispered seductively so that only he could hear.

"Say that again," he growled.

Lorelei could feel the heat of his hands on her hips through the fabric of her gown. "I shall not," she teased.

The latch of the door to the study clicked, informing Max that his daughter and Sinclair had taken their leave. "How about now?" he drawled encouragingly.

"My future husband," she whispered in his ear.

"Minx," he groaned, capturing Lorelei's giggle with his lips

Chapter Twenty-Four

The silk beneath Lorelei's fingertips was cool to the touch. She adored the way it slipped over her skin like that of the calm waters of a lake, yet when she pulled her fingers away, there was not a single drop of water. Perhaps it was a little extravagant for one day, she pondered, her eyes lingering on it longingly.

"Oh, it's divine," Ava breathed. "The white would look heavenly on you," she added.

"Do you not think it is a little too much simply for one day?" Lorelei queried.

Ava noted the longing in her voice and made a mental note of Lorelei's secret desire for the exquisite fabric. "One day that you will only ever experience once in your lifetime," she reminded Lorelei. "No, I certainly do not think it is too much, Lorelei. Not to mention that your wonderful complexion and perfect hair would look divine in that colour."

Lorelei bit her bottom lip thoughtfully. "Perhaps I shall add it to my list of possibilities."

"List of possibilities?"

"I know it sounds dreadfully dull, but I like to keep notes of what I like in case I forget it later… not that I believe I could forget that fabric," Lorelei remarked.

"No, indeed," Ava replied. "Have there been any other fabrics that have made it onto your list, Lorelei?" she enquired, continuing to saunter around the modiste, feigning nonchalance and merely a desire to simply browse.

"No, this is the first one that I have fallen rather in love with. I do not think I will find another anywhere near it."

"Mmm-hmm," Ava muttered. "What about the design of the dress, though? Do you think that fabric will suit it?"

"Well... Now this will sound boring," Lorelei began, offering a rather coy smile.

"You have me intrigued," Ava said, throwing Evangeline a look that informed her that she may want to pay attention.

"Evangeline made me a beautiful plum velvet dress, and I would like that particular design for my wedding. It was the dress I wore to the first ball where Max and I spent time together... Lady Howell's charity ball," she reminded her.

"Perhaps the skirts may be a little more sleek as it is silk rather than velvet," Evangeline interjected. "I can draw a quick sketch for you if you wish it."

Lorelei beamed at her friend. "Would you, Evangeline?"

"Of course," the modiste replied, returning the smile. "It would be my pleasure."

Ava and Lorelei gathered at the small table tucked away in the back rooms of the dressmakers, faithfully following every stroke of the pencil in Evangeline's hand as she transferred the design in her head onto paper. Lorelei was mesmerised at the sheer ease of every line she drew and the way in which she created something that resembled her plum dress yet had its own originality that would set it apart. The modiste may as well have etched it into her brain, for Lorelei could almost feel it on her body—the way the silk flowed over her skin, the way it flared and gathered around her ankles as Max turned her on the dance floor. It was exquisite.

Ava watched her brother's fiancée delightedly. "I do not think you will find any other fabric or design for your list, Lorelei," she admitted. "Evangeline knows you, for this will turn you into the bride I know you wish to be."

Lorelei nodded. "Yes, I think you are right," she replied. "Will you be able to have the dress ready in about a month, Evangeline? I know it is a lot to ask, and I understand if you cannot."

"One month is perfect." Evangeline squeezed Lorelei's hand. "You deserve this," she said. "Why any man did not steal you before now, I shall never know," she added, grumbling. "The world is mad, I tell you."

Ava and Lorelei chuckled.

"I quite agree," Ava sang. "Although the Lazenby's are rather glad that they didn't, otherwise, we wouldn't be able to claim her."

As Lorelei stepped out of the door of the dressmakers, she did not see Ava slip a letter across the counter, nor the nod of understanding Evangeline offered Lorelei's soon-to-be sister-in-law after she briefly skimmed her eyes across the page.

"One month," Evangeline called out, offering a quick wink of jest to Ava. "I shall see you then."

"Thank you, Evangeline," Lorelei called back. "It shall be the longest month of my life."

Biting her tongue, Ava smiled mischievously.

"Please don't mention my wedding gown to Cassie, Ava," Lorelei implored. "It is not that I do not want to share it with her, for I shall at some point, but I want it to be after she has enjoyed all that is to offer from her own wedding moments."

"Your secret is safe with me, Lorelei. I must say it is dreadfully generous of you, though. I cannot see Cassandra thinking the same if yours and Max's wedding were first in the order of things."

"I feel for Cassie. She does not mean to be the way she can be. She cannot cope with her own emotions, and something small can see her burn up, and then…"

"Explode," Ava put in, grinning cheekily.

"Well, yes," Lorelei replied, biting her lip as she stifled the giggle expanding in her chest. *Think of something sad*, Lorelei silently encouraged herself, afraid that her laughter would burst from her body in a snort.

Too late. A snort of laughter scraped the back of her nose. "Oh," she gasped, blushing.

Ava stopped, one arm wrapped over the front of her bodice as her upper body bobbed with mirth. The blush faded from the apples of Lorelei's cheeks as Ava's laughter infected her.

"Please don't tell Max I snorted, Ava," she pleaded, her words broken as her stomach and chest tightened around her joyful laughter. Lorelei had not laughed quite so hard since she was a little girl. It felt wonderful.

Eventually, both ladies arrived at the tearooms, both exceedingly thirsty and a little bit peckish. "Oh, look," Lorelei exclaimed, "there's Cassie and Katie… Oooh." Lorelei paused; her eyes were wide with intrigue. *"And who is he?"*

Ava peeked through the window, both women looking like naughty schoolgirls. "Ooh, I believe he is the one that Katie danced with twice last night at the Beckwith Ball.

Lorelei made another oohing sound, followed by a smile that made her eyes twinkle. "Perhaps we should have tea with Cassie and Katie. Of course, we shall have to be on our best behaviour, but you will come to realise that my biggest fault is that I love a romance story, and I can be rather nosey where other people's are concerned."

"That will explain your desire to help Cassie," Ava remarked.

"Well, yes, but also because she looked so lost in that ballroom." The memory of Cassie freezing on the spot and the fear in her eyes drained the last thread of laughter from Lorelei.

"Shall we go in?" Ava suggested. "I believe we are getting quite the audience."

Lorelei turned her head to indeed see some rather amused—and some rather haughty—expressions. It wasn't deemed correct for a lady to practically bow in front of a window so she could peer in past the window display. "Yes, indeed." She was grinning, tickled by the expressions on some of the serious faces, as she curled her arm through Ava's and led her into the tearooms.

Cassie waved as Lorelei and Ava sauntered over to the table. "We did not know you would be here," Cassie smiled. "Won't you join us?"

"That would be lovely, Cassie, but as long as we are not intruding," Lorelei queried.

"Not at all. Katie and I have only just arrived." Cassie lowered her voice. "It was an impromptu stop because she glimpsed Viscount Tilsley. They seem rather taken with one another."

"Where is your chaperone, Cassandra?" Ava enquired quite sternly. Her eyes were scanning the tables close by.

"Katie sent her away. Please don't blame our chaperone, for she did try to object, only Katie was quite forceful. I don't know where she gets it from."

Lorelei was stunned to see no humour in Cassie's

last statement. Both young ladies were not quite so aware of their own flaws, she thought, but then again, she pondered, who is truly aware of all of their flaws?

Ava's eyebrows were practically at her hairline.

Cassie chuckled. "Point taken, Aunt Ava."

Katie turned back to the table. "Oh, hello."

She looked positively radiant, Lorelei mused. There was nothing different about her attire, nor had she done anything new to her hair, but her radiance shone from her eyes with what one may refer to as nothing short of elation. Katherine Lazenby was indeed rather smitten with Viscount Tilsley.

"Oh, hello, indeed," Ava quipped. "Cassandra has informed us of your chaperone's sudden departure."

One could not fault the effort that Ava was putting in to being the stern aunt whilst observing a pink rise in Katie's face. "Oops," Katie offered, grimacing.

"Oops, indeed, young lady. Don't you tell your father about this, or he will dismiss that poor lady, and none of this is her fault."

"Will he really dismiss her?" Lorelei whispered discreetly so that only Ava was privy to her question.

Ava subtly shook her head. "It won't hurt Katie to think of the consequences of her choices, though."

Lorelei nodded in agreement.

"Lord Tilsley, may I introduce you to my aunt, Lady Ava Arlington, and my father's betrothed, Lady Whitworth," Katie announced.

"It is a pleasure to meet you both," the young

viscount offered, smiling as he bent over each of the lady's hands successively. "Perhaps I shall see you later when I call on Lady Katie?"

"You shall indeed," Ava sniffed. Her eyes were narrowed, assessing the young man. Lorelei could not determine as to whether the man displeased Katie's aunt or whether she was simply putting him on his guard so he would treat Katie kindly. As Lorelei soon found out, Ava liked to show herself as a somewhat protective aunt so that the young men do not play what she referred to as silly games with her nieces. Lorelei had to admit that it was rather ingenious.

"You can tell a gentleman's mettle if he pursues the young lady even though the aunt is a dragon," Ava had admitted on their journey back out of the city.

"You did not try that with me with regards to your brother," Lorelei mentioned in jest.

"I didn't need to, Lorelei. You had the worst test of all."

"I did?"

"Yes, you poor thing. You had Cassie." Ava smirked across the carriage. "And I must tell you, you passed with flying colours."

"Max, you are required to be in attendance this afternoon," Ava announced, barging into his study.

"Good afternoon, sister. I have had a lovely morning, thank you for asking," Max replied sarcastically.

"Yes, yes." Ava flapped her hands briefly. "This is more important than pleasantries."

Max held an expression that looked as though he was mentally trying to extract the information from her, but when he realised that she was waiting for him to say something, he simply said, "Go on."

"Your daughter is thoroughly smitten," she announced, clutching her hands in front of her skirts.

"Of course she is. She is marrying him in ten days' time."

"Not Cassandra," Ava said, correcting him. "I am referring to Katherine. I do not know what has happened to this house, but it has most definitely been blessed with romance these past few months."

Max's mouth was agape. "Are you sure? Katie insisted that she would not entertain the idea of a courtship until next season."

"Be that as it may, that young lady has been struck by Cupid's arrow, and I believe that the little cherub hit both parties quite perfectly." Ava was beaming. "He is calling here later this afternoon. I believe you will be required."

"This is wonderful, Ava. All we need now is for Jake to arrive."

"Yes, indeed. He will be here this weekend."

Max loved the way his sister dazzled at the mention of her husband's name. It was gratifying to know that she had not ended up like most women do in a loveless marriage. In fact, it seemed—although not the first time around, perhaps—that they both had been lucky. It was what he wanted for his daughters and the very reason he had allowed them to have their choice where a husband was concerned.

"How is Lorelei?" Max asked. He was waiting for Ava to give him her usual sisterly teasing smile—the one she always mustered when he asked about Lorelei. She knew it always seemed to reduce him to a green boy. It was rather embarrassing, he thought.

"She is well. We visited her modiste. Everything is in hand, although she has no idea," Ava explained.

"You're not going to tell me anything else, are you?" he asked.

"Such as? What on earth could a gentleman need to know about the dress his bride-to-be will be wearing, Max?" Ava looked rather pleased with herself as she taunted him. "It might be blue, but then again, it might not be," she sang. "It might be made of velvet." She arced an eyebrow at him. "But then again, it may be made of the most sensuous silk."

Max loosened his cravat and cleared his throat.

"Would you like to know more, Max?" Ava offered, enjoying how a vibrant pink was creeping up his neck.

"No, that will be all," he rasped.

"I thought so." Ava smiled sweetly and exited the room.

Max flomped down in his chair. "Your sister informing you that your wife may be wearing silk on her wedding day should be outlawed," he grumbled. "One's body should not behave in such a way within at least a mile of one's sibling." Max tugged on the fabric of his breeches, loosening them around his manhood, and endeavoured to think of something—anything—but Lorelei's body clad in silk.

"Oh, there was one more thing." Ava burst into the room.

"You could have knocked, Ava," Max ground out.

"Yes, I could have," she mused. "But I didn't."

Max rolled his eyes. "What is it that you want, Ava?"

"There are two things," she stated.

"Proceed," Max drawled with a mocking roll of his eyes.

Ava shuffled a little further into the room. "The first is a rather important matter, Max, for it means you must pay Lady Whitworth a visit."

"Well, I have no qualms about going to see Lo—"

"No, Max, not Lorelei… Lorelei's mother, the elder Lady Whitworth. You need to invite her to the wedding, but she must be told that it is a secret. We don't want her to spoil it for Lorelei," Ava warned.

"Yes, agreed," Max murmured, deep in thought. "I suppose I should visit her anyway, as I have not met her yet."

"You haven't met her?" Ava looked flabbergasted. "I would have thought Lorelei would have introduced you ages ago."

"It has been somewhat difficult between her and her mother since her father passed. They have only just started to mend bridges, so to speak. Then there was all the bother with Cassie. I think it was on our list to do, yet we got quite wrapped up in other things," Max explained.

"I am sure she will understand. I assume she is aware of your engagement?" Ava queried.

"Yes, I believe so. Lorelei did say she had told her. Either way, I am sure it is only to be expected," Max replied.

"Indeed."

"What was the other matter?" Max asked.

"I beg your pardon?" Ava looked deep in thought.

"You said that there were two things you wanted to discuss," Max reminded her.

"Oh, yes, I did, didn't I?" Ava was smiling. "I was wondering whether you would be in agreement if we were to give Lorelei Mama's necklace with the sapphire pendant?"

Ava waited.

"I think that is an excellent idea."

"I will tell her it is from you too," Ava offered.

"No, Ava, this was your idea, and you will be her sister, so I am sure it will mean much more if she knows that it is from you. Thank you though."

Ava nodded. "I really am leaving now, I promise." Her laughter tinkled in her wake as she bustled out of the door.

Chapter Twenty-Five

The inside of the Whitworth family home would not have been so daunting, Max thought, if he had not been there to speak with the older Lady Whitworth, whom he had not heard terribly flattering things about. Of course, they were only ever spoken by Lorelei and perhaps were all rather trivial in the grand scheme of things, but Max could not quite shake the slither of dislike for the woman who had treated Lorelei so unfairly after her father had passed. Yes, yes, Max was quite aware that grief can make one act irrationally and that his daughter had not been kind to Lorelei either, but Lady Whitworth was Lorelei's mother and, in Max's opinion, should not have treated her like that.

Max bit his tongue, reminding himself that Lorelei had managed to smooth over that rather uncomfortable period in her life and the woman seated opposite him had, for all intents and purposes, apologised to her. He would not rock the boat between them.

"I thank you for seeing me, Lady Whitworth. I do not normally make such impromptu visits, but I am afraid time is of the essence," Max offered.

Lady Whitworth did indeed resemble Lorelei, or

was it that Lorelei resembled Lady Whitworth? Perhaps it was the latter, for the older Lady Whitworth was her mother after all. The black hair she once had was streaked with silver; a thick band of it swept into the chignon atop her head. The intrusion of the paler hue drained some colour from her skin and lightened the green in her eyes. Or perhaps they weren't green at all, Max considered. Either way, he was not there to study the woman but to enlist her help, so to speak.

"I had wondered when you would visit, Lord Lazenby. One may have considered it quite rude that one's daughter's betrothed did not bother to make himself known to his fiancée's mother." Lady Whitworth sniffed as she shot him a look of disdain.

Max felt thoroughly scolded. "Yes, indeed. I can only apologise. It is no excuse, but my daughter has been somewhat of a terror to deal with these past few weeks, perhaps even months."

"You have children, Lord Lazenby?" she trilled, despite already being aware. Her irises had darkened as though she was trying to bore into his brain, to delve deeper, studying him and what he had to offer her daughter.

Max would not have expected less, he thought, beginning to lean towards liking the woman. "I have two, Lady Whitworth," he replied, trying to loop his large finger through the handle of a delicate teacup. "You need not fear though, my lady, for one is soon to be married—in another nine days, in fact—and the other, I am told, is quite smitten with a viscount."

Lady Whitworth nodded whilst pinching her lips. She looked impressed, Max mused with relief.

"I would not have expected your daughter to have become a mother to two young children," Max began, believing the lady needed to hear such words.

"Why ever not?" she interrupted. "My Lorelei would make a wonderful mother."

Max stifled the groan crawling up his throat. In his attempt to appease the woman, he had offended her. He could see how one would simply spend their lives appeasing their mother when faced with Lady Whitworth.

"I beg your forgiveness, Lady Whitworth, for I did not mean to imply that she wouldn't, but that I would not simply assume that it would be her duty with regards to Cassandra and Katherine."

"Do you intend to have more children, Lord Lazenby?" Lady Whitworth enquired. She flicked her eyes up and down his body as though she were trying to assess whether he would be capable of such a feat at forty-five years of age. "I believe you are young enough to. My daughter certainly is."

Max cleared his throat. Even Henrietta would not have assessed him in that particular way. It was rather unnerving. "My lady, I believe that that is something your daughter and I should discuss privately. However," he added, noting her attempt to correct him, "I will not deny Lorelei her right to be a mother, if that is what she wishes. In fact, I would welcome another child quite happily." Max could feel the prospect of fatherhood to a child with deep back curls and green eyes, like Lorelei's, warm his insides. He had not even considered it before Lady Whitworth raised the subject, but, he realised, that raising a child with Lorelei sounded quite wonderful indeed.

"You are smiling, Lord Lazenby," Lady Whitworth tittered. "You had no need to reply in words, for your face tells me all that I need to know, and you have made this lady very happy." Lorelei's mother's face had softened as a sense of familiarity spread out between them. "Do you know," she added, interrupting Max's thoughts, "I have waited for so long for my daughter to find a gentleman to love her in the way in which she deserves to be loved. She had a terrible experience over three years attending season after season, for they forced her to the side as a wallflower. My daughter, a wallflower? The audacity!" she exclaimed, portraying just how ridiculous it was to even consider Lorelei as a wallflower, which Max quite agreed with.

Max took another sip of tea. It was turning cold, but he refrained from grimacing; he did not want to appear rude.

"I blamed myself, but in turn I only made her feel worse. I realise that now." Regret and anguish flashed across her eyes at the memories that evidently had a chokehold on her.

Max felt sorry for the lady. "I am sure that I have

made many mistakes with my daughters, Lady Whitworth. I do not believe that whatever it is that pains you, Lorelei would want you to worry over it."

"Yes, I am sure you are correct, Lord Lazenby, but that is merely because she puts us all to shame with her wonderful heart. She is like her father in that respect," Lady Whitworth offered, smiling. "Still, I must not bore you with my woes, Lord Lazenby, for I believe you are here for a particular reason?"

Max grinned at the thought of *his* Lorelei. "Indeed, I am, Lady Whitworth, but before I divulge what it is I would like to say, I need to know that I have your full discretion, for Lorelei must not know."

Lady Whitworth pursed her lips playfully, and her eyes brightened with a sense of mischief. "Ooh, you have me quite intrigued, Lord Lazenby," she tittered.

"I need that promise, Lady Whitworth," Max implored with jest.

"You can consider yourself in possession of that promise, my lord."

"Very well."

Max launched himself straight into the crux of the reason for his visit, but before Lady Whitworth could gasp, refuse, or complain, he proceeded into great detail of how wonderful Lorelei had been with regards to Cassandra. Despite loathing to admit it, he even went to such great lengths that he felt compelled to inform Lady Whitworth of how abominably his daughter had behaved. It was all rather embarrassing, he thought as it rolled off his tongue, yet he pushed the shame aside and concentrated on his endeavour to receive Lady Whitworth's concession to attend the wedding and, of course, for her to keep the snippet of information to herself as she had promised she would.

"Oh dear," Lady Whitworth replied, chuckling. "I believe I may have been quite similar at her age."

Max remained silent. His stomach was clenching around a pool of apprehension as he waited for the woman to either agree or refuse, or perhaps even destroy everything he had planned for Lorelei.

"Still, that is neither here nor there," Lady Whitworth continued, noting the tension etched in the muscles around Max's jaw. "You wish to know whether I will attend this surprise wedding, and of course play along with your plan."

Max nodded.

"I must say, I do not think if it were me that I would wish to be excluded from the wedding plans, but it is not me we are discussing, is it?"

"No, my lady, but I must confess that Lorelei is not excluded from the plans at all, for, you see, my sister, Ava, has been casually discussing Lorelei's wishes with her, then informing me of them. The lady is rather devious, but in a good way, of course," he corrected before his future mother-in-law could misconstrue his meaning, "for she even visited the dressmaker with Lorelei and secretly arranged for the modiste to have her wedding gown ready in time." Max smiled, looking rather pleased with himself. Had you asked him, he would have happily admitted that indeed he was pleased with what he and Ava were slowly achieving, hence the reason he was on tenterhooks as he awaited Lady Whitworth's approval and agreement.

"I believe your level of consideration and fondness for my daughter is rather evident in your endeavour, Lord Lazenby," she said, a thoughtful gaze in her eyes.

"I am in love with your daughter, Lady Whitworth," Max confessed. "I would never strive to do anything that would hurt or upset her in any way."

"Yes, I do indeed believe you, and for that very reason, I will keep my promise of your secret and would love to accept your invitation to bear witness to my daughter's wedding as your guest."

Max wandered from Lorelei's childhood home with his heart practically singing and dancing in his chest. His meeting with Lady Whitworth had been the success he had hoped for. She hadn't even criticised Cassandra, which had been a pleasant surprise, but instead, she had almost sympathised. It was a relief, for no father revels in the negative critique of their child or children, even if they may have deserved it.

"Cassie, Katie," Lorelei exclaimed quietly as she looked up from her book. "I did not know you were here."

"We said we would announce ourselves," Katie replied, stretching her neck to peer over Lorelei's book to see what she was reading.

"Emma, written by Charlotte Bronte," Lorelei said, in answer to her curiosity. "It is quite amusing.

"Would you like some tea, ladies?" Lorelei added.

"Actually, Lorelei, we have come to ask if you might consider joining us on our visit to the modiste?" Cassandra offered. "I feel I need the opinion of a lady such as yourself for my final fitting."

"Oh, I would love to, Cassie. Thank you."

Cassie and Katie giggled with glee at Lorelei's eager response. "Wonderful," they chorused.

The ladies squeezed out of the door onto the street, their bubble of amiability popping and spilling its contents in a pool of easy chatter and giggles. Cassandra seemed to have a coil of excitement wound so very tight inside of her and was trying desperately to contain it, for fear of being judged with regards to her comportment.

It was rather sad, Lorelei thought, that a lady feared being judged for merely being in possession of a tad too much happiness and perhaps the release of an excited squeal or two. Lorelei grabbed both ladies' hands and led them into a quiet area where they would not be seen or heard. "You can let it out now," she smiled, her eyes twinkling at Cassie.

Cassandra did not give herself the opportunity to ask what it was that Lorelei was referring to, for when she opened her mouth all she could do was release a squeal of excitement that almost seemed to whistle as it tapered off into the air.

"Ooh," Katie breathed. "So that is what you meant, Lorelei."

"Yes. If it were I, I do not believe I would have cared who heard and what they would have thought of me, but I am much older than you ladies, and I have not got all the eyes of society trying to evaluate me for their sons." Lorelei smiled.

"Not that we are interested, of course, now that I shall be married soon, and I am sure it will only be a matter of days before Lord Tilsley speaks with Papa about Katie," Cassie replied, smiling. "However, I do not think I would ever have thought to sneak down a side street simply so one does not stir the sensibilities of London's finest." Cassie chuckled. "It was a very good idea indeed, for I thought I may have exploded back there." Cassie blushed.

"I shall be just the same, Cassie," Katie offered.

All three ladies re-entered the street, the very vision of propriety as they made their way towards the dressmaker. It was rather strange not to be visiting Evangeline, Lorelei pondered, as her mind turned to her own wedding gown.

Cassandra's wedding gown was divine. Most ladies with golden hair seemed to choose colours such as a pastel shade of blue, which she had seen Cassie wear on an occasion or two, yet as the young bride-to-be stood before Lorelei and Katie, words escaped Lorelei. The dress was a deep, rich, decadent brown velvet; every inch, designed to follow the sleek lines of her body and accentuate her bosom. Gold sparkled under the light as it trailed over the twinkling embroidered trim, highlighting the curves of her décolletage. Her skirts fanned out a tad at the sides, giving her more shapely hips, and her golden curls bounced upon the naked skin of her shoulders. Then there was the matter of her brown eyes amidst all the regality of her ensemble... Lorelei simply did not have words for how much they sparkled.

"Oh, Cassie," she exclaimed breathlessly. "You look radiant."

Cassie blushed a soft pink as she twirled a fraction from side to side. She looked at Katie, but her sister was silent, all but a sniffle as she wiped away the tear streaming from her eye.

"What do you think, Katie?" Cassie whispered across the small room.

Katie swallowed, trying desperately to regain her voice. "Y-you look like a princess, Cassie," she said, sniffling. "Actually, no, you don't look like a princess at all," she corrected herself, "for you look like a queen, Cassandra Lazenby."

Cassie was beaming. All the excitement she had released in the quiet street was happily being replaced, drop by drop. Lorelei looked to the modiste who also looked to be shedding a tear or two. The lady was thrilled at the bride-to-be's reaction.

"I think you won't need a quiet street in here,

Cassie," Lorelei assured her. To which, of course, Cassandra Lazenby simply burst.

"Is there anything that you ladies feel I should change?" Cassie asked, once composed as she turned herself towards the looking glass. Her eyes scanned her image, searching for any imperfections.

"Do not change a single thing, Cassie," Lorelei replied, walking up beside her and holding her hand. "You look beautiful, exquisite, and divine all rolled into one. I do believe your father may shed a tear when he sees you like this."

Cassie stretched across and dropped a light kiss on Lorelei's cheek. "Thank you," she whispered.

Lorelei squeezed her hand and stepped away.

Chapter Twenty-Six

Max had very much hoped that the remaining eight days prior to Cassandra's wedding, and indeed his and Lorelei's, would have sped by at a rate similar to that of the week before, but despite the whirlwind of activity, one simply could not help but notice that the hours dragged by like the devil. Those eight days could only have been described as sheer torture, Max thought with displeasure. He supposed he should not have insisted on the rather regular glances at clocks wherever he went, nor should he have been quite as devoted to the marking down of days on the calendar, for it all had him rather frustrated. Time no longer passed by in a breeze but had become as thick and dense as honey whilst his body and mind waded tirelessly through the seconds, minutes, and hours. However, as Max spread a thin line of ink through yesterday's date, he exhaled with relief that the day had finally arrived.

Apart from the one room—the library, which Ava had pushed four members of staff into, muttering something rather demanding whilst locking the door behind them—the house was a hive of activity. It was making Max's head spin.

"I have to go out," he called, striding to the door, desperation for the peace and quiet evident in his speed.

"Maximilian Lazenby, where exactly do you think you are going?" Ava called as she stood, hands on hips, her eyes boring holes in the back of Max's ink-black jacket.

Max spun on his heel to face his sister. "I was hoping to pay my fiancée a visit."

"Were you now?" she retorted, arcing her right eyebrow. "I do not see how leaving Hawethorne House will achieve that when she is here already."

Max's mouth formed an o as he watched his sister bustle closer. He had seen that look in her eyes before—she had something quite secretive to say.

"You need to help me keep her away from the library, Max," she whispered. "The lady is very perceptive, rather too perceptive if you ask me, and I can almost feel her itching to enquire as to the very reason why I have locked it. I am not the best liar, Max, as you well know."

Max raised his eyebrows.

"Do not look at me like that, Maximilian! I may be sneaky, but I am not a liar. I can do all that secretive planning and whatnot, but you know I cannot lie to someone, for I will simply make an utter fool of myself."

"Yes, all that blushing and stuttering you do when you are in a pickle could prove quite the problem," Max mused aloud. "I suppose one could *try* and occupy her," he replied as though it were a terrible chore.

Ava groaned at the lovesick, lopsided grin on her brother's face. "I don't care how you occupy her, Max, just so long as you do. It is only for another hour, and then we will need to make sure that Cassie is in that carriage heading for the church."

Max snapped to attention at the mention of the church. He was being utterly useless on his own daughter's wedding day, he inwardly berated himself.

"Do not fret, Max. It is perfectly normal to not be quite oneself on the day of their marriage," she said, lowering her voice at the mention of his wedding. "Jake has been helping me, so all you need to do is be the attentive fiancé and, of course, the attentive father."

"I can do that," he assured her.

Ava smiled with relief. "I know you can, Max," she replied, walking away, back towards her husband, Jake. He was a strong-looking man with golden hair and whose stance was rather proud as he curled his arms around Ava's waist and whispered in her ear. Ava was chuckling amidst the warmth of a rosy blush, Max noted. He watched her depart, heading upstairs to Cassandra's bedchamber, whilst Jake turned—looking rather pleased with himself—toward the locked library, where he was ordered to stand on guard.

Max searched the parlour and then the drawing room for any signs of Lorelei, but to no avail. It was the soft, contagious giggle that leaked out from the ballroom that drew his feet towards her. He should have known that she would not simply have been able to sit idly by while the rest of the household were hard at work. She was chatting with a maid who was approximately the same age as her, both of them in a happy rhythm of chatter and laughter. If Max had not known any better, he would have believed them to have been lifelong friends; the only clue that they were not was the significant difference in their attire. Max smiled to himself at how easily Lorelei would fit in at Hawethorne House and how much he knew the servants would adore her.

"Max," she breathed, turning around. The maid had nudged her gently when she had noticed him watching. "Nellie has been showing me how to dress the tables. It is all rather intricate, somewhat confusing, yet utterly fascinating. I have been having a wonderful time with her."

"So, I see," he crooned, brushing her lips with a kiss. "But I am afraid I am going to have to steal Lady Lorelei away from you, Nellie. I hope you do not mind."

"Not at all, m'lord," she replied, bobbing low into a curtsey.

"It was lovely to meet you, Nellie. I hope I see you again soon. I think you are wonderful," Lorelei offered, smiling as she placed her hand in Max's.

Nellie blushed. "Twas lovely to meet you too, m'lady," she replied happily.

Max twirled Lorelei across the ballroom dance floor, the music absent, except that which only they could hear. Lorelei threw her head back with joy as she began to hum her own tune.

"What music is that?" Max asked, his brow furrowing at the lack of recognition of such a pretty piece.

"I have no idea, Max." Lorelei smiled, then continued with the tune.

She savoured the melody, flowing over her tongue and whispering over her lips as she tried to see whether she, herself, knew what the music was. "I think I might have made it up," she declared softly.

Max tightened his grip around her waist, lifting her off her feet and spinning them both on the spot. "You, Lorelei, are wonderfully beautiful, ferociously kind, marvellously musical, and utterly delicious," he stated before pressing his lips to hers.

A flutter of nerves rippled in Max's stomach. He had had days to decipher whether a surprise wedding would be right for Lorelei, but more so whether she would be angry at him for doing it all behind her back. Ava had agreed that it was indeed a good idea; after all, it had been hers. Her words had bolstered Max's confidence, yet there was the moment when Lady Whitworth had questioned it. She had even said that she would not be best pleased if it were her. Yet, Max mused nervously, he had still bundled forward in his endeavour to marry Lorelei as soon as was possible.

"Is everything alright, Max?" Lorelei queried. She was searching his face, trying to read his thoughts.

"I was just thinking how much I want to marry

you," he growled, nestling his face in the arc of her neck so she would not have a chance to read the worry that was there.

"I would marry you today were I given the opportunity," Lorelei whispered, turning her face so that her cheek pressed against his and her lips were soft against his ear. How little she knew as to how soothing her words were, Max thought with relief, for she had eradicated his fear without even knowing.

Max cupped Lorelei's face with his large hands, his gaze filled with an unspoken devotion to her. "We have the same wish," he breathed. "I do not think this house has ever seen so much love, for we are to be married; Cassie is marrying today; and just yesterday I had a visit from Lord Tilsley, requesting my permission to marry Katie."

"That is wonderful news, Max. Katie must be thrilled."

"Katie has always been a happy child, but I must confess that I do not believe I have ever seen her quite so happy," Max grinned, lacing their fingers together.

As Lorelei and Max stepped out of the ballroom, both in the throes of conversation about the newest betrothed couple, Max spotted a twinkle of gold from the corner of his eye.

Lorelei gasped, then pulled her eyes away from the vision of beauty to observe her fiancé as he proudly watched his eldest daughter descend the stairs.

Max swallowed, then inhaled and exhaled as he

tried to release the muscles in his throat that were clamping around a swell of emotion. The sight of how elegant Cassie was had left him at a loss for words. Her poise was graceful, and her eyes sparkled like those of a young woman on the brink of an exciting new future.

"Go to her," Lorelei whispered, subtly releasing his hand.

Max couldn't move. "You look… You are a vision of beauty, my darling girl. I am so proud of you."

"Thank you, Papa," Cassie replied. The light in her eyes revealed that she felt as incredible as she looked. "Shall we go now, Papa?"

Max offered his arm to the bride and escorted her to the carriage.

Lorelei breathed a sigh of relief as the vicar announced the young couple as man and wife. Although it had not been so very long, the time and strife leading to the wedding of Mr and Mrs Sinclair had been fraught with a fragility that Lorelei could honestly say she had never quite experienced before. She had dealt with her mother after her father passed, but with Lady Whitworth, there had never been a fear of losing her through a disagreement nor losing any of those around her. The two ladies had simply fumbled their way through with a continuous sense of security, whereas with Cassandra, Lorelei likened the situation and the young woman's friendship to behave much like sand between her fingers—never knowing how long she could keep hold of the peace between them. She was never sure whether Max would have considered their engagement all too much for him because of his daughter's reaction to her. The terrifying risk of losing him had always seemed to hang precariously over her head, threatening to crash down upon her. Yet, as she peered down at her fiancé's hand, his fingers entwined with hers, she realised they had made it.

Max lifted her hand to his lips and kissed the back of it. "One down, one to go," he drawled wickedly, his words curling his mouth into a wolfish grin.

"Indeed, Max," she replied as he guided her out of the church.

The newly married couple returned to Hawethorne House, where celebrations commenced, a sense of excitement building as expectation grew for the ball later that evening.

"I have invited your mother to the ball," Max informed Lorelei as she carried out one last inspection of the ballroom. She didn't know why she was doing that, for she was quite confident the servants knew what they were doing, and it really wasn't any of her business, despite being asked by Ava to do so.

"How strange. She did not mention it," Lorelei mused. "Although I know she would have been thrilled to have received an invitation," Lorelei added.

"I thought it would be a good idea. Perhaps a chance for her to get to know us all better for when we are married," Max remarked, silently willing the guests to hurry up and fill the blasted ballroom, so he and Lorelei could slip away for their own wedding.

"Yes, I am afraid I have been rather neglectful on that front, what with all that has been going on here and the orphanage. You must think me quite a terrible daughter."

"Absolutely not," he retorted, then added, "Have you met Cassandra?"

Lorelei laughed as he pulled her to his side. "I have indeed." She sighed. "She looked very happy, didn't she?"

"I think so. I believe marriage to Sinclair will make her feel more secure, and perhaps she may not be quite so feisty," Max replied.

"We do not want her to completely mellow, Max, for every lady needs fire within her or she will be forever mistreated," Lorelei remarked.

"Well, I think it is safe to say that Mr Sinclair is quite aware of her fire, as you call it, so I am sure they will have many happy years. But what about you, Lorelei, do you have any fire in you?" Max chuckled as he nipped her ear, emitting a soft rumble of desire from the back of his throat.

Lorelei cleared her throat daintily. "Lord Lazenby, I believe you are wanted for a speech," she scolded playfully.

"Ah, yes, so I see." Max grinned, straightening his body as a tinkle of glass announced the need for silence. He abhorred making speeches no matter the reason.

Despite being a lord, he thought he would much rather melt into the background, but, he supposed, he really could not wheedle his way out of this one.

"Good evening, ladies and gentlemen, Mr and Mrs Sinclair…"

Lorelei observed the people around the table as they listened intently to Max, who stood proud at her side. The pride for his family emanated from his body with every word in rays of golden light that seeped from every pore. She was not looking at Maximilian Lazenby, her fiancé, but at Maximilian Lazenby, the father. He made her proud of the father he was, standing there, and of the father he would become to their children.

Lorelei paused. The breath from her lungs temporarily ceased to flow. She had not so much as given the possibility of children a thought. She supposed it was what was expected of a lady—of a wife. But she had to indeed wonder whether Max had even considered it, for he already had two daughters. What if he did not want any more children? she considered. How would one even be able to prevent such an occurrence as husband and wife? No one had discussed those particular aspects with regards to the union of a lady and her husband, and she had never quite plucked up the courage to query the matter, for it was not exactly the kind of subject one brings up over tea and biscuits in the drawing room. Lorelei chuckled as she imagined her mother's face in response, had she been so bold as to ask her. She was almost tempted to lean to her right and ask Lady Whitworth now for the sheer fun of it. She would be discreet, of course, but even if it wasn't as discreet as one would expect, it would have been worth it just to see her mother's spine stiffen and her face pale with awkwardness.

That would be too wicked, she thought, feeling rather amused as she pushed the idea aside. Besides, it was not really a subject she relished the thought of discussing with her mother, nor anyone else for that matter.

"Is everything alright, dear?" Lady Whitworth enquired as she began to cut her meat into tiny pieces on her plate. Lorelei thought she probably would merely push it around and rearrange the food rather than eat very much, for her mother had the appetite of a sparrow these days.

"Yes, thank you, Mama. Why do you ask?"

"You were looking at me like you were considering saying something." Lady Whitworth popped the smallest piece of beef that Lorelei had ever seen into her mouth.

"I apologise, Mama. I was simply thinking about my own wedding to Max." It was not a lie exactly, but it was enough to assuage her mother.

"Not long now, eh?" Lady Whitworth winked.

Lady Whitworth winked. Lorelei thought that perhaps her lower jaw had lost any use in the muscles surrounding it, for it would not seem to close of its own volition, so she placed her fingers beneath her chin and pushed it back up.

"Do you need to lie down, Lorelei?" It was Max; he had obviously finished the speech and was back amongst the chatter of the guests.

"No. No, I don't think so." She turned to face him, her face crumpled with confusion. "I think my mother just winked at me," she whispered.

Max mirrored her confusion, but not because her mother may have winked but because he did not know why that appeared to be a strange thing.

As if to clarify, Lorelei said: "My mother never winks, has never winked… Not ever."

"Perhaps she had something in her eye," Max replied, chortling.

"Yes, perhaps."

"I am going to steal you away during the ball. I hope that is okay?" Max announced as the guests left the table in pairs.

"I should imagine that I will be glad of the escape, Max," she replied with utmost honesty.

"Good," he grinned. "And I cannot think of anyone I would rather escape with."

Chapter Twenty-Seven

When the grandfather clock struck ten, Max's hand slipped into Lorelei's, leading her away from the remaining guests and out of the ballroom. He appeared statuesque, his shoulders broad and strong, Lorelei mused as darkness crept over his handsome features and cascaded over his back in a cape of shadows. It seemed such a shame that they had not yet married, she thought, but then reminded herself that it would not be so very long to wait now that Cassie had married Mr Sinclair.

Outside the ballroom, Ava and her husband, Jake, were waiting, and so was her mother. "What is going on? You all look rather suspicious," she teased. A swarm of emotions she could not fathom was erupting in her stomach. Had it not been for the warmth of Max's hand in hers and her mother's mischievous grin—a wink and a mischievous smile? Perhaps she should call the doctor, she pondered—her mind would have believed that swarm to be that of something terrible rather than the delicate flutter of butterfly wings.

"We have a surprise for you," Ava announced, rather formally. "Max will go with Jake and your mother to the library," she said, looking to the other three people, "and you will come with me."

Lorelei looked at Max and her mother. She must have looked worried because Ava stepped forward and assured her that there would be no nasty surprises. A little reluctantly, Lorelei followed Ava up the stairs, but after only a few steps, she looked back at Max. He was looking at her as though his heart may burst. She swallowed, for no one had ever looked at her with so much love.

"Come," Ava beckoned and led her away.

Max was, quite frankly, a nervous wreck. Preparations had separated himself and Lorelei by quite some distance across the house. He had become restless and his hands quite useless, he thought as they fumbled with the buttons of his storm grey waistcoat. He simply needed to see her face, he thought, straightening his attire and heading out of his bedchamber into the hallway.

"Ah-ah-ah, where are you going, Max?" Jake sang. Having changed his own clothes, he had decided to wait for Max before going back down to the library. Ava had warned him that her brother may act somewhat rash.

"To see my fiancée," Max barked, tugging on his cravat.

"Oh, no, you are not," Jake scolded, stepping in front of the man. "Do you not think that if Lady Lorelei had reacted badly to the news of her wedding taking place this evening we would have heard from Ava by now, or even the lady in question herself?"

Max had to concede that the man had offered a valid point. After the way she had been the first time he had met her, he did not believe she would do anything she did not want to. Max remained quiet, albeit the sound of his breath as he exhaled. It was not a sigh of conviction at his brother-in-law's words but more that of one that may aid in calming the anguish soaring through his veins.

"Do not fret, old boy," Jake offered, patting him on the back. "There is no way Lorelei will refuse to marry you tonight."

"I hope you are right, Jake. I do not think I could bear to lose her."

Jake gave Max a reassuring smile. "Let us join Lady Whitworth in the library. I believe we have kept her waiting for far too long already."

Lorelei was trembling as Ava led her up the stairs to an awaiting bedchamber. The room was beautiful, but her nerves had gotten the better of her, and she could barely take anything in other than the general colour of the décor, which was a soft powder blue set against a light oak. "Why are we up here, Ava?" she queried. She was clasping her hands in front of her skirts, one hand inside of the other, as she always seemed to do when in similar situations that warranted a bout of anxiety.

Ava walked to the closet and pulled back the door. "What do you think?" she asked, pulling out the wedding dress of Lorelei's dreams.

Lorelei gasped. "Evangeline finished my dress?" Her whole body was quivering with apprehension. "What is happening, Ava?"

Ava smoothed her hand down Lorelei's arm in comfort. "Max is waiting in the library for you, Lorelei, for he would like very much to marry you tonight. He has procured a special license, and the vicar from Cassandra's wedding is there as well."

Lorelei was lost for words. She had never wanted a big wedding, so that was not a problem. It had only been the dress that she so very much wanted to be perfect for the day, and there it was in front of her.

"And Max wants this too?"

Ava smiled profusely as she noted the addition of the word *'too'* in Lorelei's question. It was ample to tell her that the woman she was now holding the gown in front of wanted to marry her brother as soon as she could. "He does indeed."

Lorelei was desperate to marry Max, she realised as she stood with the corners of her mouth slowly curling into a joyous smile. "Then what are we waiting for?" she replied, her face aching as her happiness refused to allow her smile to fade.

Lorelei's heart was racing as she tried to slow her breathing to a steady rhythm. She was vibrating with a medley of trepidation and excitement. Her insides did not know what to do with it all, and her brain was an absolute mess of unhelpful instructions.

"Let me see you," Ava whispered, her voice strangled with what Lorelei assumed was emotion, and yet she had not even laid her eyes upon her sister-in-law-to-be.

Lorelei inhaled and closed her eyes as she turned to face the woman who would soon be her family. "What do you think?" she enquired, hiding behind the darkness of her closed eyes.

Ava did not answer.

"Ava?" The silence was concerning, Lorelei thought. Slowly, she opened her eyes.

Ava was sniffing into her handkerchief and dabbing the corner of her eyes. "Oh, Lorelei, you look like an angel," she sobbed. "I've never cried with happiness for another before, but for you and Max, I can't help it."

"Please don't cry, Ava, for soon we shall be sisters. Of course, I am looking forward to being Max's wife, but the best thing is that we shall be family. Don't tell Max, will you?" she teased, offering a wink.

A burst of amusement broke the sadness in Ava's face. "I know you only jest, but can you imagine if I did?" she replied, laughing softly as she wiped the last tear away. "He would be rather insulted, to say the least."

Lorelei grinned. "I may jest, Ava, but I hope you know that I am very glad to gain you as my sister," she soothed, picking up the lady's hands in her own and squeezing them gently.

"As I am glad to gain you as my sister," Ava replied,

her smile stretching across her face and crinkling the corners of her eyes.

"That's better," Lorelei remarked, noticing the light return to Ava's gaze. "Shall we make our way downstairs now?"

Ava quickly adjusted her own dress and patted down her skirts. "I believe that may be for the best. I have no doubt that my brother will be an absolute wreck."

"What is it with all this nervous chatter about my Lorelei not wanting to marry you?" Lady Whitworth blurted out as Max and Jake entered the library.

The woman had been eavesdropping, Max thought as he awarded her with a lopsided grin.

"Wedding nerves, Lady Whitworth," Jake offered. "Us men are all guilty of these things when we are in love with our betrothed."

"I see," Lady Whitworth replied. "Well, I can only see that as a very good sign indeed for my daughter."

"Believe me, Lady Whitworth—"

Max's words dissipated—where to he did not know, but the sight of Lorelei seemed to rush through his body, denying him the ability to think of anything but her. He could not decide whether he had ceased to breathe. Perhaps he had died, he thought, and his wedding to Lorelei was playing out before him in the heavens rather than on the earthly planes, for she looked positively ethereal.

Lorelei's hair framed her face as a few loose curls of midnight black fell softly, gently resting upon her bare shoulders. Silk of pure white caressed beneath her collarbone, swooping down and across her body, soft and sensuous against the peachy-pink deliciousness of her skin and the elegant show of décolletage. Max wanted to reach out for her and drag her towards him, yet he could not move his body, allowing only his eyes to caress her as they drank every inch of her in with a thirst he had never known before.

The light from the candles placed prettily around the room glided over her gown in a soft shimmering gold. It rippled over the river of snow-white silk as it poured over her feminine curves. She was breathtaking, Max mused.

"Do you mind all this?" Max rasped as he gestured to the serenely decorated library and then nodded discreetly at the vicar, awaiting his cue to begin the ceremony. Max had to admit that Ava had done a spectacular job, for the room did not look like the library anymore but rather that of a magical garden. If he hadn't known better, he would have suspected imps and faeries to be hiding amongst the flowers and the twinkling lights of the flickering flames.

Lorelei smiled a smile that made her eyes sparkle, relaying a message one cannot possibly find the words to translate. That alone was all he needed to witness to know that she was his.

"Shall we begin?" the vicar whispered, giving them a kind, encouraging smile.

Max nodded at the vicar. "Indeed, we would be most grateful."

When Lorelei had woken that morning, she had never expected that it would be her last morning as Lady Lorelei Whitworth of the spinster and wallflower brigade. It was an unspoken title that she had given herself and assumed she would always possess. Even as she and Max began their courtship, her mind had never quite relinquished those titles. Perhaps she had been waiting until this very moment, she thought, gazing up at the man now standing in front of her. He was whispering words in his deep, resonating voice that sent spatters of pleasure over her body as the wedding vows trailed from his lips in an invisible thread. His words weaved the tapestry of their future in the most wonderful picture she knew it would be. It made her shiver in anticipation of what life would place before them.

Lorelei followed the vicar's voice until the very moment he pronounced them man and wife. She spoke when she was supposed to and said all the right things with the aid of her tongue and lips, but nothing compared to what her heart truly wanted to say. How was one to translate the language of the heart, she wondered, when it seemed to push against her chest as though trying to gain its freedom, simply to enlighten her now husband of how much it sang in his presence.

"Lady Lorelei Lazenby," Max whispered as his mouth closed over hers. "My Lorelei."

"My Max," she replied breathlessly.

"Shall we?" Max whispered in her ear, gesturing to the door.

"We mustn't go to the ball, Max. I don't want to ruin it for Cassandra and Mr Sinclair," Lorelei said kindly.

"Oh, I have no intention of going anywhere where there will be other people," he growled cheekily in her ear.

"Oh," she gasped. "I see."

"Before you two hurry off," Ava cut in, eyeing them knowingly. Jake was at her side, pulling her close. "We have some champagne so that we may have our own little celebration."

"One glass," Max said rather sternly, causing Jake's lips to twitch at the corners with amusement.

"One glass, Max," Ava sighed, "but I think Lady Whitworth may want a few minutes with her daughter before you whisk her away."

"Mama," Lorelei cut in, stepping past Max. "Are you terribly upset that my wedding was a small affair?"

"Are you upset that your wedding was a small affair, Lorelei?" she said, returning the question.

"Not at all, Mama. I think I rather prefer it this way, with it being just us," Lorelei replied. She winced slightly, worried that it may not have been what her mother was expecting her to say.

"Then I am not upset, Lori. How can a mother be upset to see her daughter so much in love and so terribly happy?

"You were always too good for the rakes of the ton," she continued, "or any of the gentleman there. It broke my heart to see you pushed aside and labelled as a wallflower. As you know, I blamed myself, but at the same time I made you feel bad about who you were. I was positively mean, Lori," Lady Whitworth sniffled.

"But Mama," Lorelei interjected.

"Please, my darling, let me say this to you. It is a guilt that has been heavy on my heart, and I have been too stubborn and petty to admit it."

Lorelei nodded for her mother to continue.

"I'm sorry, my darling, for pushing the blame onto you. It is not an excuse for my behaviour, but I simply couldn't understand how someone so rare and beautiful as you could be treated with such contempt. In my desperation for a reason, I ended up hurting the one person I love the most. They were utter fools to have let you go, but I am sure that Maximilian is very glad that they were indeed nincompoops, for now I see that you were only meant for him, my darling."

"Oh, Mama," Lorelei sniffed, dabbing at the corner of her eye. "I do love you."

"And I love you too, Lori. Your father would be so very proud of you, as am I."

Lorelei buried her face in her mother's shoulder as she held her tightly. Every harsh word over the years crumbled between them and fell to the floor, simply forgotten.

"Come have some champagne, Mama."

Chapter Twenty-Eight

Lorelei climbed the stairs of her new home with Max close behind her. She could feel the heat of his gaze on her body, and yet she shivered. She was neither cold nor disgusted, but indeed it felt quite sinful as the pleasure trickled rapidly down her spine and spread its thin fingers over the flesh beneath her silk gown.

As they approached the bedchamber, Max must have sensed that she could no longer move, for he placed one arm behind her back and the other beneath her legs and lifted her into his arms. The piercing blue of his eyes had darkened—it was as though the day had passed in his eyes and she was staring at the night. The twinkling of the stars within them was of love and desire, making Lorelei feel as though she were the most beautiful woman in the world. Max was the only one who had ever made her feel such a way, she thought, as she shied away from his intensity.

"Look at me, Lorelei," he rumbled into her ear. "Why won't you look at me?"

Lorelei did not have a reason that would not embarrass her if she had spoken it aloud. She was no longer the woman of nine and twenty but the fragile, and somewhat vulnerable, debutante of her first season. He made her weak. *How was she to tell him such a thing without appearing ridiculous?* Lorelei forced herself to look at him.

"There you are," he rumbled, smiling wolfishly. "*My* wife."

The way he called her his wife, his possessive nature wrapped around the word 'my' fizzed and sparked through her body as he returned her to her feet. A fire had been lit within her soul, melting away the fragments of her ice-cold fragility.

As the warmth spread within her, he suddenly turned away, creating a coldness that began to coil around her; she did not want him to leave. She did not want to endure such a miserable thing.

"Where are you going?" she whispered, a sense of loss evident in the air that formed the words.

"I do not want to be presumptuous, Lorelei," he rasped.

"Have I done something wrong?" she queried, knowing that if he said yes, then she had no idea what she would do. The cold was getting closer, she wanted it to leave.

"No, of course not. It is I who does not want to do anything wrong. I do not want you to do anything that you are not ready to do, Lorelei." Max turned to face her, blasting the chill out of the room with the heat of desire, blazing in the centre of his eyes. She knew then that his words were not a statement but that of a question.

Lorelei's heart sped up. She had always assumed that a husband took what he wanted, and the wife would simply have to comply, but seeing the concern in his eyes and knowing that he was prepared to wait if that was what she had wanted, she knew it was not what she wanted at all. Lorelei did not want to wait. She wanted to be everything that a wife could be to him. In fact, she felt greedy as the hunger in his eyes mirrored her own.

"Max," she breathed, stepping forward, "I am ready. I think I have always been ready for you. Only you."

Max joined her at the edge of the bed, his hand shaking as he reached to touch the side of her face. Lorelei covered his hand with hers as she leaned into his touch, silencing the tremble within his body. "You are everything to me, Lorelei," he growled. "Can I kiss you?"

"Please," she encouraged, nodding her head.

The sound of Lorelei's voice and the tilt of her head in consent were all that her husband had needed as the confident man within him broke free, claiming her lips with his.

Max combed his fingers hungrily through Lorelei's hair, willing it to tumble from the loosened pins that had been strategically placed within it. Her obsidian curls slipped through his fingers and cascaded down her back, caressing where Max longed to place his fingers. There was not a single inch of her that he did not want to explore. All he wanted was to touch her, to feel her close to him.

Max felt humbled to his core that Lorelei could love someone like him. All this time, she had believed that she had not been good enough, but in truth, she was far more than he could ever have hoped for. The knowledge that she was his wife was intoxicating—a powerful medley stirring within him, laced with love and desire.

"Max," she breathed.

He had lost himself in an endless stream of appreciation for the new Lady Lazenby. She had stolen every inch of his soul and every beat of his heart. Without her, he did not think he would be able to breathe. He took another step closer to her, almost closing the distance between them as Lorelei slipped her hands beneath the cotton of his shirt. Max's muscles tightened and flexed at her touch. His skin tingled beneath her fingertips and palms, sending a wave of unadulterated pleasure to his loins, where he hardened only for her. He let out a groan of appreciation as he cupped her breast, her body instantly bending backward as her spine arched with an unspoken offering as she yearned for more.

Max curved his large body over hers, scraping his teeth gently over the lobe of her ear. His lips lingered briefly, then proceeded in a trail of hot kisses over the long line of her exposed neck, creating a path to her collarbone and then to the swell of her breasts. Satisfaction broadened his shoulders as he listened to the sweet sound of her breath catching, followed by a soft moan as she called to him.

The sweet, rounded, floral fragrance of orange blossoms and lemon washed over him as his heart thudded with love beneath his ribcage. Lorelei was his, he reminded himself as his large hands possessively cupped her posterior, pulling her against him, knowing she would feel just how much he needed her.

"Max," she gasped. "I need you."

Lorelei's gown and petticoats fell to the floor in a cloud of pure silk, lace, and satin, swiftly followed by a rather silly little chemise, he thought. The curves of the woman in his arms and in his hands did not require the rigid ridiculousness of a corset, for she was perfection. She had insisted on throwing society rules to the wind in the name of comfort, for which Max was rather glad as she stood before him in nothing but the pale peachy-pink tint of her skin.

"Good god, you are so beautiful," Max growled, slowly lowering her onto the bed. His shirt hung open, caught in the breeze from the window as it revealed the taut, refined muscles of his chest and abdomen. His breeches were unbuttoned, he noted, where Lorelei had already been, and the back of them were dragged halfway down his backside, where her hands had wandered beneath the fabric, squeezing and pulling him closer.

Lorelei's eyes roved over him as he slipped the shirt from his shoulders and removed his breeches. She was biting her lip again as she silently invited him to lay with her. Max's skin shivered with pleasure as their bodies met, skin to skin. Her breaths came in short bursts as she curled her legs around his waist. She was writhing beneath him, begging without words, but he would not hurry something so special. He wanted their wedding night to be everything it should be, to show her something that was far beyond what his words could ever express. Max wanted to worship her and show her with his body how much he truly loved her.

"Soon, my love," he soothed softly, shifting his body until he was above her, looking down upon her, tormented by the waves of passion crashing over him. "You are the love of my life. Lorelei. I love you so much, and I do not wish to rush this with you."

"I love you too," she rasped, her eyes sparkling with raw emotions.

Unable to look at her any longer for fear that his heart may leap from his chest, Max began a slow, teasing descent down the centre of her body, delicately brushing his lips from her heart to her navel and then to the warmth between her thighs. Lorelei let out a slightly suppressed squeal, but Max placed his large hands over the insides of her thighs, holding her in place. "Shhh, Lorelei." He smiled wickedly to himself as his words blew onto the soft curls between her legs, only proving to make her squeal again.

"Max," she protested weakly, without any conviction in her voice. "Ma-"

Max leaned in to taste her, silencing the sound of his name as it began to bleed from the back of her throat, curling around a chorus of approving sighs and moans of encouragement until her body began to buck beneath him, trembling with wave after wave of release.

"Oh, that was… " Lorelei swallowed, her throat devoid of moisture from what she could only describe as the most delightful torture—its tail ends still rippling through her. She had had no idea that such a pleasure was possible.

Max was grinning triumphantly and rather wickedly at her, she thought, as she tried to regain her composure. Her breath was emanating from her lungs in short, sharp bursts.

"I have not quite finished with you yet, Lady Lazenby," he grinned, waggling his eyebrows. "That was merely the beginning."

"Really?" Lorelei's stomach fluttered in anticipation.

"Indeed, my love."

"Oh, well, in that case." She smiled teasingly and pulled him down on top of her. Feeling every inch of him, her body begged for more.

Despite not having the conversations with her mother, Lorelei was not so naïve as to not know in which way a husband and wife were supposed to be joined. She had always assumed that when the moment arrived, she would be frightened of such a deed, especially after some of the frightful stories she had unwittingly overheard from the old dowagers of society—those who found it quite necessary to inform others around a table of how the marriage bed had been so terribly difficult for them. They had made it seem like a chore rather than what she was currently in throes of. Lorelei realised that perhaps they had not loved their husbands as she loved hers.

The word husband sang like a nightingale in Lorelei's mind as she lowered her hands to the back of his legs. She dragged her fingernails lightly over the back of his thighs and over the taut, pert muscles of his bottom, noting how they clenched at her touch, prompting his hips to tilt forward until they were touching hers, his body quivering against her.

"Max, please," Lorelei begged. "I need all of you."

Max's gaze was a furnace of desire as he heeded her words, answering her call with a sensual kiss. His tongue glided between her lips, deepening their kiss as he positioned himself between her legs. "I will be gentle, Lorelei, I promise you," he whispered lovingly as his hand grazed the side of her face.

Lorelei returned his touch. "I trust you, Max."

Max was slow to begin with, evidently terrified that he would cause her pain, but, she thought, he needn't have worried, for she already knew they were meant for each other. For all the stories, tales, and unwarranted warning that others had unapologetically bestowed upon her over the years, it appeared that she had found something rare with Max, as they had connected in heart, body, and mind. Everything about their intimacy had been beautiful, she recollected whilst laying in his arms. Max's eyes were closed, a smile teasing his lips as she curled closer into him.

Lorelei believed that she would indeed like married life very much.

Cassie ran through the entrance of her marital home without a care in the world, despite being quite aware that she had neglected to tell her new husband she simply had to go out because it was imperative that she see Lorelei. But, as she entered the carriage, she remembered that she did not even know where Lady Whitworth lived, and so, in turn, did not know where Lorelei was currently residing.

Cassandra Sinclair ran back into the house.

"Benjamin!" she called, panting as she pushed open the drawing room door. If she wasn't holding a letter from Lorelei in her hands, she may have cooed over the décor like she had the night before, but she was feeling rather frantic indeed.

"What is it, my darling?" he crooned, leaning in to kiss her.

Cassie melted into his arms, then admonished herself for allowing him to make her so terribly feeble with a simple kiss. She shook her head. "Not now, darling. We simply have to find Lorelei," she said beseechingly.

"It is supposed to be our honeymoon, my darling," he replied, leaning in to kiss her again, but this time he merely met the air as her hands pushed against his chest. "Oh, come now, Cassie," he groaned.

"Look at this," she blurted before he could begin working on manipulating her into another kiss. Cassandra simply would not allow herself to be distracted.

"Where did you find this?" Benjamin Sinclair queried, giving the parchment one last perusal.

"It was positioned at the back of my dressing table. I am afraid I did not see it last night as we were somewhat distracted." Cassie blushed profusely.

The confusion of the correspondence in Benjamin's hand melted away. A wicked smile had spread across his face, taking its place as he remembered the previous night's activities.

"Oh, you are incorrigible," Cassie scolded playfully. "We must be serious. We really must find Lorelei."

Benjamin sighed. The look of excitement and helplessness in his new wife's eyes were all that was needed to melt his resolve, he thought, fetching his hat and coat. "Perhaps we can ask your father," he suggested.

"Oh, yes, of course. I knew I married you for a reason," she jested as she took his hand and hurried him from their house.

Max and Lorelei ventured from their bedchamber a little later than either of them was used to. Lorelei had tried at least twice to make herself presentable but was quickly distracted by her husband's wandering hands.

"The servants will talk," Lorelei chided, offering him her best withering gaze.

"That won't work on me," Max replied, grinning like a cat that had lapped up the last drop of cream. "Besides, you need to keep *that* out of your admonishing gaze if it is to work," he added, waggling his finger towards her eyes.

Lorelei looked confused. "And what exactly is *that*?" she queried, resting her hands on her hips playfully.

"Oh, I don't know; perhaps it's that look that tells me you want to strip me of my clothes again," he said quite seriously. His eyes were sparkling with the humour he was trying to contain.

"Oh, really?" she sniffed, turning her back to him so he couldn't see *that* look in her eyes. "Is that so?"

"Indeed, I believe it is," he drawled seductively in her ear. He was so close, his breath whispered down her back. "Saucy minx."

Lorelei spun quickly on her heel in an effort to face her husband and deny the name he had just called her, but she had forgotten how close he was, causing her to lose her balance.

Max caught her in his arms as laughter erupted from him, his happiness washing over his new wife.

"You are radiant when you are vexed, my love," he drawled, pulling her up against him.

Lorelei smiled. "Yes, well, I have a feeling that I may be radiant quite a bit around you," she said, grinning. "But if you could allow me to be less vexed and thus less radiant, I would love something to eat. I am famished."

"Your wish is my command, my love," Max replied, offering his arm. "Shall we?"

"Where is everybody?" Lorelei enquired, scanning the room. She had never seen it quite so empty. Of course, she knew Cassandra would not be there, but there was also Ava, Jake, and Katie to consider.

"I believe they are trying to be discreet and make themselves scarce as it is our first morning as Lord and Lady Lazenby," Max replied, picking up a piece of toast and buttering it generously. "Dear lord, that sounds so good to say," Max added.

"Yes, it certainly does have a rather lovely sound to it," Lorelei remarked, taking her first sip of tea. "Oh, this is good," she sighed.

"Papa!"

"Did I hear Cassandra?" Max asked, his brow furrowed, looking to Lorelei for some clarification.

"I believe you did. If not, then this house is haunted with someone who sounds remarkably like her." Lorelei pressed her napkin to her lips and began to push her chair back so she may open the door and find out.

The door burst open with the aid of the butler, automatically willing Lorelei to sit back down, so she did.

"Cassandra, what are you doing here?" Max questioned. His eyes were wild with concern. "Whatever is the matter?"

"I need Lady Whitworth's address, Papa. I simply must see Lor-" Cassandra's voice broke off as she eyed Lorelei at the vast table. "Ooh," she breathed.

"Perhaps I shouldn't be here," Benjamin muttered, turning towards the door. "None of my business and all that," he added, ambling further away from what he believed would be rather awkward for his father-in-law and the man's future bride.

"No need, Sinclair," Max barked. "Cassie, Sinclair," he continued, "I would like you both to meet my wife."

"You are married?" Cassie mused breathlessly.

Lorelei nodded. Her stomach was doing that funny little dance it usually did when she never knew how someone would react.

"When?"

"Last night, toward the end of the ball," Max replied, giving her a steady look.

"But didn't you want a big wedding, Lorelei?" Cassie asked.

Lorelei shook her head. "I simply wanted to marry your father."

"Before you blame anyone for intruding on your

wedding day, Cassandra," Max interjected, "you must know that Ava and I planned it as a surprise for Lorelei. Lorelei, of course, did not know, as she had insisted that we wait until after your wedding so your day would be all about you. She didn't want to take the attention from you."

Cassandra looked at her father and then at Lorelei. The colour had seemed to drain from her face. "You did that for me?" she rasped, her attention on Lorelei. "Just like you did this?" Cassandra held up the piece of paper. "I found it this morning."

"It is my wedding gift to you both," Lorelei whispered, afraid that it may be the wrong thing to say.

A tear slipped from Cassie's eye and trailed down her face. "Oh, Lorelei, I don't know how I can thank you." She placed her arms around her father's new wife. "Thank you," she sobbed. "All this after I have been so rotten."

"No, you haven't, Cassie," Lorelei soothed. "We had our moments, but that has passed. I could not see you and your husband struggle when I no longer needed my own home."

Benjamin Sinclair stepped forward. "Thank you, Lady Lazenby," he offered, his voice a little deeper than what was the norm.

"Please, we are family now; you may call me Lorelei or Lori," Lorelei offered. "And please don't feel that you need to keep that house, for you can sell it if you wish and buy one that you both love. I do not want you to feel you are restricted by my gift to you both."

It seemed that Max's honeymoon with his wife would be rather short-lived—at least for a few hours anyway, he thought as he reached under the table and took his wife's hand. The intrusion of his daughter and her husband had trickled from odd sentences into conversations as they were seated around the breakfast table.

Max was relieved to see how Cassie's had blossomed in the last month or so, and it was a pleasure to witness how she had softened towards his wife. Max blew out a breath at his thoughts, for it was not possible for anyone to not soften towards Lorelei. She made kindness seem as easy as breathing. He looked at the deed at the side of Sinclair, tied with a red ribbon—a reminder of Lorelei's gift to them. A house, he mused, something that most would have fought over so others may look upon them and evaluate their worth, but there she was handing it over simply because his daughter and her husband needed it more than she did. In a perfect world, it made perfect sense, but in a world as particularly imperfect as it was, she had broken through its tough exterior to add a sparkle of perfection.

She was perfection.

"Darling," Sinclair called to Cassandra, "perhaps we should leave the happy couple to their honeymoon?"

Cassie blushed. "Oh, yes, of course."

Lorelei wondered whether the young lady was blushing because she was thinking of things that no daughter should be made to think of about their father and his new wife, or whether it was at the thought of her husband and their honeymoon. She rather preferred to imagine it being the latter, or she may have found herself on the rather crimson side as well.

"Thank you again, Lorelei," Cassie said, dropping a kiss onto her cheek. "You really are the most wonderful person."

Now Lorelei was blushing. "You are very welcome," she replied.

"We shall have to meet often," Cassie suggested as she began to walk away.

"I would like that very much," Lorelei called after her.

No sooner had the door closed than Max had pulled her onto his lap. "I have just been robbed of an hour of our honeymoon," he whispered, sounding rather disgruntled, in her ear.

Lorelei giggled. "I would not call seeing your daughter happy being robbed of anything, Max," she chided, turning to face him and curling her arms around his neck.

He growled. "I beg to differ, Lady Lazenby. I had plans for that hour."

"Taking the air with me?" she enquired teasingly. "Reading? Or perhaps-"

Max did not give Lorelei the opportunity to suggest

any more ludicrous things to do on one's honeymoon. They were utterly preposterous, he thought, chuckling at her cheeky ways as he lifted her off his lap and threw her over his shoulder, then carried her toward the stairs. "I will show you exactly what I had planned, Lady Lazenby," he drawled wickedly, taking the stairs two at a time.

"Our children will have green eyes and obsidian hair," he told her as he turned the doorknob to the bedchamber.

"I think they will have blue eyes," she argued, her fingers curled in the fabric of his jacket as she held onto him.

"No, you are quite incorrect, Lorelei, for they shall be green like yours," Max retorted.

"Is that so?" she giggled, pretending to fight her way out of his grasp.

"It is indeed. However," he remarked, lowering her on to the bed and quickly discarding his shirt and breeches, "it is imperative that I must have my wicked way with you on multiple occasions so that we may find out."

"Oh my," Lorelei gasped. "It sounds terribly important."

Max climbed on top of her; every inch that he moved seemed to unfasten some item of clothing from her body. Lorelei did not know how he had managed it, but by the time he was crawling above her, she wasn't wearing a morsel of fabric.

"Oh, it is very important, my love," he crooned, nestling into the arc of her neck. "A legal requirement, so I've been told."

"Well, in that case, Lord Lazenby," Lorelei answered, stifling her happiness as it attempted to burst from her in an overwhelming desire to laugh, "you best come a little closer."

Epilogue

Lorelei's dark curls had lost their bounce where they had been dampened by the efforts of childbirth. Max had heard her call out for it to be over with, and he had wanted nothing more than to hold her and make everything better, but he had not been allowed in the room. So, when the door opened and the maid beckoned him in, he didn't look back to see whether the seat he had been sitting on had fallen backwards, despite the crashing sound it made. It didn't matter. He needed to see his wife.

He knew she would have told him she looked terrible, for she had never been very complimentary to herself, but as he gazed at her across the room, she was a vision of strength, radiance, and beauty.

"One of each," Lorelei announced, lifting her head so she could gaze at Max, watching as he sauntered into the bedchamber.

"Twins?" he questioned, feeling rather confused when there was only one baby in his wife's arms.

"No, not twins. Thank heavens. I meant one blue, one green. Come and see," she encouraged, smiling.

'Dear God, she is beautiful,' Max thought apprecia-

tively about his wife.

Max's chest tightened with even more love as he gazed down at their son. He wondered how he could fit so much of it in his heart when all it seemed to wish to do was burst out of him.

The little bundle, made purely of whatever miracles were made of, had one blue eye and one green. Both seemed to gaze up at him with so much curiosity. Max could not stop the tears from welling in his eyes. "He's perfect," he said, emotion cutting through his voice. Max thought his son was the most beautiful little boy he had ever seen. He wondered whether *beautiful* was the correct terminology for a boy, yet one could not call a tiny little baby *handsome*, he thought; therefore, he knew that *beautiful* was indeed the correct description.

"You do realise," Lorelei said, "that this means neither of us win. I believe our son has outsmarted us."

Max chortled. "Oh, I don't think he has, my love, for I think we have both won."

"Yes, I believe you are indeed right, Max. We have won." Lorelei kissed their son's head. "We need to think of a name for him."

"I was thinking that perhaps we could call him George," Max suggested. "What do you think?"

"Do you not want him to have your name?"

"Well, I had thought of it, but then I thought to myself: What if he should get scolded by his mama? I do not want to hear my name bellowed across the house," he answered with a wry smile.

Lorelei tapped him gently on the shoulder. "I do not bellow," she retorted with humour.

Max kissed the top of her head. "I only jest, my love, but I do prefer George, but only if you wish the same."

"I think George is a lovely name. George Lazenby. However, I do think we should still give him your name as his second name," she added with a glint of mischief in her eye.

"And pray tell, why is that?" Max asked, knowing he may come to rue his curiosity.

"Well, if he's very naughty, then I shall need to extend his name to the fullest when I'm bellowing."

Lorelei couldn't help the laughter that poured from her as she gazed upon her husband and son. She was so terribly happy and knew that she would always need to release some of her happiness to allow for much more, for her body could only hold so much. Sometimes, she would give herself a little pinch, for it seemed as though it was all a dream—a dream that was meant solely for her. It was a dream that she was most grateful for, for gone were the titles of *Wallflower* and *Spinster*—they had been swept away in a tidal wave of time.

Now she, Lorelei, held the two most precious titles of all as Max's wife and George's mama.

The End

Books by the same author

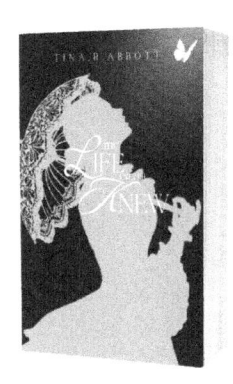

Printed in Great Britain
by Amazon